No More
Happy Endings

- Eight Short Stories -

Alastair MacDonald Hart

Cover design by Scott Gaunt: scottgaunt@hotmail.co.uk

ISBN: 9798856156163

PublishNation
www.publishnation.co.uk

Dedicated to:-

All those affected by war and hunger,

No matter where in the World.

Contents

Francis Was Confused.

Francis was confused. This was nothing new; Francis had spent most of his life in a state of confusion. He was not alone however, most of the world's population was living in a state of confusion, but I will concentrate on Francis as he is my friend.

It was a bright Tuesday morning, or was it a Wednesday? Francis and I were walking his border collie, or was it a husky? In the park, though it could have been down by the river, or it could have been the pub though this was unlikely as we did not drink.

Anyway, Francis had been watching the Prime Minister on a broadcast from Downing Street. He had been explaining in detail what we should all be doing in the face of the crisis we were all living with. Francis was confused. Don't worry I said, we are all confused by the Prime Minister these days. You are not alone.

That seemed to make Francis feel better, or it could have made Francis more confused. I will need to think about that now, I'm confused.

2

A Safe Place

It had been a whisper at first, a stray sentence that had blurred in with all the other terrible news shooting across the world. Angela had first heard about Covid-19 while in a shop. The news had been playing over the radio, speaking about a film premiere that had been delayed for fears of the illness that was sweeping the world. Like so many other people she had not imagined that it could impact her life all that much. After all, she remembered Mad Cow Disease, Swine Flu, Bird Flu, as well as the scares about Ebola and other things. None of them had touched her life. Of course, it would be unfortunate for the people who were affected by it, but it seemed strange that a major film would be delayed.

Of course, things spiralled quickly from there. She hadn't imagined that one day she would have her last meeting at work, or her last trip to the shop without a mask and without any regulations on how many people were allowed inside at any one time, or how impossible it would become to not have an impromptu drink, or how she would have her last session at the tennis club.

Sitting at home, gazing out of her window, she could see the grassy lawns, a burst of colour amid a melancholy scene. Usually there were people clad in white running back and forth across the lawns, neon green balls rising and falling in the air. There was nothing outside, nothing at all. Even the kids who clustered around street corners were absent. It was as though all life had been stripped from the world. The world had stopped as though it was a defunct machine that had had its power sapped, every part of it fading into obsolescence.

The worst part was that nobody knew how long it was going to last. The news kept talking about the 'new normal,' as though that was a phrase that made any sense. Normal had gone out of the window a long time ago. Everything that was deemed non-essential had been shut down. Restaurants and pubs and bars were now just blank buildings, a reminder of what used to be. Any shop that did not sell food was closed as well, meaning the bustling high street was barren. They may as well have been living in a ruin or a tomb, the echoes of life fading into a whisper.

People were struggling to know what to do about their jobs. Were they going to survive? Was the government going to give them help? They had introduced a furlough scheme to allow employers to keep paying wages while they stayed at home. Angela was able to do some of her work remotely, but it wasn't the same as being in the office.

She also found that without being in the office her work was largely meaningless. While Angela had never been an extroverted person, she now missed the brief conversations at the water cooler, or the bland murmurings while waiting for the kettle to boil. She also missed the background noises of the photocopier churning, and the faint hum of the computers, as well as the chattering keyboards, all of which blended together to form a cacophony.

The silence had never been more noticeable.

Her days had always been filled, but now as she worked from home, she realized that without the distractions of her colleagues she could be done with work far sooner than she had been before. It made her question two things; one was how much time she had wasted at work, and the second was how long she could go without losing her mind. With all this time on her hands, well, it made for idle work and her mind quickly ran away with itself. It was curious that whenever this happened it always found a dark corner and overturned the biggest humiliations and fears of her life. She never lost herself in bright, shimmering fantasies, and never cosied up with the triumph of her past glories. It only ever seemed to be that she had to focus on her failures, as though her mind's default setting was one of despair.

Then there came the furlough scheme. This ensured that she was going to be paid while not having to go to work, and indeed she wasn't actually supposed to work while being furloughed, but there were occasions when the boredom became severe and she had to fire up her laptop and work on a few documents. Management still wanted there to be meetings as well, saying they wanted to foster a sense of community among the workforce, although she suspected they just wanted to keep an eye on people. Although the furlough scheme offered some security, it was also hazy and vague with nobody knowing exactly how long it was going to last for. It was as though everything was hanging by a thread, and all it would take was one snip for it all to fall apart. At least she wasn't spending as much money as before though, for there was nowhere to go. She was worried about the articles that predicted an economic crisis following the pandemic, with the cost of living expected to rise and a period of austerity to ensue.

That was a story for another time though. There were already too many things to worry about.

The less she worked the more pointless it all seemed, and she wondered if she could even go back to work. She had been deemed 'non-essential' by the government, but it seemed paradoxical to her that she was allowed to remain in the comfort of her home whilst getting paid, while these essential people were forced to continue working and not being given any benefit for doing so. It wasn't as though they were given a pay rise. Angela began to develop a form of survivor's guilt, and any time she went to the supermarket she had to turn her face away in shame.

Work was one of those things that people defined her life by, and now that it had been taken away she had to find a new definition, but it was difficult to come by.

The walls of her apartment resembled a prison. The winter approached, bleaker than ever. The air was suffocating. She wasn't even allowed to go out for a walk. People were allowed half an hour exercise a day, or as well as essential food trips, but she couldn't justify going out every day to a supermarket, and nor did she wish to.

The fear was that going out could entice the virus and make things worse. The news was filled with statistics about how many people were getting infected and dying, and how the hospitals would soon be overwhelmed with casualties. There were hours where Angela was glued to the Internet, reading accounts from people in other countries to see how they were handling it. Some governments were putting their heads in the sand and people were suffering, with rising figures of the dead.

Others were enforcing strict, authoritarian procedures, punishing people who stayed out past curfew.

The world was supposed to be entering a new golden era of progress with technology, but it seemed to Angela as though it was sliding into another Dark Age. People on the Internet agreed. A new term had been coined, called 'Doomscrolling,' which was where you constantly looked at depressing and bad news. The problem was that this kind of news was everywhere. Sure, there were some glimpses of hope as people said that a vaccine would be possible, but there was no telling when, no timeline as to how long people were going to have to wait to get their lives back to normal.

Some people suggested that this was going to be the way things were going to stay for the foreseeable future. They even suggested that it was all a government hoax because what they really wanted was for everyone to be isolated like lab rats, to work in their tiny homes and not enjoy an iota of leisure because the government wanted to make humanity a slave race.

Angela didn't agree with this, but what worried her was that she could see the logic. Spending so much time by herself was turning her mind into rubber and there didn't seem to be a way to stop it. She could read a book or watch TV, but in the back of her mind there was still the same bell tolling, the same grim truth that clung to her heart.

They spoke about social bubbles as well, groups of people that you were allowed to see safely to stop the spread of infection. Most people treated this as family, but Angela was far from hers. They were up north, separated by miles of roads and train lines that were all defunct at the moment. The other people she knew all had their families, so Angela didn't fit into any bubble at all.

She had never felt more alone, not in all her years. What made it worse were the government messages claiming that we were all suffering together, or the inane messages from celebrities who lauded a united mindset. But it was easy for them, being isolated in their mansions with no worry about financial insecurity, not like the rest of people who wondered if things were ever going to get better. In fact, many of the projections suggested that even if the world did recover from the pandemic, it would only get worse, with the economy suffering most of all. Angela was a prudent woman and had always had a sensible mindset when it came to money. She did not treat herself to many luxuries, but soon enough she would not be able to treat herself to any luxuries at all.

And so she looked longingly at the tennis court again. It was the one form of exercise she enjoyed, and she could feel herself growing flabbier by the day as she fell out of the routine of playing regularly.

Angela pulled on her coat and decided that she needed to go to the shops and get some fresh air. She walked outside, digging her hands into her pockets, and took a route that went past the tennis club. She half expected a police officer to emerge from nowhere and declare that she was undergoing non-essential travel, and that she should return home immediately. Occasionally she saw someone walking a dog. They crossed to the other side of the street, heeding the government advice to remain apart.

Angela paused outside the tennis court. The paint was fading, the grass growing. It almost looked unreal, as though this was all some set on a theatre stage that would soon be taken down. She closed her eyes and remembered the feeling of the reverberations running up her arm as she hit the ball, or the satisfying ripple of the net as her opponent misjudged a shot. The only thing remaining was the smell of the grass. There wasn't even the surly groundskeeper here to tell her to clear off. She wondered about him and all the other people who used to come here. Were they missing it as much as her? Were they struggling as badly as her?

It was as though all her tethers to the world had been severed.

Angela dragged herself away with heavy steps. One of the more depressing things that the pandemic had taught her was how empty her life truly was. Aside from work, she enjoyed tennis and that was about it. She had tried to cultivate her culinary skills, but buying the current equipment to cook anything more than pasta was expensive and she simply didn't have the room in her current kitchen. She was not creative, and while she liked reading, she didn't wish to spend every day with her nose in a book. TV shows and movies had lost their lustre. She watched them with envy, for they only served to remind her how simpler life had been before lockdown had struck.

She made it to the store and fell in line with the queue, which stretched around the car park. Never before had she had to queue to get into this shop. Other people were grumbling about one thing or another. She never had much time for strangers, but this was about the only way she could get human contact nowadays. As she approached the door, she slipped her mask on and went inside. There were arrows on the floor, indicating where shoppers should walk in order to maintain social distance. At first Angela had tried to follow these guidelines, but it was impossible when nobody else did. Despite the shop being largely empty somehow people still found a way to bump into her or get to one of the shelves she needed.

And speaking of the shelves, she was faced with emptiness. A lot of the basic food stuffs were always sold out. There was constant restocking, and her diet had devolved into what it had been when she had been a student. She loaded up her basket and then headed to the checkout, pitying the cashier, who still had to work with all of this going on. It didn't seem fair that some people, like her, could stay at home while other people still had to work, yet saw no tangible reward. It wasn't as though they were going to get a bonus for this extra work.

When she paid for her shopping and carried it out, she slowed her pace, almost wanting to make this trip last longer because she could go nowhere else but home.

*

Later that evening, Angela lay on the couch and held her phone above her head, waiting for her Mum to call. They had always enjoyed a lot of contact, and now it was one of the few ways for Angela to speak to someone other than herself. Her mother, Amanda, had taken to calling at 8pm on the dot every night.

"Hey Mum," Angela replied.

"Hello love, how are you today?"

Angela sighed. "Oh, you know, the same as every day, I guess. It all just blurs into one. To be honest I'm starting to wish that I could hibernate and just sleep this thing out until spring."

"They're saying right now that they think this could stretch into next summer. Now I heard that the heat wasn't very good for it, so hopefully it will kill off this virus. If we can just hunker down and make it through the winter then we should be fine."

"Yes, yes, I suppose so. I hope so anyway," Angela said. Her parents tried to look on the bright side of things, while Angela found it difficult to see anything other than oblivion ahead.

"So, what did you do today anyway?"

"I went to the shop. I walked past the tennis courts. I wonder if they're going to be able to open again. It's really strange, Mum. You look around and it's like the world is empty."

"I know, I was talking to Doris today and she was saying how her son hasn't left the house this entire time! He's been too afraid. I wouldn't like to think what his place smells like."

"Yeah..."

"Have you spoken to your neighbours at all?"

"No."

"Oh, I thought you might have given the situation. It would be nice to make friends with them."

"I don't think anyone is making friends with anyone. I sometimes have video calls with friends and people from work. It's just... it's not the same. I never realized how much I would miss actually talking to people."

"I know, I suppose it's alright for us since we're used to going a long time without seeing you in person," Amanda said. Angela rolled her eyes. It was just another in a long line of veiled insults where she made clear her disapproval of Angela's decision to remain in London after University instead of returning to her native north.

"You know that I had to do this for my career. The opportunities just aren't the same up there."

"You did it because of Harry, I know you, and look how that worked out."

Angela pressed her lips together and blinked slowly. Sure, at the time Harry might have played a small part in her decision, but she couldn't have known that things were going to end badly.

"By the way, your father has asked me to ask you if you have thought anymore about moving back up here considering the circumstances?"

"I just don't know if it's feasible Mum. And I don't really want to throw away my career right now either. If I move back home I'm accepting defeat."

"Well, that's not quite true. What about the talk of working from home? If you did then you could work here! It would be so nice to have you back again."

"Where would I work Mum?"

"Well, from your old room. We've left it just as you used to have it. You could come back and it would just be like old times," she spoke with a smile, but to Angela it would basically mean that the last few years of her life had been pointless, and she had accomplished nothing.

"I'll keep it in mind, although I wouldn't have thought Dad would want me back. Didn't he say he always wanted to turn my room into a place for his model railway?"

"Yes, well, then he looked at how much a model railway would cost and that dream is put on the backseat for the time being."

"Is he wearing his mask yet?"

Amanda rolled her eyes. "Don't get me started on that."

"You have to be strict with him Mum."

"Don't you think I know that? You try being strict with him. Once he's made his mind up about something he won't let it go. He doesn't like the way it makes his glasses fog up, you see, and he heard from some cousin of his that they don't make much of a different."

"What, Jo?"

"Yeah."

"He mentioned that to me last time. Of course, they're not going to make that much difference in a hospital where people already have Covid and where they're all close together anyway, but it might be different for Dad. He needs to be careful."

Amanda sighed. "Then perhaps you should think harder about moving back here. You could keep on at him because Lord knows I've run out of patience."

Angela wasn't about to return home to be her father's babysitter, but it annoyed her that he wasn't following the proper protocols. "Doesn't he understand that these things only work if everyone follows them?"

"Of course he does, but then you have those stories about all the people in government who are breaking the rules and complaining about masks, so he thinks why should we have to follow it as well? And on that point I actually agree with him. I don't see why we should have to suffer when so many of the people in charge get to swan about as though the rules don't apply to them."

While Angela agreed with her mother, that wasn't really the point of things. She pinched the bridge of her nose and tried her best to remain calm. "Mum, that shouldn't have anything to do with it. I agree that it's unfair, but Covid doesn't care about fairness. It doesn't care about anything. People have to take it upon themselves to be safe otherwise other people are going to suffer and I've heard so many horror stories. I don't want you and Dad to fall ill as well. Until we get the vaccines there's no defence against Covid, the only thing that we know is that older people are more vulnerable to it."

"There's plenty of life in your father and I yet. Things aren't as bad as they seem Angela. Now have you been going out for walks regularly?"

"I try, but I don't like to spend too long outside."

"It's really a shame that you can't be here because at least then you could come into the garden. I don't know what I would do without my little breaks outside. Even though the weather isn't nice it's still good to have a change of scenery. I really don't know where the world went wrong, you know? When your father and I were younger we didn't have nearly this much trouble getting a house."

"I know Mum," Angela said. Soon after this she ended the call and sighed. It did seem to her that she and the rest of her generation had been born at the wrong time. There were global recessions, constant stories of corruption, unjust wars being fought in far off lands, and now a pandemic that had the world in its grip. It was one long tragedy, and it was easy to see why the constant generation were getting jaded. With rent the way it was Angela wasn't sure she would ever be able to save up enough money to own her own house, not without help from her parents, and definitely not at London prices. At some point she would have to leave again. She had assumed it would be to head south, but if the pandemic continued would it really be so bad to head up north again?

To Angela, life had always been a way of steady progress. You were supposed to leave home and soar like a bird taking flight from a nest, never to return home again. Yes, there was plenty of literature that spoke to a longing for home, but unlike Odysseus, who battled gods and monsters to return to his beloved Ithaca, Angela did not wish this for herself. Perhaps it was because she had not achieved anything of great importance in her own life and so returning home would not be a triumphant march of a solider coming back from a conquered Ilium, but a browbeaten, depressed sight of a wretch who had wilted under the glare of life. She was not yet thirty, still with her whole life ahead of her, and yet where that should have shone with promise it now only glowed with a frantic ember of despair, for what could she accomplish in this world that was shutting down? All the opportunities she had been promised when she was younger had been taken away one by one, and she wasn't sure if they were ever going to be given back. All the world did was take and take, as though it wanted to gorge on the hopes of a generation, and it was yet to have its fill.

*

Days blurred into weeks and weeks blurred into months. Time became elastic. In some senses it crawled so slowly, the hours eking by and the hand of the clock ticking with a sense of doom, caught in some strange parallel world where every second was repeated. Nothing was accomplished, nothing was achieved, and yet so many days were behind her now, piled up like unwanted Christmas presents. Somehow, they had gathered, as though she had been waiting for them all at once and then she blinked, and they rushed past her.

In truth she knew that this was not the case, but it became so hard to keep track of time. It was fluid around her, moving of its own accord. In bed her thoughts would not let her rest, so sleep did not come easily. She would lie there in the dark, staring at the glow of her phone screen with bleary eyes, gazing again at the news from around the world, pitying people who she would never meet for their losses, getting angry at those who ignored the truth that was staring them right in front of their faces. How could they be so ignorant as to create conspiracies when people were dying? How could anyone be so callous?

These emotions would take hold of her and whirled through her body, creating an intense storm that left her trembling and exhausted. There were so many feelings that simply had nowhere to go, so they rolled and rampaged around inside her and then she was spent, but still she could not sleep until the small hours of the morning. Now when she woke up the sky was a cold grey, the sunlight hidden behind the monochrome curtain. The roads were still empty, the promises getting farther and farther away.

What little trust had been left in the government had ebbed away to a thin streak of watercolour paint that could be washed away easily as more scandals came to light of people in power carrying on with life as normal despite asking others to make great sacrifices. The health service groaned under the weight of the pandemic and the weekly applause was not enough to buoy the hearts of those who strained to keep working and keep people healthy. News and misinformation were rife, with people claiming that a vaccine was close, but with nothing concrete to show for it. The country was rife with people aching to see each other again, with businesses falling over the brink from which there was no return, and people in a constant state of stress and worry about their livelihoods. Supply chains were growing narrower, with less and less food at the supermarket. People had to be told not to hoard supplies like staple foods, toilet paper, and hand sanitiser. It seemed like common sense to Angela to not take anything more than you needed, but society was built on greed, and too many people were out for themselves.

So much for being in it together.

The video calls with her work colleagues occurred less frequently, for people had grown tired of them. Even though she could see all their faces there was something missing about the whole endeavour, something about physical interaction that could not be replicated by technology. Angela had never considered herself a luddite and had always tried to keep up with the latest in technology, thinking that each new advancement was a wonderful addition to the world, but she was beginning to have a new appreciation for the world that had come before. There was something quaint and simple about the idea of her parents going to the local pub every Friday to meet their friends. It was a habit that had fallen out of favour with the younger generation, and now the pubs were empty tombs.

She walked past the tennis court as well. The lawns now were so overgrown that it was impossible to see the white paint. It may as well have been any other garden. She tried practicing her tennis strokes, but her arm ached and they did not want to move as naturally as they had before. Her body was regressing, unlearning everything that she had learned before.

Shopping had not become any easier. People had adjusted to this new normal, but they didn't like it. They still grumbled and moaned and everyone was more curt. They were all frustrated, but with no common enemy to unite against they spat and snapped at each other, like alligators from rival broods who competed for territory. It meant that Angela did not want to spend more time out than she needed to, and she certainly was not going to find any solace in her fellow man.

The only constant she had in her life were her phone calls with her mother, and even though she never had much to say or update her mother with, she still enjoyed the connection it gave her. She didn't know how people who had nobody coped with everything. Mostly she lay there motionless while her mother chatted away, acting as things were just as they had always been. Angela had been thinking about why her parents had been facing things differently than she was.

Part of it, she thought, was that they already had their home and had many years of work under their belts. They had achieved things and had money in the bank to soften the blow of this economic crunch, and their hopes were not dashed by the pandemic. Their home was more than big enough for the two of them. They were ensconced with warmth and had plenty of space to do whatever they liked, while Angela was stuck in a tiny flat where the walls seemed to inch more towards her every day. She wouldn't have been surprised to find that one day she awoke in a coffin.

But there was another reason as well; they had each other. Angela had never been a bleeding-heart romantic who became swayed by all the cloying, saccharine movies that gave men and women everywhere idealized dreams of romance, but neither did she distance herself from the idea entirely. She wanted companionship. She wanted someone to trust more than anyone else. She wanted to be part of something bigger than herself, and she had hoped that someone would have come along by now to change that.

There was one guy at work she had been flirting with before the pandemic started, and as soon as lockdown had begun she chastised herself for playing it cool. They continued chatting online, telling each other that when it was all over they would grab a drink. But then the lockdown dragged on and it became impossible to maintain that flirtation when nothing was going to result from it. It did not help that neither of them were good company anyway, they just regurgitated the same dire news they read on the Internet and only made each other depressed. It soon petered out, and she was left alone again.

If this was going to be the way forward then how was she ever going to meet anyone? How was the human race going to survive?

It seemed unthinkable that this could be an extinction level event, but what if they were all living through the end? There were people out there who clung to this idea and even revelled in it, but Angela only grew more depressed. Everything seemed hopeless and dark thoughts entered her mind, thoughts that she should end it before it became even worse. There seemed to be no hope of climbing out of this slippery hole, and even if a vaccine became available they would be paying off the debt of the pandemic for generations.

Would it really be so bad if an entire generation offed themselves? They were already plagued by anxiety and depression, by lowering fertility rates and increasing financial disparity. It had only been a matter of time until the world reached its breaking point, and the pandemic had accelerated its ascent.

What was more galling was the way faceless, soulless corporations were being treated. Companies went bankrupt because of lost revenues yet were said to be too big to fail. They were bailed out with more money the government said it did not have, a safety net that was not offered to regular people. No, apparently individuals were small enough to fail, and fail they did. They were allowed to fall into poverty and starvation and homelessness. It said something about a society when the people in power were eager to rush to the aid of a corporation instead of an actual person. And yes, they could justify it by saying that they were saving the jobs and thus in turn preventing people from suffering, but why did it have to be mutually exclusive? Why could only corporations be saved and not individuals? Were people worth less because they could not employ others? It seemed cruel that everything was in service of profit.

So far Angela had been able to rely on her income from her job, but rumours had been floating for a while that things were going to change. Without an end in sight businesses were starting to think about winding up. Were there going to be layoffs? Was the company going to cease existing as a whole? It was as unclear as the fate of the pandemic itself and it only added to Angela's stress.

She just wished someone would make a breakthrough, or someone would have some good news to share. Surely people would not be able to continue living like this indefinitely.

There had to be a breaking point somewhere along the way, if they hadn't reached it already. So much was asked of them, so much, and the new dawns did not bring a new hope. It was just an endless mess of sorrow that poisoned her mind and made her groan as she dragged herself to bed. She pulled the sheets over herself and every night she prayed that she would wake up from this terrible nightmare, that somehow she would wake up as a fifteen year old again with all of her best days ahead of her, blessed with ignorance about the true state of the world, yet with the knowledge that she should enjoy every day while it lasted because they were not going to last forever.

She thought of all the boys she would love and all the things she would do, all the money she would spend instead of saving because what was she saving it for?

*

Just when Angela thought that she could not take any more another blow was dealt to her. Amanda called her early in the afternoon, which was strange as she was so consistent with her schedule.

Angela knew that something was wrong immediately. She could tell by the look on her mother's face.

"Mum, what's going on?"

"Well, I don't want to worry you dear, I'm sure it's nothing, it's just that... well... your father had to be taken to hospital."

Angela's heart caught in her throat. "What do you mean he had to be taken to hospital? What with?"

"Ah, well, it seems to be Covid."

The dreaded word stabbed Angela's mind. Colour drained from her face and her knees went weak. Despite the pandemic raging around the world she and her family had remained protected. She and her family had remained shielded. It wasn't supposed to reach them. It was only supposed to hurt other people.

Angela knew how illogical this was, yet it was the way she felt nonetheless.

"What happened?"

He couldn't stop coughing and he was struggling to breathe. They have him on a ventilator now. He's in the best care though, and the nurses are working hard. I'm sure he's going to recover. He's still a healthy man."

All Angela heard when her mother spoke was a woman in denial. Angela swallowed the lump in her throat and tried to keep her voice steady. "What happened Mum? How did he catch it? Did he ever start wearing a mask?"

"I don't think it's really important how he caught it."

"That's a yes then. I told him to be careful! I told him he couldn't just ignore this advice."

"You know what your father is like. Nobody could tell him to do anything."

"And this is the result," Angela shook her head. There was a dispiriting expression on her face. "I thought you were going to talk to him."

"I did talk to him Angela, but I can't force him to wear a mask. Please don't be angry with me. I'm only telling you because I thought you would want to know. It's probably not even going to be that serious. I bet he'll be out of hospital in a couple of days and everything will be back to normal. I've been reading about a lot of people who have caught Covid and it's been like a bad cold, if that."

"Not when they're on ventilators Mum. That's when you have to take it seriously," Angela groaned. She pressed her hands against her forehead, trying to ease away the crown of tension that squeezed her scalp. She felt hollow inside, as though all the best parts of her had been ripped away. Then something snapped inside her.

"I'm going to come up there Mum."

"What? But you can't."

"I don't care about non-essential travel. This is essential to me, damn it. I can't just sit by and wait for you to keep calling me. I can't, not when he's in the hospital. I should be there with you, and with him. I'm your daughter, I shouldn't be so far away," she choked on her words as she spoke, not realizing until this moment how badly she wanted to be nestled in the embrace of her family once again. Life had never been the grand adventure that she had wanted it to be. It had just been one long grind, and she longed for the days when she was taken care of, when all her meals were cooked for her and she didn't have to worry about the bills or the roof over her head, she only had to worry about trivial things like homework. What a paradise it was, and how she had squandered it at the time, wishing with all her might that she could be older.

If only she had known the curse of age. There had been warning signs of course, like the fable of Peter Pan. Time was a hunter though and it had caught her in its grip years ago. It had just taken her until this moment to understand the savagery of its blow. Now she trembled, with tears in her eyes because all she wanted was the thing every scared child craved the most; to go home.

"You can't love, that's what I'm trying to tell you. The hospital has a strict policy about visitors. Nobody is allowed in, not even me. I brought some of his personal effects and had to wait in the car park for someone to come and collect them. If you drove all this way you'd only be told to wait in the car park while some nurse comes out and tells you something you could have figured out over the phone. It's not worth it, especially if anyone catches you driving all this way. You don't want to be fined or anything."

Angela wasn't sure if the rumours about the police fining people for traveling were true. She suspected that it was just a way to deter people from making long trips. However, the risk was not worth taking as she could not afford a fine at this time.

"I just don't know what to do Mum. I feel so far away right now."

"I know love, I know, but like I said I'm sure it's going to be okay. He's got far too many things to do yet, and goodness knows he likes annoying me too much to stop now," she chuckled and once again reassured Angela that things were going to be fine, but Angela did not have as much faith.

The world continued to turn and the news did not get any better. Every day Angela called her mother expecting to hear news that her father had been discharged from hospital, but it never came. He was still on the ventilator, still under care of the nurses, and Angela could do nothing but worry.

There were other things that drew her attention as well, like the sharp knife in the kitchen drawer. It was sleek silver, the handle made of hefty wood. The blade was sharp and was meant to cut through gristle. It could probably make short work of bone as well. One evening she had kept herself busy by sorting out the kitchen drawers when she had come upon it. She held it aloft, drawing it through the air before her eyes, as though she was expecting to pierce the veil of the world and open a doorway to somewhere else, somewhere magical, but of course such a thing lay only in the realms of fantasy.

The grim reality though was that this knife could be a key to another world, only that the lock was her flesh and to unlock that door she would have to pierce her own skin and let blood pour out while her soul slipped into whatever lay beyond this place. If there was something better then it was a risk worth taking, while if there was nothing then she wouldn't care at all anyway, and if there was something worse… well, what could be worse than this?

She had never been the type of person for whom these shadowy thoughts entered her mind before, but after being barraged with awful news for months on end it had all taken its toll and a way out did not seem as unpalatable as it had done before. There was nobody to save her from the terror of her own mind, and nobody to remind her what life was worth living for. Her parents would be upset of course, and this was perhaps the one thing that prevented her from making that final slice across her flesh, but the longer she stared at the blade the more she was tempted, and the more she was tempted the more the idea played on her mind. It was like a seed that grew within her, the roots stretching out through the confines of his mind and touching the very core of her soul, spreading dark, bitter poison throughout.

It was easy to live when possessed with the distractions of the world, when she had a job to exhaust herself and TV shows to blunt her senses. The pandemic had given her nothing but time, time to think and wonder and worry, time to stare at the unmasked face of the world and see it in all its gaudy horror. She had read somewhere that if the mind had been allowed to fester for too long then it would eventually go insane, driving itself mad with the absurd reality that nothing really mattered at all, that life was an existential horror and the only way to get through it was to turn away from the truth, to gorge on drugs like love, but once seen this could not be unseen, and how was she ever going to break free of this curse?

There were hours when she would sit there with the knife resting against her wrists, the point so close to cutting that all it needed was a little pressure and the process could begin.

Coward.

She spat the word in her own mind. She was so close, so close to breaking free from this vile cocoon, so close to liberating herself from this world without hope.

How much more could she take?

The truth turned out to be not much at all.

But still, she did not take that final strike. Still, she did not make herself bleed. Still, she remained, one kernel of hope existing in the back of her mind, perhaps a remnant of the child she used to be, perhaps just a mindless shred of innocence she had managed to cling onto when the world had crumbled apart. Either way it was there, and it was this that prevented her from giving up entirely.

This, and her ties to her mother.

Perhaps that was the only thing holding the world together now, a web of dependence from parents to children, acting like a safety net to prevent people from falling away. It wasn't fool proof of course, but it had served to catch her.

But then something else happened.

It was late at night. After another long session of doomscrolling Angela had finally fallen asleep. Her tousled hair was mussed and greasy, for her efforts at washing herself had grown less frequent, not seeing the need when it wasn't for the benefit of anyone else, and she was blind to her own odour. Her mouth hung open and drool trickled down one cheek. She was startled awake by the buzzing phone, the vibrations first becoming a part of her dream, before coaxing her back into reality. At first, she was not aware of the time and so did not think anything of her mother calling her, but she did when she heard Amanda's frail voice, a voice that sounded old and wounded.

And then Angela knew that something dire had happened. Bad news only ever came at night, riding on the wings of a raven. It struck like an assassin's dagger.

"He's dead," Amanda choked.

Angela stared into space, holding the phone limply. It wasn't supposed to be this way. The Covid deaths had been statistics, but now they had become a personal tragedy.

"Mum…"

"I couldn't even see him, Angela! I wanted to… but they told me it was too dangerous. They told me it wasn't safe. He had to die alone Angela. He had to die without me there to say goodbye and I… I just want him back. I just want one last moment with him. It's not fair. It's not fair."

Angela could not do anything but agree with her mother. It wasn't fair at all. And now she would have no chance to see her father again. There would not be another argument, another chance for him to lecture her about a mistake she had made, nor another of his silly jokes or affectionate hugs or long-winded diatribes about the latest sporting event. It was all just gone, and it wasn't that she immediately mourned the loss of him, because it still hadn't sunk in yet that he was really gone; it was more that she mourned the things that would never happen again. It was another piece of the world that Covid had stripped away. Slowly and surely all the things she was looking forward to doing again were being picked off one by one, leaving her with nothing.

And now she was alone from her mother when her mother needed her the most. She was locked away from her family.

"Mum… I'm coming to see you."

"No love, no I'm alright, really. I don't want you getting in trouble. I have the neighbours and they're all there for me. We're there for each other. You should take care of yourself. I'm sure that this will all be over soon and we'll be able to see each other again."

"I don't know that this is ending any time soon Mum. I think we're going to have to get used to living like this for a long time. And I'm not sure I can do it anymore. I should have been there to see him. I should have been there and I couldn't because of this stupid lockdown and these stupid rules."

"You're always the one saying that we should be following the rules," Amanda said, a weak laugh breaking through the sorrowful tones.

"When I thought they would make a difference, yes, but what are they doing at the moment? They're only making things worse for people. People are still dying, people are still suffering, and we don't even have the comfort blanket of our family to count on. I hate to think of the way he felt in that hospital, alone. Did he know that I loved him?"

"Of course he knew," Amanda said, but Angela wasn't so sure.

"I can't remember the last time I told him. I can't remember…" she trailed away and then the tears came. They poured sweet and clear and hot, trickling down her cheeks and landing in her lap. Her mother cried as well. They were so far apart, yet they were connected in this union of sorrow. Eventually Amanda had to leave and Angela was plunged into silent darkness, the shroud of the world falling over her like a cloak. She thought about getting the knife again, but knew she could not. Her mother was already dealing with one loss. Angela wasn't going to be another.

Yet she knew that something had to change. This could not be allowed to continue. She was being deprived of everything that made life worth living, and when that happened what was left? She couldn't be happy here. She had to make a change. She had to find some way to fight through the pandemic because she was going to die one way or another. If her physical body didn't perish then her soul would, and she could feel that it was on its way there. She hadn't caught Covid, but she was still a victim of it. This virus took many forms. It didn't just ravage the lungs, it also leeched away life and made it impossible for happiness to thrive.

No more.

No. More.

*

The following few days were a blaze of tears. Angela stuffed her clothes into a bag and flung them into a car. She had had enough of her surroundings. She had lost too much and had put up with too much. She had reached her limits and now it was time to face them. She threw as many of her belongings as she could into the car and then slammed the door to her flat.

She wasn't sure if she was ever going to return.

She drove past the tennis courts and took a lingering glance. The grass was long and the place looked abandoned. It didn't seem as if it was ever going to reach its heyday again, and she had grown tired of waiting for it to open once again. Even if it did it would not be the same. Too much time had passed. The people would no longer be the same, and she would not be able to play to the same standard. Things would never go back to the way they were, no matter how much she hoped for it to be. How would she even be able to justify the cost when the price of everything was going to rise?

She pressed her foot on the accelerator and left everything behind. The tennis court and the other familiar sights receded into the background as she drove away from the place that had been her home for the last number of years, but it had never truly won a place in her heart. It had never called her like the north called her.

The roads were barren. She gripped the steering wheel tightly as she tried to distract herself with music, but there was always at least one song that reminded her of her father, and she fell into sadness again. She blinked away her blurred vision and was grateful for the lack of traffic as it meant she was less likely to crash.

The fields of England slipped past her as she ascended north, quiet and solemn, as though they were mourning too. The cities remained dark and silent where once they had buzzed with life and bright lights. There were moments when she became worried that the police would pull her over for questioning and send her back to London. She wasn't a government official so it was unlikely that they would take pity on her, but she didn't see herself as violating the rules. She was returning home. She wasn't going to see anyone because she didn't have anyone to see. She didn't have Covid, and she wasn't going to pose a danger to anyone.

And even if she had, well, that hadn't made a difference to her father.

She arrived at the church where the funeral was being held. The scant makeup she wore was already running, leaving black streaks trailing down her cheeks. The church was hollow, its silence brooding and heavy.

"Where is everyone?" Angela asked.

"Restrictions," Amanda said. It was her and a few other relatives, a small gathering for a man who was so much larger than life, and deserved so much more than this. Covid was still taking. Angela went to hug her mother, but Amanda stepped back.

"I'm not sure we should," she said in a hushed whisper, casting a wary glance around at the other guests. There were still rules in place about close contact. People had to grieve alone. Angela clenched her fists and nodded, embracing all the pain that throbbed inside her.

"I'm glad you're here love. He would be too," Amanda said.

"I just wish I had been here sooner."

"You're here when it matters. He knew why you couldn't be here. It wasn't your fault. You were following the rules. You were doing what you were supposed to be doing,"

Amanda said, but Angela felt like that was scant consolation when it didn't make much different. Would things have been any worse if she had gone into hospital to say goodbye to her father? Would any lives have been saved, any deaths prevented? When nothing she did mattered, did it really matter what she did?

They walked into the chapel and Angela had to endure the most painful funeral. She was reminded of the man her father had been, and shared memories that she had of him as well, but the church should have been packed to the rafters with his old schoolmates, his work colleagues, and the people from the bowling club he frequented. This was not a true representation of his life at all, and if this was what his funeral was going to be like then she dreaded to know what her own was going to be.

There would only be the birds tweeting their soulful song, utterly oblivious to the way the world was being destroyed.

Angela cried a river that day. It was as though all the rage and the emotions that had been building up since the beginning of the pandemic were finally being released and they flowed out of her in a torrent, hot and harsh, leaving deathly ash within her, making her feel empty.

She had to nod to the other relatives who had attended, unable to hug them. Angela had never liked forced displays of affection, but now when they were taken away from her she craved them badly. How she wished that things had been different.

They didn't even have a wake. It was such a hollow celebration for a man who had always been so vital, and a hollow death as well. She wasn't sure that any death had any grand meaning, but this one was just empty. It was almost as though it hadn't happened at all. The world was still lost in its despair and he now became one more number added to the sum of the Covid victims, a number used to herald the end of modern society, a number used as weapons by both sides of the debate, those who urged for a vaccine and those who claimed that things weren't as bad as the media was making out.

Well Angela knew that things were just that bad because she had been touched by Covid, but she did not have the energy to be angry with it anymore. Nothing she did made the slightest bit of difference, so what was the point in being upset with it? She could no more be upset at this than she could be at an avalanche that was submerging her, or a tide that was drowning her. It had taken everything she had and she had no more to give. She was exhausted, drained, and devoid of anything resembling hope.

When she returned home the first thing she did as soon as the door was shut was fall into Amanda's arms. Until that point she hadn't known how much she needed that hug. The simple embrace took away all of her anguish and her misery. It gave her strength and courage, and she draped herself against her mother for what seemed like an eternity. She shuddered with sorrow.

"I can't do it anymore Mum. I just can't do it."

"I know sweetie, none of us can."

"It's not right. He shouldn't have had a funeral like that."

"I know, but we'll give him a proper send off when people are allowed to gather properly again. I've already spoken to a lot of his friends and they've all agreed to come."

"But what if it's never over Mum? What if this never ends? There's no way out. It's like we've all walked into a tunnel and none of us can see the exit. We keep being told that there's going to be one, but they keep moving the goalposts. I just don't see a way where we can get through to the other side of this. This is it. This is our lives now."

"There's always a way to make things better Angela, always. We just need to be strong and wait this out. That's what your father would have wanted."

"But I'm not strong enough. I've been waiting all this time and I can't wait anymore. I just want to give up. I want to let it all go," she whimpered.

Amanda leaned back and looked at her properly. Their eyes met and Amanda sighed, shaking her head.

"This has been really tough on you, hasn't it?"

Angela nodded.

"Look, stay here a while. There's no need for you to go back to London, is there? This is your home. This is where you belong. Go and get yourself cleaned up and I'll make you some food. You're safe here and things are going to be alright again. I'll take care of you."

Angela could not have argued even if she had wanted to, for she lacked the strength. She dragged herself upstairs, the paths of this house imprinted in her blood. Her feet shuffled across the floor as she went into the bathroom. She turned on the shower. The room quickly filled up with steam and the water screamed as it left the showerhead. Angela stepped in and surrendered herself to the hard, biting water. It swept over her skin, cleansing her of the grime and sweat that had built up over her flesh. She held her face under it and lost herself to the sound of bubbles and the scent of coconut body wash, wanting to stay in there forever because it was better than what awaited outside. She allowed herself to wallow in the warmth of the shower before she turned it off and walked through the steamy haze. She grabbed a soft towel. She smiled, for this was like staying in a hotel. She held it around her body and wiped herself dry. With every sweep she felt as though she was brushing away one more bit of sadness.

When she opened the door, she realized that Amanda had left her some clean clothes. She pulled on the long nightie and headed downstairs, where a plate of cheese and toast was cooking. It was such a simple meal, and yet somehow in all her years of living alone Angela had not been able to perfectly copy the recipe. All it took was one bite for the flavour to swim in her mouth and bring back a wave of nostalgia. She let out a small moan of satisfaction.

"Nobody can make this like you can Mum," she said.

"Sometimes it's just the simple things in life that are the most important," Amanda said, stroking Angela's hair before she took a seat at the table as well. "Do you feel better now?"

"I guess so. I just miss him, and I hate how it all happened, and I just want this pandemic to be over. It feels like we're all just having to miss out on the moments that matter. This is our life. It's the only one we have, and it's all just moving by in a blur. I don't know what else we're supposed to do. I don't know how we're supposed to get through it."

"Just one day at a time. That's what your father said. He didn't have much patience for it at all. I wish he had been more cautious though."

"Me too. It's not even worth being angry with him now though. It's not going to change anything."

"I'll be angry enough for the both of us," Amanda said. She reached out and clasped Angela's hand. "It'll be okay Angela, I promise. I know it might not seem like it at the moment, but as long as we're alive then it's all okay."

Angela looked into her mother's deep blue eyes and felt ashamed. She vowed never to tell Amanda how close she had come to throwing away her own life, and how that urge was still deep inside her somewhere. It was only her love and concern for Amanda that prevented her from going through with it.

"So what are you going to do Angela? Are you going to stay here, or are you going to go back to London?" Amanda asked.

Angela had made up her mind before she left. "I want to stay here Mum. This is my home," she said weakly.

"You can stay here for as long as you like. It'll be nice to have you around again, especially with your father home. I was beginning to go stir crazy by myself."

Angela smirked because she knew how that felt. It had happened to her after all. Perhaps being at home with Amanda again would restore some of the sanity that she had lost. She was already feeling much better for someone to take care of her, and maybe that was the only way to really make it through this pandemic with your hope and your heart intact; to have someone looking after you. Life was too short to be lonely, and Angela did not want to have to cope by herself again.

If retreating home was going to give her that confidence, then so be it.

After eating she went into her room, which was indeed as her mother had left it. She set her bag down and began to unpack, thinking about how her life was moving in reverse. The pandemic was still out there, suffocating the world, and she would probably be jobless soon. The future was bleak, and the fact that a young woman was returning home was not a sign of a prosperous society, but Angela could not make it through life by herself. She needed to feel the comfort of home, to be young again and rely on her parents. She liked knowing there was always going to be a meal on the table, and that the house was always going to be warm.

But deep inside there was a malaise that would never go. The pandemic had changed the world, and it had changed her. She was colder inside now, and sharper. She was jaded and could not see any way for her life to get better now. She would be stuck at home for the foreseeable future, living life in reverse. But this is what life in the pandemic was like, robbing people of their lives and their freedoms, and with the treacherous future that lay ahead of everyone it was not as though she was going to find her feet again.

This was where she had been born and had grown up, and it was likely where she was going to die as well.

The pandemic had robbed a generation of their ambition and hope, and the echoes of this were going to ripple through the future. Angela was tired of fighting. The only thing she could do was give up. The pandemic had won, but at least she had found her safe place. She would never leave it again.

An Unpleasant Family

Chapter One

Detective Chief Inspector Ben Edwards strode through Baywood police station, his heavy hand thumping against the door. Constable Sunita Khan was sitting at the reception desk, her black hair tied back into a tight ponytail. There was a strained look on her face.

"I'm really sorry for disturbing you boss," she said in an apologetic tone. Ben exhaled as he placed his hand on the desk.

"Don't worry about it. He really says he won't speak to anyone else?"

"Yeah, says he wants to share something with an old friend."

Ben grunted a laugh and rapped his fingers on the desk. "We were friends? That's news to me. Still, I guess I can't pass up the opportunity. I'll see what he has to say. How long has he been waiting for?"

"About half an hour now," Sunita said, turning around to look at the clock behind her. Ben glanced up at it as well. He pressed his lips together and nodded curtly.

"Then he can wait a little bit longer."

Sunita flashed a mischievous grin. Ben winked at her and then turned, walking through the doors that led to the interview rooms. He passed them all and instead went to the break room, where the coffee machine was located. He poured the thick liquid into his mug and took a sip, sighing as the caffeine jolted through him. The slender frame of Mark Thatcher appeared shortly after this. He too poured a mug of coffee.

"I hear we have a special guest in the nick," Mark said, pushing his spectacles up the bridge of his nose with one finger.

"Oh yeah, I'm going to make sure to give him the VIP treatment."

"What do you think he wants?"

"I have no idea. Maybe after all these years he's found religion and he's going to change his ways," Ben said. Both men laughed.

"Think there's trouble?"

"There's always trouble where the McKay's are concerned. Heard that even his son is getting in on the action now," Ben exhaled sharply and shook his head. "At some point you'd think the cycle would be broken. Haven't they learned their lesson by now?"

"What lesson? They've been in and out of prison, but they keep reoffending. I heard the old git got a fine for driving without paying his car tax. It's in their blood to dodge the law. Some people are just beyond help," Mark took a long sip of his coffee. The slurping sound made Ben wince. Mark might as well have scraped his fingernails down a chalkboard.

"That's not very progressive of you. Remember we're supposed to give people the chance to change, no matter how many times they prove us wrong," Ben rolled his eyes. Mark chortled.

"The world has gone mad. Sometimes I wonder why we bother to try and hold it together."

"If we don't then who will?" Ben replied rhetorically. Mark arched his eyebrows and gave a helpless nod. It did indeed seem sometimes that they were fighting a losing battle, the war of attrition getting the better of them. Ben had entered the police force as a wide-eyed young man, eager to make the world a better place and protect the innocent. It hadn't been exactly like that though. Over the years he had seen prisoners move through the revolving doors of prisons, and how many criminals did not serve the time that they should have. He knew he was becoming jaded, and yet had no idea how to stop it.

What was the point of upholding the law when so many people knew how to bend it? There were people out there who should have been locked up yet were allowed to roam free because they had simply paid a fine. The victims had to live with the terror and the fear. That was the true-life sentence, and there was no escape from it. During his career Ben had only been certain of one thing; the world was backwards.

And yet he was still banging his head against the wall, because this was the only thing he could imagine doing. He'd thought about hanging up his badge many times, but he knew he would feel powerless. This job was an addiction, but there was no support group for him.

"You want any help in there?" Mark asked.

Ben took another long gulp of coffee and then poured the rest down the sink. The stain faded quickly, although there was always a shadow left.

"Not right now. I'll see what he has to say. If you hear a lot of kerfuffle then maybe come on in," Ben patted Mark on the shoulder as he walked out of the break room. He scratched his chin as he walked towards the interview room, pausing outside the door as he composed himself. He had seen Alfie McKay far more often than he ever wanted. That was the problem with this job; he was forced to associate with criminals. He saw them more often than his own friends.

Then he paused.

What friends?

A grim thought began to seep through his mind, but he shook it away with a curt nod. It would not do to think of such things now. He pushed open the door. Alfie was pacing towards the rear of the room and he glared at Ben as the Inspector entered.

"Where the fuck have you been?" he spat.

Ben sighed. It had started just the way he thought it would. "If there's one thing I've admired about you over the years Alfie it's your way with words. I'm so glad your mother taught you manners."

"What are you saying about my Mum?" Alfie turned and slammed his hands onto the small table. Ben had learned a long time ago to not be threatened by this type of histrionics. He sank into the seat and leaned back, sighing wearily. He and Alfie were of a similar build; both of them were stocky, although he was slightly trimmer than Alfie. They were the same age, for they had gone to school together. Approaching forty now, Alfie's body was reaching that middle age spread, his belly rounded by alcohol and his face flushed crimson. His hair had receded dramatically, so that now his head resembled a cue ball. He was still a large man though. Ben always remembered him being large, even at school. He had matured physically far soon than the other boys in the class and had used this to his advantage.

That advantage had slipped over the years though.

"What do you want Alfie? Is this just a social call?"

"No, it's not a fucking social call. Do you think I want to come here? This place makes my skin crawl, what with being around all you uniformed twats," Alfie said.

Ben opened his mouth and shook his head. He then slapped his thighs and rose from the chair, turning towards the door. "Right, if you're going to speak like that then I don't have any interest in listening to what you have to say. Why don't you just go back to whatever hole you crawled out of Alfie. I have better things to do with my time."

His hands curled around the handle of the door when Alfie spoke again.

"Wait." This time Ben heard something in Alfie's voice that he had never heard before. It was pitiful desperation. Every instinct in Ben's body told him to leave Alfie to whatever hell he had devised for himself, every instinct but one. There was still that core part of him that made him a good police officer, the part that had not been entirely eroded away.

Inwardly he cursed himself for what he was about to do, but he turned and sank back to the table. Alfie seemed to calm down as he too took a seat.

"If we're going to do this Alfie then there needs to be some ground rules. You're not going to speak to me like that again. This is my turf, alright? I'm the big dog around here and you're going to treat me with respect," Ben wagged a finger in front of him and then pointed it to the table. Alfie wore a sour look, but he nodded in agreement.

"I'm just on edge, that's all," Alfie said.

"So why don't you tell me what's going on. Do you have information about a crime for me?"

"I'm no snitch," Alfie jerked back, his voice rising sharply. Ben arched his eyebrows and shifted in his seat, making out like he was going to leave again. Alfie's posture immediately softened. He lowered his voice and held out his hands in front of him, spreading his fingers to gesture that he was going to keep things under control.

"I'm sorry, I'm just on edge," Alfie said. Ben tilted his head, unsure if he had actually just

66

heard what he thought he just heard. Alfie McKay did not apologise to anyone. In fact, it might well have been the McKay family motto. Ben bit his tongue however, not allowing the snide comment to sneak past his lips because that would only exacerbate the situation.

"It's about Joe," Alfie continued. "He's missing."

"What do you mean missing? Did he run away?"

"No, he didn't run away. What would he want to run away for? I've given him everything he could have wanted!"

"I'm just trying to ascertain the nature of this Alfie. There's no need to take it personally," Ben said in a calm tone.

"Yeah, well, it's hard not to take things personal when your son goes missing. I just… I just want him back, alright? He's the only thing I've got in this world."

It was as though Alfie transformed before Ben's eyes. Instead of being the hardened criminal, the schoolyard bully, the man hewn in the image of his father, Alfie was a pitiful, scared man who was worried for his son. For all that Ben despised the man and what he represented, the law was there for him as well. Some might have said that this was justice for all the misery that Alfie had doled out through the years, but Ben did not serve karma. He served the laws of the country, and it meant he had to try and help Alfie.

"Alright Alfie. Let me get someone in here and we'll get the information down. Ben opened the door and called out for Sunita to join them. Her flat shoes skipped along the floor as she hurried from behind the reception desk to join them. Alfie seemed annoyed that someone else was being involved, but he did not complain.

"Okay then Alfie, tell me what's been going on? When did you last see Joe?"

Alfie sniffed and clasped his hands together. He gazed towards the table, and his voice trembled. "Three days ago. He said he was going out with mates. Sometimes he stayed round their house. I liked to give him his freedom, you know, he's a young man and he deserves to be out in the world without his Dad breathing down his neck, but last night we were supposed to go to the match. It was a cup game, and Joe loves the cup, especially when we have a good chance of going through. Thought he would be back, but he wasn't. Tried phoning around his mates, but they all said they thought he had come home. It's not like him to stay away. I asked them if he was with a bird, but they all laughed. I don't know what was so funny, but I guess there goes that theory. Thought the only thing that he would miss the footy for was a woman, so if he's not with one of them then were could he have gone? He's not answering his phone, he's not been seen down the local. It's like he's just disappeared off the face of the earth and I can't… I can't bear to think of what might have happened to him," Alfie's voice cracked again. Ben glanced towards Sunita, who was rapidly writing down all the information. Alfie was perhaps the last person who deserved sympathy, and yet Ben couldn't help feeling it anyway.

"It's been three days, so we can officially declare him missing. I'm going to need the name of his friends so that we can contact them."

"But I've already spoken to them. You think they would lie to me?"

"I don't know what to think, but I know that I need to follow every lead. I will do my best to find him Alfie."

"I know you will. That's why I asked for you specifically. We might be on opposite sides now, but at one point we were on the same team. I hope you don't forget that," Alfie's eyes flicked up and met Ben's in a level gaze.

"I'm a copper Alfie. Past loyalties don't come into it. I do my job because it's the right thing to do. I help people who need it, and if Joe needs it then I'll help him too," Ben replied tersely.

"Yeah, well, just make sure you don't forget where you came from. Find my boy."

Ben nodded and then he and Sunita took down all the pertinent information about Joe and his associates. Then Alfie left, and Ben breathed a huge sigh of relief.

"What did he mean when he said you and he were on the same team once?" Sunita asked.

"It was another life, a life before all this. We played on the same rugby team. I guess he thinks that gives us some extra sense of comradeship."

"Does it?"

Ben smirked. "I didn't like him then and I don't like him now, and I'm sure the feeling is mutual. But if his son is in trouble then we need to find out why. Start collating all the information. Let's try to track his phone first, and I'll see who he spoke to last. Knowing the McKay family, he's just under some rock somewhere. I wouldn't be surprised if this is all a waste of time." However, there was a part of Ben that knew it might not be a waste at all. People disappeared from the world all the time, and often it's because they were taken against their will. But if Joe had died then Ben needed to prepare for what was next, because then Alfie would be unhinged.

Chapter Two

Alfie pushed against the faded paintwork of the door and ignored the broken armchair in the front garden. The stained wallpaper carried with it a musty smell, and damp stained the ceiling. He walked into the lounge where his father, Cyril, was sitting with a blanket over his knees. Horse racing was on the TV, and Cyril's attention was firmly focused on the race, up until the horse he backed faltered and receded into the back of the racing pack.

"Bunch of useless bastards," he said, scrunching up his betting slip and tossing it on the floor.

"You should really put that in the bin," Alfie said. Cyril swung his head around and stared at him with beady eyes.

"What are you saying to me? You sound like your mother."

"Yeah, well, if she were here maybe this place would be cleaner."

"That's woman's work. You should have kept a hold of your wife then we wouldn't have this problem."

"She was never my wife," Alfie said bitterly.

"Oh yes, well, that always was your problem Alfie. You never could seal the deal."

Alfie glared at his father and tried to ignore the cackling laugh that filled the room. He huffed as he bent down and picked up the rubbish. "I went to the station today," he said, his words heavy.

"Getting a train are you?"

"No. I got a copper."

The laughter ceased immediately. Cyril stared at Alfie as though he had just uttered a curse. "What the hell do you think you're doing boy? You actually went to them?"

"Of course I did! I can't find Joe anywhere."

"Then you're not looking hard enough." Cyril waved a dismissive hand in the air. "He's probably just disappeared in a girl's tits for a few days, and more power to him for that. It's about time the men in this family showed some balls. It skipped a generation with you. I remember when I was your age I had a different girl every week. If it wasn't for my body failing me then I still would now."

Alfie swallowed a lump in his throat as he braced himself against the ugly image.

"All his friends say he's not with a bird. I'm worried about him. I know he's tough, but the world is a dangerous place. What if he's in danger?"

"Then you should do a better job of protecting him. We don't need no coppers meddling in our affairs. You can't trust them as far as you can throw them. Bunch of swots, the lot of them. If you want to find Joe then you get your ear to the ground and you knock some heads together. That's the way we used to do it in the old days."

"I'm going to Dad, but I thought it couldn't hurt to get the coppers on the case as well. They might be able to stir something up. And they have all this technology they can use nowadays to track people as well."

Cyril was not convinced though. He shook his head and waved his hand through the air again. "You know this is all your fault. You should have taught him better. I tried with you, I really did, but you just couldn't take anything in."

Alfie pressed his lips tightly together. "It's not all my fault Dad. Maybe if you hadn't gambled away all your money then we wouldn't have to live in this dump."

Cyril narrowed his eyes. "If you wanted out you could have gotten out a long time ago. Don't blame me for the fact that you haven't made a success of yourself," he barked.

Alfie shook his head. There was no winning with the old man. He turned on his heels and walked away. Hopefully Cyril would be asleep by the time he got back. There was an old adage that crime didn't pay, and as Alfie had grown older he had seen the truth of that. He used to think his dad was the grandest man to ever have lived for he always flashed his gold chains and watches, dressed in the finest clothes, and was the talk of the town as he always got a round in. But over the years Alfie had come to learn that this had all been an image fuelled by Cyril's ill-gotten gains, and he kept this appearance going even when he should have been more sensible. If Cyril had been more prudent with his money then

Alfie might have had a better chance at life, but Cyril let it all slip through his fingers, preferring to live fast and die slowly.

And now Alfie was trapped in the same life. He did a deal here, got some cash out of hand there, but it wasn't anything to be proud of. He'd been in and out of jail for petty crimes, but it was the only life he had ever known. He'd even tried to get a job, but had been sacked on the first day for punching his boss.

He just wasn't made out for the working life, which was ironic considering he was a part of the working class. But that was just one thing that had never made much sense to Alfie. He often felt at odds with the world, and it seemed as though other people knew the rules to a game they were all playing. It's one of the reasons why he hated school. He knew the other kids and the teachers were laughing at him because the words never made sense to him, always jumbled up as though they were dancing before his eyes. The only way he could get respect was to earn it by being the strongest, so he did. He took it from them and made sure that they always knew there was no messing with him. Even the teachers had been afraid of him towards the end of his tenure at school, he remembered one of them pitying the world because Alfie was going to be unleashed upon it, as though he was some animal released from the zoo.

The only thing he had ever enjoyed and been good at in school was sports, but a career in that field had been blighted by his love of alcohol and greasy food. It had always felt as though the world was against him, and this feeling had never changed as the years passed by.

Even now, as he walked along the estate and gazed up at the azure sky he knew there were people out there enjoying this beautiful day. Not him though. The days and the nights were things to be endured and toughened out, the world a measure of harsh discipline that was always dealt out towards him, and he was never given any respite. He had tried to make things easier on Joe, but that had been hard too. Alfie had never learned how to be a good parent. There had never been anyone to show him a better way.

He passed gardens where kids were playing. Their laughter was the sweetest sound he had ever heard, for it had not been made cynical by the passage of time. These kids would become jaded in their own time, falling into the same of cycles that plagued everyone else. It was impossible to escape this world. There were people out there who lived in fancy houses and worked in skyscrapers, but they might as well have been aliens to Alfie.

He had been walking for the better part of an hour when he began skulking through the quiet streets of the suburbs. The houses here had neatly kept gardens and there was barely a stone out of place. He kicked a pebble along the path, groaning in dismay when it skidded off the kerb and disappeared down the drain. He dug his hands in his pockets and sighed as he approached a small bungalow. He pursed his lips and breathed to calm himself as he walked up the path to the door, and then he pressed the doorbell. It had a melodic chime that soared through the air, and then the door opened, but only a crack.

Rachel looked at him with her pink lips and blue eyes, always dolled up as though she was going to star in a movie. She was still the most beautiful thing he had ever seen though, and he was always plagued by regret whenever they saw each other.

"What do you want Alfie? You know you're not supposed to be here. If Gary finds out that you're around-"

"What's he going to do? Run away and call the coppers on me again? I'll gladly spend another night in the nick if I get to bloody his nose. I don't know how you can cope living with him. He'd bore my tits off," Alfie rolled his eyes, while Rachel scowled.

"He's a good man, a far better man than you could ever hope to be. Do you think you could have given me this house? This life? He takes care of me Alfie. That's all a woman wants in the end."

"I think a woman like you wants more than that," Alfie said, his voice dropping an octave. A shimmer of desire flashed across Rachel's eyes. "Just like you wanted more when we were kids. Remember the way you used to put a pillow over your mouth so that your parents wouldn't hear you moaning?"

Rachel glared at him. "That was another life. I'm a different woman now."

"I bet Gary doesn't even know how to touch you," Alfie said. By the look on her face he had clearly touched a nerve. She clung to the door and used it as a shield. He wondered what would have happened if he had burst in and taken her upstairs and reminded her of what he could do better than Gary. The furious, passionate energy burned through his body, but he knew it would only lead to trouble. She would enjoy it, but then she'd blame him and he still wouldn't end up with her because ultimately she was right; he couldn't give her this house or the life that Gary had. She chose comfort over love.

"You'd better tell me what you're doing here Alfie before something happens that we're both going to regret."

Alfie's lip curled. She knew just how to get under his skin, and how to tempt him with forbidden flesh. He wasn't as young as he used to be and he certainly wasn't as trim, but there was still a lot of tension between them. That tension changed though as he revealed why he was there.

"It's about Joe. Have you seen him over the last few days?"

"No, he's been with you. Why?"

"Because I haven't seen him either. I'm worried he's gone missing."

Rachel opened the door more widely as she heard this, her face wearing an expression of shock. "What do you mean he's missing? Where has he gone? What have you done to him?"

"I haven't done anything," Alfie scowled, wondering how everything always seemed to be his fault.

"You know that he's sensitive Alfie. You can't just have a go at him all the time. I bet it's your bloody father again putting ideas into his head, isn't it? I knew I should have tried harder to keep him away from you," Rachel rolled her eyes.

"He's my son Rachel. You can't do that," Alfie said. "I'm on the case anyway. I just wanted to see if you had heard from him."

"No, I haven't. And what do you mean you're on the case? Are you a copper now?" Rachel laughed.

Alfie turned crimson, but he bit his tongue. "No, I'm not, but I have asked them for help."

"Oh right, like they're going to help you. After all the trouble you've caused them over the years? Why on earth would they do that?"

"I have a…" Alfie was about to say 'friend', but he realized that was perhaps being a tad too generous. "I know someone there. Used to play rugby with him. He'll do me a solid."

"Oh, friends in high places. Shame you couldn't have used a contact like that to get out of trouble before."

"Well, he's the straight shooter kind of guy. He doesn't bend the rules. But he's going to find Joe, and I'm going to find him as well, no matter what. Nothing is going to stop me."

"Well, you'd better, because if you've lost my son then there's going to be hell to pay Alfie McKay. You've made a mess of your own life, you'd better not make a mess of his as well. He deserved better than having you as a father."

Alfie bore the brunt of the words and did not retaliate. He turned around silently and allowed the anger to simmer inside him. His hands clenched into tight balls and he grinded his teeth so tightly they almost shattered.

Chapter Three

Ben stood upon muddy grass, looking down at the lake. The diving team were sifting through the water, casting their nets in the hope of fishing out the phone. The breeze was cold, the sky a cool shade of blue, and the world quiet around him. The scent of grass was refreshing, a welcome change from the grimy stench of the city.

"You think we'll find anything here?" Sunita asked. She was an able deputy, quick witted, intelligent, and determined. Ben had assigned her to help him.

"I hope we do. This is where the trail ends after all. It might be that we find more than a phone."

"Like a body?"

"Exactly. And then we just have to find a killer."

"It's never a dull day…" Sunita said, shifting her weight between her feet.

"You would have thought people would have better things to do than kill other people. With all the possibilities available in the world there are still people who want to hurt others. It really does boggle my mind."

"I'd have thought you'd have gained a better understanding of the criminal mind given how many years you've served, boss," Sunita said with a grin. Ben wondered if she was taking a jab at his age. The joke was on her, because nobody escaped the passage of time.

"I think not understanding them is the main reason why I've been able to do this job for as long as I have. If I started thinking like them… I worry that it would be a slippery slope."

"Maybe he just wanted a fresh start. Can't imagine it was a happy life with Alfie as his Dad."

"No, these things tend to be passed down through the generations. Alfie never had a good time of it either."

"No?"

Ben shook his head. "His Dad is Cyril McKay, a real character. Used to be notorious for cracking safes. It was said that once he broke into every bank in the region and that he was Britain's richest criminal."

"What happened to him?"

"He got arrogant. Eventually the locksmiths created more advanced locks and new security systems came into play. I always got the impression that Cyril thought he could keep robbing banks all his life, as though they would just let him waltz in and bankroll his future. He spent like there was no tomorrow, and eventually he had nothing left."

"So, all of that glitz and glamor was for nothing."

"Exactly. Still, in his heyday he was a big deal, and I'm sure he thinks that those days were worth it. He just never cared too much for his son."

"Makes you wonder how different the world would be if parents loved their children."

Ben snorted and nodded. "I don't think it would be the worst thing in the world for a parenting license to be introduced, although I have no idea how the hell anyone would go about policing it."

"I'm sure they would find a way," Sunita replied. It was then that one of the diving team emerged from the water and waved their hand in the air. They were clad in diving gear so as not to contaminate any of the evidence. Ben and Sunita rushed down to the edge of the lake as the diver presented his findings. It was a slim phone, modern. The screen was cracked. Water seeped out of it. Ben tried to turn it on anyway, but of course there was no luck.

"Get this back to the lab and see if you can get anything off the drive. Any scrap of data is going to be important. Everyone else keep diving. It's likely that this is Joe's phone, but we can't be sure, and we won't know unless we get information off of it. The work isn't done yet," he yelled, clapping his hands to encourage them even though the work was hard going. He and Sunita had somewhere else to be though.

*

They pulled up outside a dilapidated, brooding house. Ben beat his fist upon the door and bellowed his name, while he got his badge out to show whoever was opening the door. He heard a patter of footsteps and then a back door opening. He cursed under his breath.

86

"Watch this door. Make sure nobody comes out. I'll be right back," he said.

He ran alongside the house down a narrow alley and kicked the back gate down. Wood splintered as he smashed through like a charging bull. He had lost a yard of pace, but he was still in good shape and sprinted forward. As he crashed through to the garden he saw legs dangling over the garden wall. Blood pumped through his body and he gnashed his teeth as he followed the path, and ended up having to do a hurdle dash through other gardens. Dogs barked and cats screeched, but he ignored them all as he vaulted the fences in pursuit of his quarry. The younger man was all limbs, flailing about as he tried to escape. He twisted his neck back at one point and seemed shocked that Ben was keeping pace with him. He was quickly running out of gardens, so veered to the right. Ben followed. The ground sloped down and led to a long road which turned to the left. Ben was afraid that if this boy escaped from his sight then he would find a way to disappear. Ben found another gear and increased his speed, yelling at the top of his lungs for the boy to stop running.

Inquisitive people peered out of their windows and doors, eager to see what was occurring. Ben ignored them all. The panicked boy did indeed go to the left and tried to climb up a brick wall to get into a garden, but this one was too high and he was unable to access the garden with a smooth movement. When Ben found him, his legs were scrabbling against the bricks trying to throw himself over the wall. Ben put both his hands on his legs and yanked him down. The boy yelped as he plummeted down and landed on the concrete pavement, his teeth chattering and his bones juddering. Ben was panting heavily. His cheeks were red and his forehead glistened with sweat.

The boy's name was Davey. He cowered before Ben.

"Now why are you running away from me?" Ben said, flashing his badge.

"You can't arrest me! I haven't done anything wrong!" he cried. Ben grimaced.

"I never said anything about arresting you. But a guilty conscience will serve you well in life. Keep listening to it and maybe it'll keep you out of trouble, at least after today," he said, reaching down to grab Davey by the scruff of the neck. Davey began to struggle and tried to wrench himself free, but Ben wasn't having any of it. He slammed Davey against the wall, driving the breath from his lungs.

"If you want to make things difficult then by all means, make them difficult Davey. Because I can make things difficult too," Ben growled. The thinly veiled threat was heeded, and Davey hung his head, shrugging Ben's hand away. Ben did not allow him to stray far though, and pushed him towards the car where Sunita waited for them. She straightened when she saw them approach.

"Get him inside. We're going back to the station with him. I think he could use a reminder of why it's always better to listen to the police instead of running away," Ben said. Davey looked surly as he sat in the back seat. He dug his hands in his arm pits and held his gaze out of the window, watching the blurry world outside. Ben glanced back towards him, finding it depressing how so many young men threw their lives away by falling into crime. There were so many better things to do with their lives, and yet none of them wanted to take the hard way out.

*

They were sitting in the interview room. Davey had a glass of water in front of him. He had a scruff of a beard and gaunt, deep-set eyes. His hair was tousled and thick, his clothes baggy. His nose was a sharp point.

"Who do I have to talk to about making a complaint about police brutality?" he said.

Ben snorted. "You've been watching too much TV. This isn't America. We don't treat our citizens badly."

"You pulled me off a wall!" he cried.

"Yeah, but gravity did the rest of the job. Make a complaint to Newtown if you must," Ben said. Davey stared at him with glazed eyes. Ben sighed and shook his head. "Look Davey, you're not in trouble and we're not arresting you. If you had just opened the door then you wouldn't have gotten yourself in this situation. I don't care whatever petty little scheme you have going on right now because there's something more important I need to talk to you about. It's about Joe McKay."

As he mentioned the name Ben watched Davey carefully. Davey shifted his eyes to the left and his tongue darted out to lick his lips. He adjusted his position and leaned forward.

"I don't know who you're talking about," he muttered.

Ben laughed. "You know when I said I could make things difficult Davey? If you want, I could look into your schemes. I'm sure we have a cell free tonight, maybe tomorrow night as well, hell, maybe we could host you for a week. I'm sure you'd like that, right?"

Davey gulped. "What do you want to know?" he asked with a resigned tone. Ben settled down, glad that he was finally getting somewhere.

"That's better. Maybe you're not as stupid as you look. It's come to my attention that Joe has gone missing. You're one of his friends. Any idea where he might be?"

Davey shrugged. It was always difficult in cases like these to get information for people who had grown up thinking the police were their adversaries. Ben softened his tone and tried a different tack. "Look Davey, I know you don't like me and you don't like what I represent. Your life would be a hell of a lot easier if me and my kind weren't around, but the fact is I have a job to do and at the moment I'm the only one who can help Joe if he's in danger. There are different kinds of criminals out here, right, what if Joe has fallen victim to one of them? I'm not here to arrest you or him or uncover any little plan you have going on, I just want to find out what happened to him because if he has been kidnapped or worse, then I have a really big problem."

"You think he might have been killed?" Davey asked, sitting up extremely straight. Ben wished that he hadn't jumped straight to that conclusion, but if it was going to scare him into telling the truth then perhaps it was worthwhile.

"Frankly I don't know what's happened. The best case scenario is that he's just gone somewhere to lie low for a few days, but if not then, well, we don't know what could have happened. It's why I need to know what you know, or if you don't know anything then tell me who would know. When was the last time you saw Joe?"

Davey sniffed and ran his hand through his hair, thinking about his options.

"Do I like… do I get favourable treatment if I help you?" he asked.

Ben glanced towards Sunita and offered her a grim look. "I guess there really is no honour among thieves, is there? I would have thought you'd want to help your friend for the sake of his own safety."

"I just thought I'd ask. There's no harm in asking," Davey muttered, and then decided that it was in his best interest to be truthful. "I saw him a few days ago. We were just hanging out. We weren't doing anything wrong," he said, which Ben took as proof that they were concocting some scheme.

"So what were you doing?"

Davey shrugged. "Just playing games and stuff."

"Right, and did he mention anyone he was going to see, or anything he was going to do? Was there anything he said that points to who might have taken him?"

"Not that I can think of."

"So he didn't have a girl he was going to see?"

When Ben asked this a wide grin came across Davey's face. Ben recalled how Alfie had said that people had laughed when he'd asked if Joe was with a girl. "What's so funny Davey?"

"It's nothing."

"I don't think it's nothing at all."

"It's just… well… Joe doesn't like girls. He never has."

Ben leaned back as he considered this new piece of information. "But he likes men?"

"Well he's gotta like something," Davey snorted. "Everyone knows apart from his Dad. It's been a bit of a joke between the lads, like, how can anyone be that blind?"

This started a whole new troubling line of enquiry. "Okay Davey. Was Joe seeing anyone then? Did he have any dates arranged?"

"He never really liked to talk about it. Kept himself to himself you know, and if you ask me that was the best thing because I didn't want to know anything about it. I'm all for them, you know, but the thought of actually

94

doing it makes me, well..." he visibly shuddered. Ben remained placid.

"So, you have no idea if Joe was seeing anyone or not?"

"I mean, he was on his phone a lot when we were hanging out. I caught him smiling a couple of times. I never asked him what he was doing though. Like I said, I didn't want to know, and I figured he could handle things himself. If he ever needed help he knew that we were all there for him. You can ask the others as well and they'll all tell you the same thing. If Joe was seeing someone then nobody would have known about it, and nobody would have known who he was."

Then a strange expression came over Davey's face. It was as though a light bulb had gone off.

"What is it Davey? What have you just thought about?"

"It's nothing really..."

"I'm not sure about that at all. Anything can help. Remember, this is for Joe."

Davey sucked in his breath. It was clear that he was really struggling with trusting the police to this extent. "It's just that recently Joe he, well, he started getting more cash. He began flashing it down the pub and stuff and getting rounds in. It was more than we ever scored from..." he caught himself before he revealed one of his illegal schemes. Ben would have let it slide anyway. In times like these it was important to choose his battles carefully. "Anyway, yeah, he wasn't shy about flashing it about, but when we'd ask him where he got it he'd only ever wink at us. The only thing that makes sense is that he was getting it from other guys, maybe older guys? I don't know..."

"You've been very helpful today Davey, thanks a lot."

"Just don't tell anyone I've been here, alright?" he said, adjusting his clothes as he rose and glancing at the door. Ben held it open for him, making sure Davey knew that he wasn't being held prisoner here. Davey was wary, thinking that this might have been a trap, and Ben assumed he was going to breathe a sigh of relief as he stepped out of the door.

"So this has opened up a new angle to the case," Sunita said once Davey was out of earshot.

"You're damn right, and I'm ready to assume that Joe hasn't simply gone missing. I think there's foul play here. If he was meeting strangers, then any one of them could have taken him." Ben pinched his temples and tried to ease the band of tension that was quickly appearing. He then got a call from the tech department. They had managed to retrieve something from the phone.

Chapter Four

Alfie had been skulking around the neighbourhood ever since he had seen Rachel. He'd been to the local bars and asked them if they had seen Joe, but none of them had any news to report. It just didn't make sense. How could he have disappeared off the face of the earth?

Rage boiled inside him and he wanted to lash out in every direction. If someone looked at him wrong he growled at them, baring his teeth like a feral dog. He drunk beer after beer to try and douse his emotions before he staggered back home, the walk taking longer than it should have because he was swaying from side to side, the world spinning around him as though it had lost all measure of control.

There were only two possibilities in his mind. Either Joe had run away or he had been killed. The first didn't seem like Joe at all. He was happy... wasn't he? Maybe Alfie had never given him the best chance in life, but he had tried his best. He had always been there for him, well, except when he was in prison, and he had tried to teach him how to get by in the world. Joe had shown a natural aptitude for crime, something that had been passed down from generation to generation. He was going to be the latest McKay to run roughshod over the city, and he had a good group of mates to do it with. The future was going to be bright for him, so why would he want to walk away from that?

Rachel claimed that he was sensitive, but Alfie had never seen that side of him. Joe had always enjoyed going to football. He roared with the rest of the crowd and got really into it, especially with his favourite players. Sometimes Alfie was sure that Joe like some of the players more than the game itself. Was there something that Alfie was missing about his own son? He would be the first to admit that he wasn't the perfect father, but he tried his best and that counted for a lot. Joe was his best friend when it came down to it, so he couldn't believe that Joe would have wanted to run away. Surely if things had been that bad then Joe would have come to him first to talk about it?

But then the other possibility was that he had been killed, and this was too bitter to face. Alfie felt sick as the thought entered his mind. His stomach twisted, and he had to steady himself against a wall as bile rose from his throat. If anyone touched his son like that God help him… his hand clenched into a tight ball and he was ready to declare war against the world. Who the hell would have been stupid enough to dare touch his son?

When he lurched home, he found Cyril still glued to the TV. "Any luck yet?"

"No," Alfie replied. The single word was elongated as it came out in a slur.

"Well, I'm glad to see you're putting your all into looking for Joe."

Alfie glared at him. "You could do a lot more than just sitting there and watching the horse racing. Have you not lost enough money yet?"

Cyril glared at him. His eye twitched. Even though Cyril was approaching 70 and spent most of his time glued to his chair, the years had given Alfie a deep-seated fear of him. Alfie still remembered the beatings of his childhood, the times when Cyril had hauled his wailing body along and then clipped him around the ear or put him across his knee and spanked him. All Alfie had ever known was violence. His life was defined by it. Even now, years later, one look was all it took for Alfie to feel as scared as a child again. It was the one thing he had never passed on to Joe. He had tried it once, when Joe was very young and had been raising havoc. Alfie had decided to take matters into his own hands and done as his father did. He pulled Joe across his legs and then spanked him.

It hadn't felt right at all, and afterwards Alfie hated himself because he remembered how much he had hated it. It made him feel less of a man.

And that feeling had pursued him all his life. There was always a sense that his father was better than him in every way, even if that wasn't borne out in reality. But as long as Cyril was there he would always cackle and hoot and loom over Alfie like a dark shadow, always drenching him in negative words, making him feel worse about himself, making him feel subhuman.

"If I thought Joe was in trouble then I'd be out there ripping up the trees and bursting into every house until someone told me something useful. I wouldn't be leaving it to the hands of the coppers. Joe is tougher than you ever were Alfie, and he can cope with more than you can. He reminds me of myself. I think whatever I had must have skipped a generation."

Alfie went rigid with tension. He vibrated on the spot, all the trembling anger running through him, reverberating dramatically. If he was braver then he might well have attacked his father, although the last time had not gone so well for him. That had been almost twenty years ago, when he had enough of Cyril's cackling and accosted the older man. Cyril had made short work of him though and left Alfie on the floor, his lip bleeding, his eye swollen and dark. It had left Alfie humiliated and there he knew that he would never outdo his father. A limit had been placed upon his life, a tower erected, a peak he could never reach.

And now he was failing his son, finding himself unable to wrest the unsteady world out of control. He had tried so hard to protect Joe, but still this had happened.

Before he could step forward and unleash his anger on his father, Alfie's phone rang. The intense emotions were enough to break his drunken state for a brief moment and offer him some clarity.

"Hello?" he asked, turning away from Cyril.

"Alfie, it's Ben. I think you need to come down to the station."

"Have you found him? Is he alright?"

There was a moment of grim hesitation before Ben spoke again. "I think you need to come down here. I don't want to talk about this over the phone."

Alfie was not filled with confidence by Ben's tone, nor his reluctance to share information. If he had found Joe then surely he would just tell him the good news? Whatever was left of his drunken state quickly dissipated from his mind and he sobered up immediately.

"I need to go out Dad," he said, not bothering to tell Cyril where he was going. Cyril didn't bother to reply. Alfie slammed the door of his squalid house shut and strode towards the police station, hating that he had to go to the heart of the enemy to find out what happened to his son.

*

When Alfie arrived, he was greeted by Sunita, the receptionist who always seemed to have a smirk on her face. She might have been pretty if she hadn't been a cop. It was easy to read the emotion in her eyes, and the message wasn't good. She disappeared behind closed doors to fetch Ben. He came striding out. Alfie couldn't help but compare himself to the man he had once shared a locker room with. Back then Alfie had been the strongest, and in his adolescent haze he had always assumed that he would stay the strongest. But the other boys grew stronger and taller and quickly enough the advantages that Alfie had enjoyed had been eroded, aided by the fact that Alfie had fallen into bad habits. Ben was one such kid. Alfie remembered him as a runt at school, but now he was anything but. He looked like a man who was in control of his life, a man who had found his purpose.

Alfie wished he could have been so lucky.

104

"What's going on Ben? Have you found him?" Alfie asked.

"I want you to come back here with me," Ben said.

Alfie cursed under his breath. "This is the problem with you people. You never give a straight answer."

He walked through the back of the police station. Officers they passed gave Alfie dirty looks, for they knew who he was. He glared back and showed them his teeth, for he was not afraid of any of them. Frankly he wished he could show them what he was capable of because he knew they all thought of him as scum of the earth, as though he didn't matter at all, but he did matter. He still had a life. It wasn't his fault that it was a crap one.

They entered a dark room. In the middle of the room was a computer. Ben sat down and offered Alfie a chair as well.

"What is this?" he asked.

Ben took a deep breath before he began speaking. "We managed to locate his phone. It had been broken and thrown into a lake. As of this moment we do not know if his body is there as well. We haven't found it yet, but I

105

still have a team sifting through the lake. My guess is that if his body was there then we would have found it by now, but I can't be certain."

"Okay, so what's on the phone?" Alfie asked, his gaze darting towards the computer.

"Well, we weren't able to retrieve all of the information on it because of the damage suffered, but there has been a recording. I want you to listen and I need to warn you that you might not like what you hear," Ben said.

Alfie braced himself, wondering what on earth could have been on Joe's phone.

There was a muffled sound of breathing. Fabric scraped against fabric. Joe sounded as though he was in a hurry. Then he stopped suddenly. He was panting.

"Joe?" another voice said.

"Yeah, that's me," Joe replied. Alfie's heart was in his mouth as he heard his son's voice. But who the hell was this other man?

"It's good to meet you. You're even cuter than your pictures."

"I wish I could say the same. I didn't realize that you were paranoid about your appearance. You can take the mask off now."

106

"I'll take the mask off when I'm good and ready. Part of the reason why I'm doing this and paying you so much is for discretion."

"Sure, so where do you want to do this? You got a place nearby?"

"Oh Joe, why are you in such a hurry? Is there no art to romance anymore?"

Joe laughed. "I think this is the farthest thing from romance. I'm only here for one thing, and I know you are too."

"Indeed, but do you know what thing that might be?" the question lingered in the air. Was this playful flirtation? But that didn't make any sense. Joe wasn't bent.

"I know, and I know I'm fucking good at it and I'm worth every penny you're going to pay."

There was a slight chuckle from the other man. His voice had a rasping quality to it. "There's just one thing I need to do before we continue Joe. I need to check that you're not wearing a wire."

"A wire? What the fuck are you talking about? Why would I be wearing a wire?"

"I have to be careful you see Joe, the world is still dangerous for men like me and unfortunately there have been a number of times where people have tried to play jokes on me. Are you playing a joke on me Joe?"

"No, of course not."

"Then you won't mind if I have a look," the man said, and he evidently made a move towards Joe as there was another burst of static. Alfie could imagine his son twisting away from whatever the hell this was. Joe cursed and tried to get this other man off him, but then there was a thumping sound, and Alfie imagined this was where the phone had changed hands.

"Oh Joe, Joe, Joe, what do we have here. I thought you said you weren't going to be like this?"

"I'm not like that. It's just for my own personal security. I didn't mean anything by it. I'll delete it after we're done."

"I'm afraid that's not good enough. You've been a very naughty boy, and you know what happens to naughty boys, don't you?"

"No wait, put that away..." Joe said. Alfie's heart broke as he heard the terror in Joe's voice. Then there was a cry of pain and the sound of something tumbling to the ground.

That something was Joe. There were gasps and moans of agony, and then the attacker brought the phone closer to his mouth. "I'm going to smash this phone and throw it into the lake, but I know how resourceful the police are nowadays so if they find this then I'm going to leave a little message that I want passed on to Adonis. Tell him that I'm here now and I'm better than he ever was. I already have more victims than him and nobody even knows! But I'm tired of hiding in the shadows. I want you to know that your work has been outdone Adonis. You are nothing any longer. You are but a relic of a past that no longer has any place in this world. Now it's my time, because I'm better than you."

The recording ended with a crunch, which must have been the heel of a boot crashing down upon the phone. Then everything was blank.

"What the fuck was that?" Alfie asked, the words punching the air. "Who the fuck is this guy? What was he doing with my son? Who is Adonis?"

Ben breathed deeply. He pulled the laptop towards him and closed the lid.

"We believe that your son was meeting men from a dating app and charging for his services."

"What kind of services?" Alfie asked. Ben just stared at him, and as the silence lingered the truth started gnawing in Alfie's mind. He shook his head and uttered a denial, but the more he thought about it the more he knew it to be true. "He can't be. He can't be. My son ain't queer."

"I know it must be hard to believe, but according to the friends we spoke to it was quite common knowledge among them that Joe preferred the company of men."

"But he can't... I mean, he came with me to football every time. He was never like them."

"I don't think there are signs. I think plenty of gay men enjoy football. I'm sure there were even men like that on our rugby team. Let's face it Alfie, what could be more gay than grunting and tackling men and then showering with them after the game?"

Alfie remembered how there were times when he had to guide Joe's attention to the action when he had focused on one of the players. In fact Joe had always loved masculine things, and now Alfie realized it was because he liked the men, not the things themselves. How had he been so blind?

"I never knew… he never told me…"

"Can you blame him?"

"I wouldn't have judged him for it," Alfie sneered. "It's just different, that's all. And anyway, we don't know that he's gay. He could have just been doing this for the money."

Ben gave him a wearying look. Alfie swallowed the awkward lump in his throat. "How long has he been doing this for?"

"We're not sure, a few months."

"And he never told me…" a million things were running through Alfie's mind, but perhaps the thing that hurt the most was the fact that there had been this secret part of Joe's life that he had never shared with his father. Alfie had always thought of them as close, as two partners in crime, more like buddies than friends, but now he wondered if he had really known his son at all.

Ben's voice was terse. "What's important at the moment is that we find him. I need to know if there's anything that might give us a clue to where he might be. Whoever he's with is dangerous and any time we waste is... well..."

"He's fucking dead isn't he."

"We don't know that."

Alfie lifted his gaze and looked Ben straight in the eye. Ben's gaze was unwavering. How he had changed over the years, this man who was now in possession of such dignity, such confidence. And how Alfie had diminished. There was no power, no control. His own son had been taken away by this strange masked man and Alfie had no idea how to get to him. His hands trembled as all he wanted to do was get his hands around that man's neck and wring it tight until all the bones snapped, but he was powerless. Joe was the only thing that mattered, and he was gone.

"I'm going to be coming over to the house to look into his room. I'll do the same at his mother's as well. If there's anything to find then we'll find it Alfie. I'm just sorry this has happened."

The thought of the cops traipsing through his house was not an appealing one, but Alfie merely nodded mutely.

"Who is Adonis?" he croaked.

Ben licked his lips. "Adonis is the name of a serial killer that was never caught. 20 years ago he preyed upon young men. He would take them home, poison them, and then leave them slumped against walls. He was never caught. One day it all just stopped. Nobody knows if he died or if he was caught for some other crime and was locked in prison, or if he just stopped entirely of his own accord. But he created quite the reputation for himself in the circles of those who like unresolved mysteries."

"So whoever did this to Joe… it's just a message to this Adonis?"

"Seems that way. Seems like there's some rivalry going on here, which means that Joe might not be the last victim. We need to find Joe so that we can stop any other men from being hurt."

Alfie sniffed and rose to his feet. "I don't care about anyone else. I just care about Joe. And you'd better find him Ben, because otherwise there will be hell to pay," Alfie turned and stormed out of the police station, the thoughts still whirling through his mind.

How could his son be gay? He tried to shake the thought away, and then wondered how on earth he was going to tell Cyril. Not only that, but Cyril was going to have to come to terms with the fact that the police were going come to their house. As he walked home, Alfie peered into every shadow and every alley, and he looked directly into the eyes of every stranger, wondering if they were the one who had taken his son. Anger boiled inside him as though he was a star ready to go nova. All it would take was one spark.

Chapter Five

Ben took a heavy sigh as Alfie left.

"Did that go as expected?" Sunita asked.

"I'm not sure what the hell I expected to be honest with you. I'm just glad he didn't reject the idea of us coming to his home."

"For everything you said about him, it seems as though he does care about his son."

"Joe is the only thing he has," Ben's words caught in his throat. He never thought he would have been envious of a man like Alfie, but despite it all Alfie still had one thing that Ben didn't: a family. It had always been something that had been on Ben's agenda, but the career had always come first. There had been women through the years, wonderful, sweet women with loving hearts who had tried as best they could to forge a life with him, but it always ended the same way, with them drifting out of his bed and leaving the sheets cold and empty. The job he had and the life he lived did not leave much room for anything else.

"Keep working. I'll be back later. I need to take a break," Ben said as he too walked out of the station.

Ben drove away from the cluster of houses out towards the perimeter of the city where it was quiet. The houses here were spaced farther apart and the air seemed sweeter. He pulled up outside a building with a bag of gravel and a skip in the front garden. He pulled some keys out of his pocket and opened the door. Silence greeted him. The wallpaper was in the process of being stripped. The kitchen floor was non-existent as it had been pulled up so that the pipes could be examined. The lounge was devoid of any personality, and the pale light shone through the wide, curtainless windows. This place was an empty shell of a thing. It was soulless and could not be called a home at all, but one day it would be again. Ben already had the image in his mind. He knew what colour paint he wanted on the walls, and what type of furniture he wanted to adorn the room. He knew where he was going to place the sofa, and on which wall the TV was going to be mounted. One day this place would shine again and it would make people happy; it would give them a place to feel safe and secure, a place where they could make memories.

It was the hobby that had turned into a career and now gave him respite from the grim reality of the world. It had all started when he was just a junior detective. After one criminal was taken away Ben wondered what happened to his house. He was told that it was being put up for auction, and given the state of it, the place wasn't going to fetch much. Ben had squirreled away a good amount of savings because he didn't have anything else to spend his money on other than cheap takeaway, so he bought the house and renovated it. He found that he liked this creative feeling flowing through him, and loved knowing that he could turn something ugly into something beautiful, something that somebody would want. His day to day life was surrounded with so much misery that it felt good to be able to create a ray of sunshine bursting through the bleakness, and since then he had gone on to renovate a number of properties. He spun them all and had a small fortune in his bank account. If he really tried then he might well have been able to retire, but he knew that was never going to be possible.

He would always be a cop, right until the day he died. He was a man of perpetual motion and if he stopped for one moment then all the thoughts in his mind would come crashing down. While he stood between the bad people and the good people he could pretend that his life had purpose and meaning, and if he ever stopped then he would be consumed by guilt, knowing that all these crimes were still happening. He could never turn a blind eye to them.

But at least he was giving something back. He placed his hand against a bare wall. The rough texture scratched his palm. He closed his eyes and in the recess of his mind he could hear children laughing as they scampered about the hall, he could see the loving smile of a father as he watched them, and it brought a wistfulness to his soul to think of this life that he would never know.

*

The next day, he met with Sunita and they drove to the McKay residence.

"Do you think we're going to find anything there?" Sunita asked on the way.

"It's as good a place to start as any. Has there been any luck with the phone?"

"Unfortunately not, and we've had some people sign up to the app in the hope that we might come across the assailant, but as yet we've had no luck. Given that the victim mentioned that he was wearing a mask we hoped his picture might have stood out, but he could have deleted his profile, or he might even have a stock image that he uses on the site and then sends private pictures elsewhere. I'm always waiting to hear back from the company about the way they store data, but they're being reluctant to share at the moment. Their whole thing is about privacy."

Ben scowled. "I understand the need for privacy, but if it costs people their lives then is it really worth it?" he muttered.

Sunita looked out the window. "I've never heard of Adonis before this."

"Well, people don't like to talk about their failures. It's easier to let the past lie."

"Were you involved?"

Ben smirked at her, tempted to ask her how old she thought he was. Then he thought better of it. He did not need reminding of how many years had slipped away.

"My old partner was involved. It always ate him up inside that he couldn't get the guy. He was convinced he knew who it was."

"Then why wasn't he caught?"

"No evidence. The guy was ahead of his time in covering his tracks. And then we assumed he died. There was a letter delivered to us, from Adonis. He said that he was dying and that he had lived a good life, a happy life, a life of freedom. Even at the last he wanted to mock us. I remember that day well. Gus brought in a bottle of whiskey and told me we were going to drink. I thought he was happy at first, but then I realized he was drinking to try and forget. He told me that this job was hard because when we grow up we always believe that the good guys win and the bad guys get punished in the end, but that's just not the truth of the matter. Sometimes they get away with it and die knowing that they never got caught. We finished the whole bottle. The

120

next day Gus wasn't at work. He'd taken retirement. I never saw or heard from him again. I think that case broke him. I guess it would break any man. What's the point of this job if we can't bring people to justice?"

"Have you ever reached that point?"

Ben's grip tightened on the wheel and his eyes turned to steel. "Not yet," he said.

They pulled up outside the house and walked up the unkempt garden. The musty damp smell greeted them. Ben hammered his fist on the door, once again afraid that it was just going to crumble under the slightest touch. The door opened and Alfie stood there. A dark shadow was under one eye and his lip was cut and swollen.

"Is there anything you need to tell me Alfie?" Ben asked.

Alfie just looked away.

"Who is it?" a craggy voice called from the lounge.

"It's the detective dad. I told you they were coming," Alfie cried out. Ben pretended not to hear what Cyril said in reply. Alfie and Sunita entered the house. They walked into the lounge. Cyril was sitting in a chair, resting on his cane, staring at Ben with beady eyes. His gaze then turned to Sunita.

"Oh, you didn't tell me you were bringing entertainment as well. Come and sit by me love. I can tell you stories of old that nobody else would ever know," he let out a wheezing laugh. Ben knew his reputation, but wondered how his charm had ever worked on women.

"They're just here to help Joe, Dad," Alfie said.

Cyril's thick fingers curled around the heavy wooden cane. "They don't help anyone. They just stick their noses into where it's not wanted. Alfie told me all about what's happened, including the message. I remember when Adonis prowled the streets. All you cops were too busy nicking people like me when you should have been out there dealing with the real danger. Then again, if you let us in on the problem maybe justice would have been served."

"I don't think what you would have done can be called justice," Ben replied.

"Better than what happened to him, which was nothing. Was he ever caught?"

"Potentially, for another crime," Ben lied.

Cyril let out a dry, crackling laugh and shook his head. "It's a wonder you fools ever get anything done. Do what you came here to do and then get out of my house," Cyril narrowed his eyes and sat there like a jackal, unmoving as he waited for them to leave. Alfie exhaled a short breath and then turned to lead Ben and Sunita upstairs.

"Don't worry about him. He's just, well, you know how he is. He's not ever going to have any love for coppers," Alfie said.

"I always thought you shared that sentiment," Ben replied.

"Not if you can help find Joe. Besides, you're a copper I know. At one point we were on the same team," Alfie said. Ben's mind flashed back to those muddy, cold days where his teeth chattered and his studs sank into the grass. Playing rugby was a respite for him as it became the only time when Alfie's ire was not directed to people in his own school, but to their opponents. He relished the battle like a warrior of old, and thumped into bodies, leaving them trailing behind him. It had been a sight to behold.

"You want to tell me how you got that black eye Alfie?"

"Just walked into a door," Alfie mumbled. Ben didn't believe that for a second. In fact he remembered Alfie coming to school with a lot of bruises. When he was younger, Ben had always assumed these were from fights that Alfie had gotten himself into, but he suspected now that it had been Cyril. It was amazing how so much violence could be found within the household. He hoped the same attitude hadn't been passed down to Joe as was so common. Fathers emulated sons and violent begat violence. It was all a cruel circle from which so few people were able to escape.

They trudged upstairs, ignoring the mould on the walls and the piles of clothes on the floor. Ben began thinking about what wonders he could work with this place. It would be a hell of a challenge, but would at least give him something to keep himself occupied.

Alfie stood at the door to Joe's room and opened it. The smell was musty. The curtains had been closed for goodness' knows how

124

long. There was a small, single bed with a narrow mattress. A chest of drawers stood against one wall. There were toys and models on it, arranged in a haphazard manner. On the back of the door hung a calendar depicting topless women. It was still stuck on the first month of the year.

"Guess I never needed to buy him that," Alfie muttered darkly. The other walls were adorned with posters of football players, their powerful leg muscles swelling, their masculine glory captured in these pictures. "I can't believe I missed it."

"I guess you weren't looking," Ben said. Alfie put his hands on his hips.

"If he had told me maybe I could have looked out for him. I could have told him that it was dangerous and that there were easier ways to make money. Christ… if he wanted cash I could have…" he then thought better about what he had been about to say given the presence of two police officers. Ben and Sunita put on rubber gloves and got to work, trying to find anything that might have been a clue. Sunita was rifling through the drawers and exclaimed when she reached far back and pulled out a wad of notes, all wrapped together tightly. Joe's earnings.

Alfie looked agog, and then he became crestfallen. "How many men must he have met to get that lot?" he asked.

Ben thought it best that he did not offer an answer. Ben had been searching around the perimeter of the room and found himself near the window. He pulled the curtains back and winced at the mould that had gathered around the windowsill. The room looked entirely different as light spilled into it, more like a boy's room than a man's. Joe seemed to be too young to be involved in this sort of life.

But it wasn't that which caught Ben's attention. It was something outside. He saw a man standing across the road dressed in a dark coat, staring at the house. As soon as the curtains were flung open, the man began to move away. Something about it did not seem right. Ben's tightly honed instincts snapped and he turned, marching out of the room. Alfie was full of questions and started following him, while Ben told Sunita to stay in the room and keep looking.

Ben found himself outside. He peered into the direction of where the man had gone and noticed that there was a narrow alley cutting through a park. He broke into a sprint. Alfie's heavy footsteps crashing behind him. Ben darted through this path and saw the man at the other end of the park, walking at a good speed. He had not broken into a run yet. Ben increased his speed and pulled out his badge, waving it in the air, crying out that he was a police officer. The stranger took notice, but he did not stop. He only started running.

However, despite him having a head start, he did not seem like the athletic type. Ben and Alfie's long legs carried them across the park, much to the bewilderment of parents with children and owners with dogs. The dogs loved it too, assuming that there had been some game that they had not been invited too, but were eager to join. Ben used his momentum to carry him across the fence and he landed in stride, keeping his pace. The man ahead of him was labouring, having to drag himself forward. He turned into another alley, but there was nowhere for him to run.

Ben caught up with him and pushed him into the wall. The man yelped and then slumped to the ground. His cheeks were red and puffy, while sweat glistened upon his brow and cheeks. He shook his head and his words were lost in his breathless exhaustion. Alfie joined Ben within moments and his face looked like thunder. His fists were tight and his words were curt.

"Is this the bastard? Where's my son? What the fuck have you done with him? If you've killed him-"

Ben turned and glared at Alfie. He put his hand on Alfie's chest and pushed him back a couple of steps. "Alfie, get yourself under control. We're doing this my way."

Alfie looked as though he might have wanted to challenge that, but he did not. Ben turned back to the man, who was holding his side, wincing in pain.

"What's your name and why were you running from us?" Ben asked.

"Please… please… I didn't mean any harm. I'm not a bad man. Please…"

"I'm Chief Inspector Ben Edwards and you're going to answer my questions or I'm

128

going to haul you down to the police station and we can do this in an interview room. It's your choice. Now tell me your name and why you were running."

The man nodded and held up his hands in surrender. Once he gathered his breath he was able to speak properly, although his words were still punctuated by haggard inhalations. "I'm Simon Grayson I'm just… I'm just an ordinary man."

"Ordinary men don't run from the police," Ben reminded him.

Simon nodded. "Okay… look, I was just… I just wanted to see if he was there. I thought maybe he was afraid that I was stalking him or something and that he had called the police on me, but I wasn't, I promise! I just happened to figure out where he lived and I just wanted to check up on him."

"You're talking about Joe?" Ben asked.

Simon nodded again.

"And how do you know Joe?" Ben asked, although he suspected he already knew the answer.

"We were lovers."

Behind him, Alfie made a guttural noise. Ben pressed on. "Tell me more. What do you mean you were lovers? Surely if you were lovers then you wouldn't have been afraid of him bringing out a restraining order on you?"

"We were lovers once. I... I wanted more, but he didn't. It's the same old story isn't it, you give someone your heart and they throw it back in your face. I just... I thought it could be different with him. I kept telling him that what he was doing wasn't safe. It was going to lead him into trouble one day. I would have taken care of him. He could have been happy with me. But he didn't want that."

"What do you mean he could have been happy?"

"I would have given him anything. He was so... so beautiful and so passionate. But at the same time he could be so cruel. The way he looked at me the morning after when I asked him to stay, when I told him that I loved him... I knew he pitied me. I felt like such a fool, but can I be anything else? I just wanted to see him again, to explain to him and try and make him see that I can be better than I am. I could be the man he wanted me to be. But I haven't heard from him again. I haven't even seen him. I thought he might have been avoiding me."

"So you did some digging and found out where he lived and you thought you'd pay him a visit."

"It's not my proudest moment, but you know how some people can just get under your skin? It all seemed so real. That night we shared, it wasn't just about our bodies. It was about our feelings as well. I can't believe he would have shared those things with anyone else. We really connected." Ben did not try and dissuade him of this notion, but it seemed to Ben that Simon was deluding himself and seeing things that weren't there. It often happened with lonely people.

Ben then asked him about the masked man on the dating app, which was where Simon had met Joe. Simon said he didn't know anything. "It's always a risk for us though," Simon confessed. "There are always people out there looking for us. I've been beaten up enough, or made fun of by people pretending to be something they're not. You'd have thought that by now the world would be a safe place for us."

Ben dug his hands in his pockets and then gave him a warning, telling him to keep to himself. Simon nodded and scrambled away after wiping the dust of his trousers. Alfie looked at Ben in disbelief.

"You're just letting him walk?"

"Why would I do anything else? He didn't commit a crime, he was just looking for some companionship and he let himself get carried away."

"What if he knows something?"

"If he knew something then he would have told us. Come on, the killer is still out there. We need to get back," Ben turned around and this time trudged back to Alfie's house rather than sprinted. His mind whirred though. How many people were on this app. It must have been like a free buffet for a serial killer, so many victims at his disposal, and he could search through them at his leisure. It made Ben's skin crawl. With all the new forensic technology at their disposal he had always seen it as an ally to the police, but it could be dangerous too, with criminals able to master it just as easily.

He glanced towards Alfie as they walked along. Despite all that had happened, Ben did feel sorry for him. He couldn't imagine what it would be like to go through this. Perhaps that was another reason why he had never settled down.

They returned to a surprising sight. Cyril was slumped on the stairs, his cane having fallen down to the foot of the stairs. He was cursing, calling Sunita every name under the sun, while she stood above him, her hands raised.

"What's going on here?" Ben asked.

"Police brutality! That bitch almost killed me! I'm going to sue you for every penny!" Cyril cried out.

Sunita had an unimpressed look on her face. "He came upstairs and made inappropriate comments towards me. Then he tried to touch me. I saw it as a threat and I defended myself."

Ben suppressed a smirk. "The world has changed Cyril. You can't take what you want any longer. You have to ask for it. It's not too late for you to learn some manners you know," Ben said. Cyril had a dark look on his face as he crawled down the stairs and grabbed his cane. He used it to raise himself into a standing position again. Ben knew that if Cyril had been twenty years young this would have probably ended in a fistfight. As it was, Cyril skulked back into the lounge muttering under his breath.

"Keep out of trouble Alfie. I'll find who did this," Ben said. Alfie then shut the door and Ben hoped that his promise would not turn out to be a lie.

*

"I'm sorry for what happened in there," Sunita said.

"No, I'm sorry for leaving you alone with him. It's easy to forget the kind of man he is when he's that old. I'm just glad you were able to deal with him."

"Not the first time, sir."

Ben nodded.

"Did you find out anything?"

"Nothing other than Joe was meeting men, which we already knew. This one had taken more than a brief liking to him though. I wonder how many other people fell in love with him?"

"I just can't understand why he would have got involved in this."

Ben shrugged. "Makes sense to me. He was brought up with the family he has, given this skewed mindset of what a man should be. He saw a way to use what he had to exploit others and get money for it. It's the same playbook that Cyril and Alfie used, so why should Joe be any different? The only problem is that he didn't think about the consequences, or maybe he did and he just didn't care. They've always liked to take risks."

They took the short journey to Joe's other home, where he lived with his mother, Rachel, and her partner, Gary. The difference between this house and Alfie's was stark. The garden was neat, the house clean and orderly. The bins had their own sheltered home, keeping them out of sight. The door was sturdy, and when they went inside they found themselves greeted by a pleasant floral fragrance. The colours of the home were calming and tranquil.

Rachel was anything but. Her hands trembled and her lips were chapped from where she had been biting them. There were dark shadows under her eyes. Ben had already called ahead, so she had been expected them. She made them some tea.

"Have you found anything?" she asked.

Ben caught her up to date on the case. It was only fair that she knew as much as Alfie.

"Did you have any idea that he was involved in any of this?"

"No I... he kept to himself a lot, you see. I always knew he would be trouble. I hoped that since we had split up he wouldn't turn out to be like Alfie, but he is his father's son. I assumed he was getting in some kind of trouble, but not this... never this. I had tried so hard with Alfie to change him and it had taken so much out of me that I didn't want to go through it again. I couldn't. But now I think maybe I should have."

"Try not to blame yourself. What's important is that we try to find Joe. Do you have any idea where he could be?"

Rachel let out a dry laugh. "I have no idea. I never knew where he was. I tried to make a

136

nice home for him, but he always preferred to stay with Alfie. I was never his favourite."

"And what about your partner, is he here?"

Rachel shook her head. "He has to work. His job has long hours. I don't mind really because it pays for this place. I never thought I'd ever end up in a house like this, but it would be nice if he was around a little more."

"And how was his relationship with Joe? Did Joe feel welcome here?"

"Of course," Rachel said, her features pinched in a defensive expression. "This is his home." She then relaxed and exhaled a sigh of acceptance. "They never really got on of course. I think Gary always expected him to be better behaved than he was. He left most of the disciplining to me. I'm not sure Gary ever wanted to be a father, but he wanted to be with me so he's given it a good go. Maybe if he had been more interested then they might have struck up a bond, but Joe was old enough to resent any man who wasn't his father. He worships Alfie so much and I've never understood why really, but there we go. I just… I just wish he had trusted me enough to tell me about all of this. I would have understood. I would have spoken to him about it."

Her voice cracked on emotion and she had to look away, for she was on the verge of tears. Ben glanced towards Sunita. He then asked Rachel if it was possible for him to look into Joe's room. Rachel nodded. She was a pitiful figure, sitting there huddled on the sofa, clutching her cup of tea as though it was the only thing that anchored her to the world. At least Alfie had Cyril to keep him company, although perhaps it was better to be alone.

Ben walked up the carpeted stairs. He peered into the rooms as he passed. The bathroom was gleaming white. Pictures of flowers hung on the walls. The beds were made and devoid of any clutter. It was almost as though this place was a show home. He then made it to Joe's room. It was almost as though another person lived in here, compared to the room he had at Alfie's. There were no posters of men on the walls, in fact there was nothing that showed any hint of personality at all. The bed had not been slept in, there was a gaming console in the corner with a flatscreen TV, as well as shelves of books, which had probably gone unread. It was clean though, and comfortable. In fact this whole house should have been a paradise to Joe, and yet his bond with his father was so powerful that Joe preferred to stay in the dilapidated, musty house. It would never fail to amaze Ben how powerful emotions could be, and how much they could change the course of someone's life.

It made him think about his own father as well, and how that particular relationship had sent him on the path he had eventually begun walking down. He shook the thought from his mind as he rifled through Joe's drawers. In these drawers there was no money, only clothes. They were all soft and trendy, and had hardly been worn. Ben wished to find Joe not only to save his life, but also to have a talk with him and try and make him understand how he had two different paths to walk, and one of them was much better than the other. It was always hard though with two imposing figures like Cyril and Alfie in his life.

Ben went back downstairs. Rachel had calmed down a little. Sunita was always good at speaking with people.

"I didn't find anything in his room. Rachel, is there anything that you could tell me about Joe? Was there anything he might have mentioned in passing about where he was going or who he was talking to?"

Rachel wracked her brains and seemed disappointed when she couldn't come up with anything. "I'm really sorry, but there's just nothing. It's like he wanted to keep this whole part of himself hidden from me. I always thought that I knew him better than I knew myself, but it's not true, is it? He's really his own person, and I'm just the person who gave birth to him."

"I'm sure that's not the case," Sunita said. "I'm sure that once we find him and he comes back he'll realize how much you mean to him, and how much he means to you."

Rachel smiled weakly. Ben didn't get a chance to say anything else to her though, as the door opened and Gary entered the room. He had a quizzical look on his face. He was a plain looking man, the kind of man you wouldn't notice if you sat across from him on a train or something like that. He had an easy smile though, and a smooth voice. It was easy to see why someone like him would have appealed to Rachel, especially after the tumultuous relationship with Alfie.

"Oh good, you're home," Rachel said, and moved to Gary's side. An arm wrapped around her back, as though it was always meant to be there. He did not take his eyes off Ben and Sunita though. Ben introduced them. There was a slight hesitation in Gary's movements, although that was common when the police were around.

"I don't suppose there's anything you can tell us about Joe?" Ben asked after he and Rachel had updated Gary about the current situation. Gary sank to the sofa and leaned forward, wearing a concerned look.

"I wish I did, but I'm sure that Rachel has told you he and I were never that close. I tried, you know, I really did try, but he was always his father's son. I can't imagine the kinds of things Alfie was saying about me when he was looking after Joe," Gary's voice became terse, and it took a calming hand from Rachel to soften his voice. "Look, I'm not going to lie to you, I've never had any respect for Alfie, especially not after the stories I've heard from

Rachel. I've tried to give her and Joe the best life I can, but at some point you have to accept that people are going to make mistakes. Joe preferred to live with Alfie and he made it clear that I was never going to be anything more to him than his mother's boyfriend. I made my peace with that a long time ago. I wish things could be different, but unfortunately there was never anything he was going to tell me that he wouldn't have told his mother or father. I was never anyone important in his life. I'm sorry that I can't be of more help," Gary said.

Ben had suspected as much. He thanked Rachel for their time and then left with Sunita. By now it was late in the day. The sun was beginning to set and the sky was streaked with red. It was another collection of moments that had passed. For so many in the world they would have been serene, but for Joe they would have been hellish, if Joe was still alive. Ben tried to guard himself against the uneasy feeling inside, but as the gnawing sense of inevitability grew inside him he knew that the more time that passed the unlikelier finding Joe alive was going to be.

Had he just failed again?

Chapter Six

Alfie sauntered into the lounge. Cyril was still sour about what had happened before.

"I can't believe you brought them here. If you had any balls then you'd take care of this situation by yourself."

"And how am I going to do that Dad?"

"Round up the men and get them to turn up stones. Eventually some slimy asshole is going to turn up."

Alfie shook his head in disbelief. "Can't you accept that times have changed? It's not as simple as it was. And how am I going to figure out who took Joe anyway?"

"There are always whispers."

"Not now, Dad. Now people use phones. It's all hidden and silent. Nobody has to say a word. Joe kept this from us, you think if it was back in the day he would have been able to do that? No."

"The world is going to the dogs," Cyril snarled. "It never used to be like this."

"Times change."

"And men are forced to change with them. Christ. Now we have women who can fight back as well. What the hell is this world coming to?" Alfie let the comment slide. He wasn't afraid to admit that seeing his father sprawled over the stairs had brought him immense satisfaction. After all the beatings he had endured it was pleasing to see Cyril getting a taste of his own medicine, especially from a woman. The humiliation must have been severe. But Cyril wasn't done talking.

"But it's all your fault. I should have made sure that you were a better father. Maybe Joe wouldn't have turned out that way."

"What way?" Alfie asked, growing an edge to his voice.

"You know what way. Bent."

"There's nothing wrong with the way he is Dad, just what he did."

"There's everything wrong with the way he is. It got him into this mess, didn't it? It's all your fault, pandering to him this much. I told you that you needed to be harder on him. There's no fucking discipline with you. It's always been your problem Alfie. You should have beat that out of him."

144

"Just like you beat things out of me?" Alfie glared at Cyril. The old rage flooded through his body and his head began to thrum. It had been years ago now, so long that it could almost have been said to be another life, but it was all that Alfie could remember. The alcohol-stained breath was imprinted on his mind, as was the impact of the fist onto his young body. He used to cry himself to sleep at night after counting the bruises on his flesh. They were always in different states, making him look like a horse with a dappled hide. Some were yellow, some dark purple, some as black as the night. They were all sore, and they were all drummed into him by the meaty fists of his father who was so angry at the world and could only take out that anger on his son.

And now Cyril was trying to tell Alfie that he had been wrong for not doing the same to Joe.

"Fat lot of good it did you. I should have gone harder. Maybe then you wouldn't have been such a failure," Cyril barked.

"I'm the failure? I'm not the one who lost a small fortune Dad. I'm not the one who forced his kid to live in squalor because he couldn't take control of his gambling addiction. You always said that you would do anything for your family, but that's not true. You only ever did things for yourself. And the only reason my life is shit is because I've had to spend it looking after you. The only good thing I've ever been able to do is treat Joe like a person, and even that hasn't been enough to keep him safe." The words poured out of his mouth like hot coals, each one sizzling and bursting with fury.

And Cyril just stared at him. But something had changed. Seeing Cyril helplessly prostrate on the stairs, felled by a woman half the size of him had shattered the illusion that had held Alfie in its thrall. No longer was Cyril this intimidating monster, he was just an old man.

"The worst thing I did was ever bring an ungrateful little shit like you into the world. Why do you think I gambled away all my money? It was because that was the only way I could get a break from your snivelling, whining mews. I tried to make you into a man, but you only ever became a kitten. You've got a faggot for a son and you don't even have the balls to go and find the fucker who killed him."

As soon as the slur left Cyril's mouth, Alfie was striding across the room, arm already swinging back. A lifetime of rage had built up within him and it was now boiling over. He saw nothing but red, and he roared as he brought his fist crashing around. It hit his father in the cheek and the chair was sent flying back. Once again Cyril was on his knees, and now it was Alfie's turn to tower over him, glowering like an angry giant. The power was intoxicating and Alfie could understand why his father had been so addicted to it, but it was better served elsewhere.

His son was in danger, and Alfie needed to find out where Joe was.

*

Night had descended on the land. The stars were overshadowed by the lights from the buildings and the lampposts. It was a world in which nothing was allowed to hide, and yet so many things went unnoticed. With every step Alfie drove his feet into the ground, shaking the very world. His fists were still clenched by his side, and he wore an angry expression.

He hated himself for what he had just done, even though if anyone had deserved that kind of treatment then it would have been Cyril. But Alfie had always had a stringent rule to never lay his hands on family, for he had never wanted to be like his father. And now he was that monster. But sometimes you had to become a monster to slay a monster.

Somewhere out there was a monster who had lain hands on Joe, who had twisted and torture him, who had used him in some game with this Adonis.

Alfie was standing in front of the door. The house shook as he hammered his fists against it.

"Rachel!" he cried. The door swung open. "Did you know?" he asked, the plea of a desperate man.

Rachel uttered a gasp. Then she looked crestfallen and shook her head.

"How the hell did this happen without us noticing?" he asked.

"I don't know. I always thought I was a good mother. Now I just... I don't know what

I'm supposed to do. Where is he? Where's our boy?"

"I don't know, but I'm going to find out. I don't care how long it takes or how many necks I have to break, I'm going to find who did this and when I do I'm going to-" Alfie didn't get a chance to finish his sentence because Gary was standing there, hovering behind Rachel, still with that smug look in his eyes. The look never left him, not since Alfie had first met him. It was a look that said 'I've got what you want'.

"You know you're not supposed to be here Alfie. Do I need to call the police?" he said. There was a practised lilt to his voice, as though he was putting on a performance.

"You'd like that, wouldn't you? Well, my son is in danger so if you want me to make a scene then I'll make a scene."

"I know you're angry, but there's no need to take it out on me. I haven't done anything. It's not my fault that the boy was given such a poor example growing up. If he hadn't idolised you so much then perhaps he would have been more open to having a good role model. I could have been a better father to him

149

than you could ever be, but he never gave me the chance."

Alfie snarled. "Don't you dare say anything like that. I've been a good father to him. I've always given him anything he has ever wanted. I've made sure that he's safe and protected and loved."

"Oh sure, I'm sure he feels protected now. Just face it Alfie, the best thing you can do for that boy is to stay well away and let the police do their job. You mess up everything you touch."

Rachel stood in between them and turned to Gary in an attempt to stop him. Alfie was already too far gone though. He lunged forward and grabbed Gary's shirt collar, pulling him forward. Gary yelped as his shoulder hit the frame of the door. Rachel gasped and cried out. Alfie slammed his fist across Gary's face, sending him to the ground. He looked up and saw that Rachel's face was ashen. Fear appeared in her eyes and she cowered, seeing not a man, but a monster.

Alfie was never going to escape the darkness inside him, the darkness that had been put there by Cyril all those years ago.

Every one of those beatings had opened up a dark scar where resentment had festered and demons had bred.

"Get the fuck out of here!" Gary cried out, blood flying from his mouth as he was held by Rachel. Alfie turned and slunk away, disappearing into the darkness, alone. It would be a long night for him, a night where he would trawl through the seediest bars and clubs, asking anyone he could get his hands on if they knew where his son was or who had taken him.

None did.

He asked them about this Adonis as well. Everyone had a story. Some of them thought it was a well-known celebrity who was protected and taken into hiding because of the fear that other people would be taken down with him, while others believed it was a cop who was given early retirement and a cushy pension to keep quiet. There was a story for anyone and the truth his hidden somewhere in this web of lies, but it was too much for him to search through by himself.

In the small hours of the night he was staggering away from the buildings that came alive at night. Never before had he felt so alone, without a friend in the world. All the people he knew were either in the slammer or out drinking. They wouldn't care that Joe was in trouble.

There was only one man who cared, and to Alfie it seemed like a great irony. But he headed towards Ben's house anyway because he didn't want to go home and face his father.

Ben opened the door. Alfie groaned. His body felt heavier than usual. He dragged himself into the house and slumped on the chair. It was all very nice here, very clean, and yet there was something about it that was unsettling as well, as though it wasn't really a place in which to live, just to exist. Ben made some coffee and brought it in.

"I'm not drunk," Alfie heard the slurred words. "Well, not *that* drunk." He belched after his first sip of coffee.

"What have you been doing tonight Alfie? I really hope you haven't been getting yourself in trouble."

"My whole life has been trouble. But no, I've just been asking around. Trying to figure out what happened to him and where he is.

Didn't find anything though. It's like you're the only one who cares. Do you know how fucked up that is? God… I remember when we were kids. You were always a swot. Always figured you'd get some job in a bank or something. Never thought you'd be a cop. Guess I shouldn't have been surprised though, not when you started playing rugby."

"I'm glad I could surprise you," Ben replied dryly.

"Why didn't you?" Alfie asked.

"What do you mean?"

"Why didn't you become a banker? You had the brains for it. I remember you were always at the top of those tests we did. You could have been anything."

Ben shrugged and tilted his head to the side. "I wanted to do something that would make a difference to the world. I'm not really sure how much difference I've made, but there we go. I knew there were bad men who got away with crimes. I wanted to make sure I caught as many as possible. I just hate that I can't get them all."

A moment of silence passed between them.

"We're not going to find him, are we, at least… he's not going to be alive." Ben opened his mouth. Alfie made him promise not to lie. Perhaps it was the ambience of the night, the intimacy that was conjured by these small hours where most people were asleep, or maybe it was just because they had a bond that stretched back to their childhood, either way, Ben chose to be candid with him.

"I'm not going to lie to you Alfie, but the chances are slim. In a crime like this the killer isn't likely to keep his victim alive for a great deal of time. He'd want to dispose of the body swiftly. I can't guarantee that of course, and I wish that I could promise you something different, but that's the most probable outcome."

Alfie's throat went dry. He had assumed this would be the case after all, but still, hearing it in such cold words was chilling.

"I know you don't think much of me Ben, but I've always tried to do right by that boy. I know I've never been the best father, but I've tried to learn. I never laid a hand on him. I never tried to make him feel less than he was. And still I wasn't able to protect him. All the

154

fights I've been in… the reputation I have and this still happens."

"There are no rules to the world Alfie. What I've learned during my life is that it's all just messed up and there's nothing we can do to make it make sense. Sometimes the people who love us the most are the ones who hurt us the most and as hard as you can try to think about it, it's never going to make sense."

For a moment Alfie thought that Ben was talking about him and Cyril, but there was a deep look in his eyes and a reflective tone in his voice. It was clear that Ben was speaking about himself, and Alfie began to wonder if they had something else in common.

"I never really gave much thought to it back then, but what was life like for you at home? I always imagined it to be perfect."

Ben wore a wry smile. "I'm not sure anyone ever has a perfect life. I certainly didn't. But I know what you're getting at Alfie." He took a moment to compose himself. "Your father and mine were cut from the same cloth. They had the same idea about discipline."

Alfie pressed his lips together and bowed his head. "I want you to know that I was never like that to Joe. I never wanted to be like Dad."

"I can see that. I can see how much he means to you. Tell me, what's it like having a son? I've often thought about it myself."

"It's the most wonderful thing in the world, and sometimes the most awful thing as well. I still remember that day when I held him in my arms for the first time. He was so small I thought I was going to crush him. All he did was make these strange noises, but when he opened his eyes you could see this whole world going on inside him and you could feel that there was this whole other person inside him, and all I wanted to do was make him happy. It was hard at first, you know, knowing that I had to give up a lot of things I took for granted. I started seeing the world in a different way as well. Never realized how dangerous it could be. All I wanted was to protect him, but over the years he got older and started doing his own thing and I guess there's not much we can do about it, is there? Maybe kids always keep secrets from their parents. It's just that my one had a secret that got him killed."

"You're a brave man Alfie, for bringing a son into this world."

"I think that's the kindest thing you've ever said to me."

"Well, nobody deserves to go through this. But I hope you use this as a lesson to change you ways. This life of crime isn't going to work out well for you."

Alfie gave a resigned sigh. "The problem is that it's the only life I know. What use is going straight going to do me? The world isn't made for people like me. Besides, it's not as though this life is working out well for you, is it?" he asked, looking around the cavernous home. Ben didn't say anything in reply to that.

They spent the next few hours reminiscing about their school years, talking about teachers who were probably retired or dead by now, as well as other students who had gone their own way and fallen into the ether while Ben and Alfie had remained behind, rooted to this area like trees, locked into this path where both of them walked parallel to each other yet remained apart. There was a part of Alfie that wondered if he and Ben were closer to each other than anyone else because they understood where they had come from and knew true loneliness. Ben might have had a good job and a prestigious standing in society, but his life seemed empty. Maybe it was because he knew how painful it was to lose things, and maybe he was lucky for that.

Alfie wasn't sure though. He still had the memories of Joe. Would he have wanted to carve them out of his mind to save himself the pain? It was a question that plagued him as he wandered back home as dawn rose around him, bringing about a new day, another day without his son.

Chapter Seven

It shouldn't have been like this. Ben was almost forty, well past the point of adulthood. He should have had children and a long-suffering wife. He should have had crushed hopes and dashed dreams and barbecues with people who he tolerated as acquaintances. Instead, he shared his nights with a convict, a bully, and yet strangely Alfie was perhaps the one man who could understand him in all the world. Talking to Alfie brought back awful memories of his past, a past that Ben tried to forget. It was never possible though. They were always there, swirling around the back of his mind like eerie oceanic creatures in the shadows of the unexplored sea. There was the sharp crack of a belt as it lashed through the air, the imprint of the metal buckle left on Ben's skin. It always took a long time for it to recede, and the pain took longer.

No score was good enough. No mark was high enough. The standards were impossible to meet and the punishment was always meted out the same way; a laborious ordeal where Ben was always told that it was never what his father wanted to do, only what he had to do, and that it really did hurt him more than it hurt Ben.

The words had always rung hollow, however.

Ben had his eyes opened from a young age, his innocence taken away by a thief in the night as he realized that there were bad people everywhere, even close to home. He had tried to tell his mother, but she had brushed away his concerns. Sometimes there was nobody to listen. There was nobody to put the bad people away.

And so he wanted to be that person.

But now there was a killer on the loose and he had no idea if he was going to be able to find them and bring them to justice. A young man had likely lost his life, and it didn't matter that he was a McKay. All that mattered was that he was a victim.

Ben went into the station on little sleep. Coffee kept him awake. He listened to the recording again and again. There was something that struck him as familiar about the voice, but it remained elusive, and in the end he listened to it so much that he couldn't even tell if he recognized something or if he was just making things up. His mind may have been trying so hard to make sense of it that it was conjuring some meaning from nowhere.

There still hadn't been any developments from the app. Sunita had nothing but bad news to tell him. Now the goal wasn't necessarily to save Joe, but to catch this man before anyone else could be killed. Ben paced around his office, trying to think around the problem and find that one bit of inspiration that could unlock the case and provide a clue as to who this man was. But Joe wasn't talking to anyone he knew about it… but what about someone he didn't know?

Ben stopped pacing. Something had caught in his mind. He thought back to when he had cornered Simon Grayson. He had been convinced that there was more between him and Joe than what there had actually been. Ben had dismissed his ramblings as little more than desperation, but what if there had been some truth to what he was saying? What if Joe had actually shared something?

He slammed his palm against his forehead and gasped, cursing at himself in annoyance because of how stupid he had been. He grabbed his coat and told Sunita to keep working on the app while he went out. Maybe there was a lead here after all.

*

Simon was nervous when he answered the door. He peered outside, likely afraid of what his neighbours might think, and ushered Ben in quickly.

"You didn't have to come all this way Detective," Simon said. The house was neatly kept. A budgie chirped on a perch, greeting the newcomer. Simon put his finger into the cage. The bird opened its beak, as though it was being threatened.

"There's just something I wanted to ask you about. You said that Joe told you certain things, things that led you to believe you had a closer relationship than what you actually did?"

Simon leaned back in his chair and wore a pensive look. "I mean, I'm not a fool Detective. I know that when you pay men for their services there's hardly going to be an explosion of love, but I did hope that something might blossom. There are so many people who are struggling in today's world and I saw the money as a sort of invitational fee. I mean, I'd end up spending almost as much on a date anyway. It did seem to expedite matters."

Ben ignored the fact that this exchange of money for sexual services was illegal. It was a murky world to become involved in and the laws were always vague. Besides, it wasn't going to help him get any closer to Joe's killer, so he let Simon continue to talk.

"But I wasn't on that app just for the physical things. I wanted to find someone to connect with as well. It's so hard to meet people, especially people who are on the same wavelength. When Joe came round I knew that there was something between us instantly. Maybe he just wasn't interested, or maybe he didn't want to bother with anything that heavy because it would have interfered with his ability to earn money, but I could feel it. I knew he felt it too. There's no way he could have kissed me like that if he didn't."

"I don't need all the details Simon," Ben reminded him gently. "I just want to know if there was anything that Joe told you that he might not have told anyone else."

"Well, after it was over he was getting ready to leave and I told him to stay. I had to promise to pay him extra for the privilege, but it was money well spent. I didn't do it so much for myself, but for him as well. I know what's it like at that age and how confusing it can be. I wish I had had had someone to talk to when I was his age. It would have made things a lot less painful and confusing, so I wanted to return the favour. I shared some of my stories, and he shared some of his. He told me why he had begun this in the first place."

"Why?"

"Well, mainly because it was easy. At first he joined the app because he didn't know anyone else who was gay and he wanted people to talk to, people his own age. What he found were older men who were willing to pay him to spend time, and once he started going down that rabbit hole he couldn't stop. I didn't get the impression that he actually liked it. I think he would have preferred to just have friends, but he didn't think he could turn down the money. When I told him that we could be friends he just smiled. It was the kind of smile that could have meant anything."

"Did he tell you about anyone he met who had been threatening him? Anyone who made him feel like he had been in danger?"

Simon shook his head. "Not anyone that he met, no. I did warn him that if he kept doing this he was going to find someone who wasn't nice at all, but Joe didn't seem to be worried. I guess it was because he was young and just thought that everything would wash off him. Or maybe it was because he had been through things already."

"What things?"

Simon put his hands in his lap and bowed his head. The budgie in the cage flapped its wings as it moved from one side of the cage to the other. "I'm not sure I should tell you. He told me in confidence."

"Simon, do I need to remind you that I'm investigating a crime here? If there's anything you can tell me that might give some insight into the crime then I need to know."

"Well that's just the thing… I'm not sure it is going to give insight into the crime."

"That's for me to decide," Ben said tersely. Simon did not offer any resistance after this. He merely sighed and looked despondent at having to give up this valuable piece of information.

"He told me that he had been abused by someone close to him. He didn't say who, and he didn't say how long. All he said was that it happened, and that's why he liked taking money because it meant that things were business, not personal. I tried to press, but he didn't want to talk about it, and I was afraid that if I pushed too hard then he would turn away completely."

"And you're sure that he was telling the truth?"

Simon nodded. "I recognize the look in his eyes," he said. Ben looked away at that moment for fear that Simon might be able to glean something about him as well. He thanked Simon and then rose, heading back to his car. His mind whirred. If Joe was abused by someone close to him then it meant there was another wrinkle to this crime, and more secrets that needed to be exposed. Maybe it wouldn't help them reveal the masked man, but it might help them understand Joe a little more.

Ben had seen victims of abuse before. Sometimes they sought out abusive situations again but this time with more control. It was quite possible that Joe was doing this, getting the men to pay him to have sex with him so that this time he was in control. Except one of the men had taken control from him again. When Ben got into the car he phoned Sunita.

"I have another lead Sunita. I just spoke to Simon again and he told me that Joe was abused when he was younger. He doesn't know by who. It could be someone he was related to, or one of his teachers, someone that he had a lot of contact with. I want you to start by making a list of all the adult males he interacted with on a regular basis. I know it's going to take some time, but see if any of them have anything on their records like this."

"Do you think the killer is the abuser?" Sunita asked.

Ben sighed. "I don't know. The fact he used a mask… was that because he didn't want Joe to know it was him? Either way, I think if we can find out who abused Joe maybe we can link that to the people he was meeting up with from the app. Maybe there's someone who looks like him. It's all we have," Ben said. It felt a little like he was grasping at straws, but there was nothing else he could do.

"Are we treating Alfie as a suspect as well?"

Ben paused for a moment. Rationally he knew that everyone in Joe's life needed to be suspected, but life wasn't always about logic. Alfie was a criminal, but Ben didn't want to believe that Alfie could do something like this.

"I don't think it's him Sunita. Look at the others," Ben said. He exhaled a low whistle as he drove towards Alfie's house and hoped that he wasn't making some mistake. But he wanted to tell Alfie this latest development because it was something he should know. Ben knew what Cyril was like, and he couldn't help but wonder if the old man had wanted to teach his grandson a lesson.

Chapter Eight

Alfie was in his bedroom when there was a knock at the door. He was still stewing and fuming with impotent anger. Every moment he spent without Joe was another moment where he had to face the reality that Joe was never going to come back. Alfie hadn't yet faced the reality of the situation. He didn't dare think about what he was going to do when it was confirmed. Joe was his future. Without him what did Alfie have?

A whole lot of nothing.

Ben was standing there. The colour drained from Alfie's face. "What do you want? Have you found him?"

"Not yet, but I did discover something disturbing. It seems that Joe was abused when he was younger."

"What? No... that's impossible."

"We don't know if it was a teacher or someone closer to him, but he confided that it happened. It's only natural that he wouldn't tell you about it. A lot of people don't want to tell anyone because they'd rather try and convince themselves that it didn't really happen."

"What do you mean it could be someone close to him? You mean like…?" Alfie didn't give himself a chance to finish uttering the thought. He was already turning around and storming into the lounge.

"What the fuck have you done old man? What the fuck did you do to my son?" Alfie roared. Cyril had been watching TV undisturbed and did not have the time to react. Alfie pushed him out of the chair and kicked his cane away, leaving the old man on the floor, huddled together as Alfie beat him and kicked him and cursed at him. Ben had to rush in and wrestle Alfie away.

"Stop this!" Ben cried out. Alfie's emotions poured out of him and he had nothing but animosity for his father.

"What did you do?" Alfie thundered.

"What the hell are you talking about? I never did anything to him," Cyril spat back as he pulled himself back into his chair.

"We don't know it was him," Ben said.

"Was it you? Did you do that to him?" Alfie cried.

170

"Do what?" Cyril was still at a loss as to what was happening.

"Joe was abused," Alfie said in a dry, cracked voice.

"And you think it was me? Oh what a high opinion you have of me, my boy. Why would I ever do that? I beat some sense into you, sure, but abuse? No, no, no, I would never sink as low as that. You dare to think that of me? If I were a younger man I'd throw you out of this house right now and make sure that you never returned."

Alfie slumped to the ground and felt as though all the breath and energy had been drained from him. His head bowed. Ben stood in between the two men to make sure that they weren't going to attack each other again.

"I just want to know where he is," Alfie pleaded.

"We're going to find out. We're getting the records of everyone who might have done this," Ben said.

"And the killer?"

"We're still working on that," Ben's words were faltering.

Cyril cackled. "You see what trusting the police has done Alfie? Nothing. All they do is come up with more and more crimes, and speak to more and more people, and dredge more and more useless things. They never do anything right. They're just a joke, and they spend more time hounding good, upright people instead of getting the real criminals. The only way you're going to find this killer is to get him yourself. It's the way we would have handled it in my day, and the way you should have handled it from the beginning. With the amount of noise they're making I have no doubt that the killer is hiding. He's going to remain hidden if he has any sense until they stop snooping around. Do you know how many people slip through their fingers?"

"You didn't," Ben said. Cyril's expression turned sour and Ben left the room, not waiting for any reply. Alfie smirked, although he wondered if there was more truth to his father's words than he would have cared to admit. Had the investigation brought more attention to the crime than was warranted? Had the killer gone into hiding? And now he had to worry about some bastard who had abused Joe as well. It felt as though a whole life had happened to Joe that Alfie hadn't been privy to, and he wasn't sure how this had happened. How had someone touched his son like that without him knowing.

The anger began to rise again, and he followed Ben outside.

"What are you doing about this? How are we going to find him?" Alfie asked tersely. Ben merely stared at the sky.

"I don't know," he admitted.

"That's not good enough. Damn it that's not good enough!" Alfie grabbed Ben's shoulder and pulled him around. He saw the same helpless look in Ben's eyes as he felt himself. Ben didn't even give Alfie a warning about touching a police officer like this.

"I know how you feel Alfie. I'm sorry. I hate that this is happening. I hate that it feels like nothing is ever going to change. I hate that there are people out there who get away with this stuff, over and over again. I don't know how it's going to stop."

"It's going to stop when we teach them a lesson," Alfie said through gritted teeth. "I know that you're all for locking people up, but at some point the justice system just doesn't work. What's the point of threatening them with jail time when they never get arrested for it anyway? They need to be taught a lesson. They need some justice. They need to have some sense being beaten into them."

Ben was silent.

"You agree with me, don't you?" Alfie said. The realization took him by surprise. There was a moment where their gazes levelled with each other. Ben did not say anything, but Alfie saw the truth in his eyes. He saw the understanding. Before he could say anything else, however, Ben received a phone call.

Chapter Nine

"I finally managed to get through to them boss. I told them that if they didn't help then they would be impeding and investigation and if more people died then they would be held liable and responsible, and a lot of the blowback would be on them for allowing these kinds of meetings and transactions to take place on their site. They didn't like that one bit. They keep track of their user's location data so they can match them up with people in their local area. I got them to send us the files so that we could pinpoint the phone that was in the same area as Joe the night he went missing. I'm sending you the precise location now. It'll lead you right to whoever did this. I'll be on my way to give you backup," Sunita said.

By 'they' she meant the developers of the app, who had finally relented in sharing information. Everyone in this world was always quick to cover their backs, and they did not want their name smeared with these scandalous crimes.

"We have a location. It's just coming through now," Ben said.

"I'm going with you. And don't try and tell me otherwise," Alfie replied. Ben wouldn't have dreamed of it. As much as he served the justice system he wasn't blind to the flaws within it, and Alfie had pinpointed some of them. His phone pinged again when the location came through. Ben and Alfie looked at each other.

"Shit. No fucking way," he said. Ben arched an eyebrow, but they wasted no time in heading to the location.

*

Alfie was hammering on the door. "Get the fuck out of the way Rachel. Where is he? Where is that bastard?" he asked as Rachel answered. Ben flashed Rachel his badge again and pulled her aside. Rachel was confused.

"Stay back. Stay out of the way," Ben ordered. Rachel's mouth slammed shut and she nodded mutely, staggering down the garden path. Ben followed Alfie inside, determined to not let him out of his sight. Ben declared himself and called out Gary's name. Alfie snarled like a wild animal who had been

176

let loose. He stormed through the house, as Gary stood in the doorway of the kitchen. He had a nonplussed look on his face.

"Can I help you?" he asked. As soon as he saw the expression on Alfie's face, Gary retreated into the kitchen and grabbed a carving knife, pointing the blade straight at Alfie. "I don't know what this is about, but I'm not letting you in here! You're a madman!"

"I'm not the mad one, you sick fuck. What the hell did you think was going to happen when you took Joe? Are you the one who touched him too? You fucking monster," Alfie raged.

"Alfie, wait!" Ben cried. Alfie wasn't going to be deterred by a man holding a knife though. He surged forward and lunged towards Gary. Gary brought the knife down in a sharp slashing motion and cut through Alfie's arm. Blood sprayed out in a red jet, but Alfie didn't seem to care. He landed on Gary and started pummelling him in the face, his fist driving back so fast that it was almost a blur. Gary was stunned and groggy. He tried in vain to fight back, but Alfie's onslaught was too much to cope with.

Ben rushed in, however, and managed to pull Alfie off. He kicked the knife out of reach. Alfie only now seemed to realize that he had been wounded. The anger had blinded him to anything else. He nursed his arm and the blood ran slick over his fingers. Ben stood over Gary, who spat out blood and glared.

"I want that man arrested. How dare he come into my home and attack me like this. He's feral!" Gary cried. He spat out again, and this time a tooth came with the blood.

"I'm not here for Alfie. I'm here for you," Ben said. "Where is the phone Gary?"

"What phone?"

"The phone you used to contact young men, to meet up with them wearing a mask, to potentially kill them."

"Where is he Gary? Where's my boy? I'm going to tear this house apart until I find him," Alfie growled.

"I don't know what you're talking about," Gary replied, a bewildered look on his face. "Whatever you think is going on here, this isn't it. I want my lawyer. I want someone sane who knows what's going on. I want-"

"Why are you here? Why are you doing this to us! Alfie, you need to keep leaving us alone. You can't come around here anymore."

"He's been here?" Gary scowled. "Why didn't you tell me?"

"I... I just wanted to forget it," Rachel shuddered in terror, glancing between these two men she had promised different parts of her life to.

"Everyone settle down," Ben said sternly, as though he was a teacher trying to restore order to the classroom. "Rachel, we're here because we got a ping on a phone. It's the same phone that belongs to the person who killed Joe."

"And it's that monster," Alfie snarled, looking like he was a dog itching to get off a leash.

"I didn't do it! You want a phone? Here," Gary pulled out his phone and tossed it towards Ben. "I have nothing to hide. I don't even have a security lock. Just swipe it and it'll open. I don't have any secrets," as he said this he glanced towards Rachel, who turned her head away in shame.

Ben quickly glanced through the various apps as well as some images. He didn't see anything that was incriminating.

"He could have wiped it! Or he could have another one," a look of realization came upon Alfie's face. "Yeah, yeah that must be it. But where are you hiding it?" he prowled around the room, looking like a bear that was on the hunt. He was big and mean and Ben thought he looked capable of tearing this place apart. Then it was as though a light bulb went off in his mind. He snapped his fingers. "The shed," he said, and raced outside.

Ben had a small torch attached to his keyring. He held it at eye level and a bright beam of light spilled out ahead of him. The garden was small and narrow. The plants were neat, the lawn trimmed to a smooth verdant layer, and at the rear of the garden was a brick shed. A broken padlock hung off the door. Alfie yanked it open.

"I don't keep anything valuable in there. This is a waste of time," Gary protested from behind. Ben shot him a wary glance, but his mind was whirring. Rachel and Gary sidled up beside him. Rachel looked as though she wanted to say something, but before she could there was a crash from inside the shed and then Alfie came out, holding a phone triumphantly, as if it were a trophy.

"See! This has to be it. This is it Gary. You are going down for a long time. You'd just better be glad that he's here," Alfie nodded towards Ben, "otherwise I'd show you what I'm capable of. You took my boy from me Gary," he snarled.

"I've never seen that phone before in my life. I barely even come down to the shed. This is all ridiculous!" Gary shook his head and held his arms aloft in the air, seemingly unable to comprehend how this was all happening.

And then Rachel spoke in a small voice. "Alfie… what were you doing here the other night?"

Alfie's face scrunched up. "What are you talking about?"

"When I found you in the garden. I yelled at you to leave. You were here, by the shed. I thought you had just climbed over the wall, but maybe you had been here for longer than that." She turned to face Gary. "It was a night when you were working late."

"I wasn't here. I don't know what you're talking about. I can't believe you're trying to protect him when we have the evidence right here," Alfie said in a despairing tone, pushing the phone towards Ben.

"Alfie, I saw you. We had a conversation. Don't even try to deny it," Rachel said.

"Why didn't you say anything?" Gary asked accusingly.

Rachel sighed. "I know things have been hard for Alfie, and they've been hard on Joe as well. Joe always thought the world of you Alfie. I wish that he had looked at me the way he did to you, and I knew that if I did anything to keep his Dad away then he would go on hating me more. I just thought you were drunk or something. You didn't seem quite right."

"Well maybe I was. It still doesn't change the fact that this man murdered our kid," Alfie spat the words out. Gary cursed under his breath and turned towards Ben.

"You had really better start doing something to get him under control."

Ben pursed his lips. "Give me the phone Alfie. This is the only way we're going to get out of this," he said. Alfie flashed a sneering look towards Gary, a look that said he had been ensnared in a trap. The phone was an old one. There was no security look. The camera was rudimentary. There was only one app, and it was the one that had been used to lure Joe to his death. Ben opened it, a sickening feeling twisting in his gut as he wondered what he was going to find on it. His gaze flicked from the phone to the people around him, this web of sorrow had drawn them all in.

The app loaded. A gallery of thumbnails was displayed on the screen, each one of them a square with different guys inside, as though they were all living in windows, waiting to be picked up. There was a message icon flashing. Ben clicked on it and a page filled with messages rippled down the screen. He scrolled down and clicked on the message thread from Joe. These messages had been brief. Others were not. In others he had sent pictures. At first glance it was clear that this couldn't have been Gary, even though the face was obscured by a mask. The build was far too stocky and tall. It was more like…

Ben's voice almost caught in his throat. He took a deep breath as he slowly moved the hand holding his torch, moving it towards his belt where a small can of pepper spray was nestled against the small of his back.

"Alfie, what tattoos do you have?" he asked.

Alfie scrunched up his face. "What? Why the hell are you asking me that now? What does that have to do with anything?"

"Just answer the question," Ben said softly.

The answer wasn't forthcoming from Alfie, but Rachel knew.

"He's got a snake running down his chest. On his stomach there's a playing card," she began, and then proceeded to describe a number of other distinctive tattoos, each one of which was ticked off by Ben as he stared at the picture.

It was Alfie. It had been Alfie all along.

"Alright Alfie. Get on your knees. Put your hands on the back of your head. You're under arrest for the murder of Joe-"

"What? What the fuck is this?" Alfie backed away. "It's him. It has to be him!" Alfie said.

Ben had no idea what was going on, but he knew the only way to bring an end to this situation was to show Alfie the terrible truth of the matter. He turned the phone and held it towards Alfie. Alfie peered at it and then he shook his head slowly, unable to bring himself to see the truth.

"No… no this can't be right. How did that get on there? How did he do that?"

"Alfie, I don't know what game you're trying to play, but it's time to stop it. You need to tell me the truth," Ben said.

"This is the truth! I would never have done this. Tell him Rachel. Tell him… you know me better than anyone. I know I wasn't perfect, but tell him I never would have done anything like this. This isn't me. I couldn't have hurt him," Alfie gasped.

"Alfie… don't you remember anything?"

"What do you mean? I know things weren't perfect, but it was just because we were young. Things could have been better if we had tried. We were both to blame really."

Rachel let out a dry, humourless laugh. "Both to blame? Alfie, have you really ignored everything that happened? You hurt us. You hurt Joe."

"What? I never would have done that."

"Alfie, you caught him kissing one of the posters of the footballer he liked. You threw him out of the room and down the stairs. He broke his damn arm because of you! It's why I can't believe that after all this time he still thinks the sun shines out of your ass. You hurt him and now you're telling me that you killed him as well?"

"What? No... I... I couldn't have. I wouldn't have. He was my boy. I loved him. I..." Alfie's expression twisted as though his features were being pulled in different directions. He staggered back and acted as though he had been punched in the gut, but really Ben thought it was just the force of the memory hitting him. He kept muttering to himself that he couldn't do this, so Ben took the opportunity to slap handcuffs on him before he became impossible to handle. Then he called for backup, and Alfie was hauled away.

Epilogue

"So this is it then?" Sunita asked as she looked at the report that Ben had typed up. Ben's shirt collar was open. He leaned his head back. There was a dull ache at the back of his skull, which didn't seem like it would ever go away.

"This is it," he said.

"Undiagnosed multiple personality disorder..." she let out a low whistle. "There's something I don't get though. How does Adonis fit into all of this?"

Ben rubbed his eyes. "Alfie was abused by Adonis. These things have a way of happening over and over again, cycling through the generations. Alfie was hurt, so he hurt Joe and other people. Maybe the abuse he suffered created this other persona. I don't know if it was a way for him to punish himself because he saw the weak child he used to be in his victims, or to win Adonis' approval, or as a way to try and outdo Adonis' legacy."

"Maybe it's a mixture of all three. I guess there's never going to be a way to logically explain the actions of an irrational mind."

"No, no I suppose there isn't."

"But his own son…"

"It must have been a breaking point for him to see his son delve into the same world. It wouldn't surprise me if there were other signs of abuse over the years."

"But why would Joe not tell anyone?"

Ben shrugged. "Probably scared. But for boys like Joe their fathers are their world. There's a kind of hero worship that happens and for some people they won't hate their fathers no matter what they've done. Look at that whole family as a case in point; Alfie never disowned Cyril even after learning everything he did."

"Do you think Cyril could have been Adonis?"

"I'm not sure, but I'm going to find out."

*

Ben found himself in the dank, damp house again. It was a house of sin and lies. The TV blared. Ben let himself in and walked into the lounge.

"What are you doing here?" Cyril asked.

"I came to ask you a question. Does the name Adonis mean anything to you?" Silence hung in the air. Cyril's gaze was glued to the screen. "I think it should. The man was a notorious abuser. I'm certain that he abused your son, and then your son turned out to be an abuser as well. These things happen to run in families so I'm just here to see if-"

"It's not me," Cyril spat. There was a dark look on his face. "He twisted my boy. I tried to save him, but there was always something a little wrong about Alfie. I wish I had been able to do more. I thought if I was strict with him… but he was already broken."

"You could have got him medical help."

Cyril laughed a brittle laugh. "Medical help? The world doesn't help people like us. It just wants to sweep us into the gutters so that we can get carried away with all the rest of the sewage."

"You know that he hurt a lot of people. He hurt your own grandson."

"They deserved to be hurt. They were all sinners."

"It's a bit rich for a man like you to be talking about sin."

"Who better? I'm more intimately acquainted with sin than you will ever be. I've made my peace though. But men like Adonis were monsters. He put poison into Alfie and that affected Joe as well. I wish there was a cure for it."

Ben could only shake his head at the sheer lack of sympathy from this man.

"So you weren't Adonis?" he asked, trying to maintain the reason why he was there.

Cyril shook his head. "No. But he won't worry you at all. I took care of him after I realized what was happening with Alfie. I took him off the playing board. You're welcome."

"You killed a man."

"Good luck trying to convict me without a body or any evidence. Seems like he had the last laugh though. He begged me to let him write a letter. Thought I'd grant him his dying wish, especially since it would rankle your lot. What's going to happen to Alfie now?"

"Nothing. That's the other thing that I came here to tell you. When he realized what he did I think something inside him snapped. He started a fight as soon as he got into prison. He let himself get stabbed and he died. You're the only one left Cyril."

Ben couldn't tell if he was imagining the wet sorrow in Cyril's eyes. It could have just been the reflection of the screen. They were an unpleasant family indeed. Unpleasant things had been done to them and they had done unpleasant things, but despite everything Ben couldn't help himself feel a flare of pity for Alfie, and especially Joe. Perhaps that was a good thing. Perhaps it showed that the job hadn't suffocated his conscience just yet. And maybe the only mercy here was the fact that the abusive cycle had ended, it was just a tragedy that it had to end in death.

Low Tech

Chapter one

"They're at it again," Mia said, rolling her eyes. Tabitha sighed and flicked away a few strands of tawny brown hair.

"Boys and their toys," she replied, casting a glance towards the other room where the murmuring voices bubbled with excitement, before she turned her attention back to the TV. It was often like this in the quiet cul-de-sac where two houses were joined as one. Mia and Tabitha had become fast friends, mostly because they had no choice in the matter. They had married two unique men, men whose bond stretched back to the very birth, and still had a hold on them now. It was a running joke that Adrian and George spent more time with each other than their wives. Sometimes, late at night, when Mia and Tabitha were alone in their beds, the joke lost its humour and it actually became a sad state of affairs.

However, there was nothing they could do about the status quo. The bond of these men went beyond brotherhood. It was forged in time, and their souls were inextricably linked. Even their first date with their eventual wives had been a double date, their weddings a joint one. Everything they did had to be done together, and now in their mid thirties it showed no signs of changing.

Mia and Tabitha shook their heads and sighed as they knew that another night would go by when they would not see their husbands.

*

"Look, see, it takes a record of my heart rate and then it uploads it to this app," George said as he pulled out his phone, holding it alongside the fitness monitoring device he wore on his wrist, "so that I can keep track of it. With all this data I can see where my peak times are, when exercise is most effective, and I can see how it dips. Look, this is where I had that cold," he pointed to a dip in the graph, a wide smile stretching across his face as he was so proud of his new device.

"And what are you going to do with all this data?" Adrian wore a sceptical look and had his arms folded across his chest.

"What can't I do? Think of the implications; I can chart my bio readings throughout the years. I can see where I'm most productive and most active, and I can tailor my schedule to this. I can also see when I'm flagging and if my performance dips then I know that it's likely I've got a cold coming, meaning that I can take medicine before I start truly suffering from it, which also means that I'll recover quicker. This is going to change my life. You should really get one too."

"I don't know. I'm not sure that I like how invasive it is. I'm fine with the one I have already. It does everything yours does, but it doesn't collect all this data on me. And really the only thing I use it for is the pedometer."

George rolled his eyes and uttered a derisive snort. "Then all the data you're going to collect about yourself is going to be faulty. You're not going to be able to make any serious conclusions because you can't trust the input. This is basic statistics Adrian. I can't believe that you would be so close minded about this."

"I'm not close minded, I just get a little freaked out when I hear about all the data these companies are collecting. I mean, sure it's going to help you with your exercise regimes and all that stuff, but aren't you worried that the company has this data too?"

"And what are they going to do with it?"

"I don't know, they could try and take advantage of it, like maybe they'll see when you're thirsty so they'll send an advert towards you."

"Which means that I'll be able to get a drink there and then. I really don't think it's as bad as you're making out. You've been listening to too many fear mongering articles. Come on, when has more technology ever been a bad thing? It's just fear of the unknown that is holding these people back. We need to look to the future. This is the way the world is going. People are becoming more connected with technology and it's becoming more of an integral part of our lives. I thought you more than anyone would have been able to understand that and see the benefits."

Adrian exhaled slowly. "But we have to look at what we're losing as well as what we're gaining. There are so many warning stories out there of how technology can go wrong. There's something essential about humanity that we risk losing if we keep diluting it with all of this technology."

George waved his hands in the air dismissively. "You've never been able to get rid of the humanist streak, have you Adrian? The only reason we think there's something special about humanity is because we're egotistical creatures who can't believe that we just arose and evolved because of chance. Deep down everyone wants to think that we were curated lovingly by an intelligent designer who set up the world as our playground and gave us everything we could have ever wanted, but that's just not true. We're as much of a random element as everything else, and our existence only happened thanks to chance. Everyone keeps trying to make sense of it, but it's pointless. There's nothing inherently special about us Adrian, and the longer people cling to the belief that there is, the harder it's going to be to move forward."

"And you think giving up everything you are to technology is moving forward?"

"Of course! I'm only worried that it's going to take too long. I mean, we might have forty years left if we're lucky, maybe fifty if medical technology continues to increase, but at that point are we going to be cognizant enough to really enjoy the benefits? Are you really telling me you wouldn't like an eye implant that could see all the spectrums of light, while also zooming in on something far away, no matter how small? There could even be a display where it shows information about whatever you're looking at, and it could take screenshots so that you can revisit memories and recall them as they actually happened. Now eye-witnesses would be the most reliable pieces of evidence when criminals are prosecuted. And that's just with the eye! Imagine everything else."

Adrian continued to shake his head. "As much as I love technology I just can't come to the same conclusion as you George. There has to be something special about us because we're the only life forms on earth to have developed consciousness. Surely that says something about us? Sometimes our flaws define us as well. If we all have these implants then what's going to differentiate us? If we're augmented by technology then surely there's going to be no need for athletic competition, games of skill would always be solved and only end up as draws, there would be no need for competition anywhere."

"New games would arise. New ways of competing would come to the fore, ways that we can't begin to compute. It wasn't so long ago in the grand scheme of things that people believed the four-minute mile was impossible, but that barrier was broken. I'll grant you that humans have always been great at one thing; breaking down barriers and pushing the limits of what is achievable. All I want to do is push that to the next level. Let's see what we're all capable of once we're augmented by technology."

"Or let's just lose that drive as the technology overwhelms us. Isn't there a danger that we're not going to get the balance right?"

"Maybe, maybe, but that's why there are tests and oversights and things. I'm sure that all the major companies are doing research right now into it and they'll develop a way for us to use it safely."

"I think you have more faith in them than I do."

"Well, that's always been the way, and don't forget, you've always made the wrong choice when it comes to tech," George teased. Adrian sighed. To outsiders their discussions often seemed like full blown rows, but really they were just positing different viewpoints and defending them with all the force they could muster. They never lost sight of their friendship, and despite their differences of opinion they remained firm friends. It had been like this throughout their lives, beginning with arguing over who was better; Mario or Sonic.

"I just worry that eventually we're going to give so much of ourselves over to humanity that we won't have anything left. If all of industry is automated, then people are going to be out of work. And sure, maybe by that point we'll have some kind of universal basic income where people can have their needs met so we won't have billions of homeless, starving people out there. I get that. But eventually the records are going to be pushed so hard that eventually they aren't going to be broken at all. There's going to be absolutely no mystery to the world, and I'm not sure I want to live in a world like that."

"Then you're one of the people who are standing in the way of progress, and I would have expected better of you."

Adrian shot George a withering look. "Okay then, let's take things like art and literature. If what you're saying is true then at some point writers and artists and poets and anyone else who is in the creative arts is just going to be redundant, because eventually an AI is going to be developed that can create coherent stories in the blink of an eye," Adrian snapped his fingers to punctuate his point. "So if industry is taken away and if the arts are taken away then what are we going to have left? Are we just supposed to laze around and make babies, to what end? What is our purpose going to be? We need something to drive us forward."

"That's the beauty of it; humanity needs to reframe what it thinks the meaning of life is. We don't need a purpose any longer because we will have created something that can do everything for us. We won't have to have any of these burdens. We can be zen and simply focus on the moment in which we exist. There won't *be* anything else to do."

"I fail to see how this life is desirable in any way."

"Because you're not opening up your mind," as George said this he made a motion with his hands that made it look as though he was opening up his scalp and scooping out his brain. "This is what I'm saying. It's as though we've all gotten addicted into thinking that this is the only way to live, but it's not. We're so far down the rabbit hole that we can't see any other possibilities. We need to take a step back and open our eyes again to everything that is possible, because there are things that we just can't fathom, and yeah it's going to be scary because it's something different to what we've always known, but fear should not stand in the way of progress."

"Fear isn't always something to be ignored George. It's as much a part of our instinct as anything else. It's helped us during our evolution, and we shouldn't just ignore it when something feels deeply wrong."

"We should when all the data is telling us that it's wrong. We are flawed beings Adrian, but we can correct those flaws. I get it, okay, you've been brought up on a diet of dystopian movies where technology has run amok, but those movies were written by humans who were scared and who couldn't grasp the concepts of what benefits this could all bring. It's just propaganda, and I know that you think of yourself as someone who isn't going to be influenced by that, but anyone can be."

"I'm guessing in your world AI wouldn't write movies where it's the bad guy," Adrian muttered.

"It could write anything. It's not going to be biased against any type of person and it's not going to be putting forward any agenda. I understand that there's still some reluctance to accept that AI could be better than humans in the creative fields, but if it's better then it's better, surely at the end of the day it's the quality that should matter, not who made it? Isn't that what equity and equal opportunities is about? It takes me back thinking about when the orchestra in America started having blind auditions because they found that the judges were biased against women. After the blind auditions began taking place, they could not judge anyone on who they were, but only the quality of the piece they were playing. Isn't that what we should strive for, for the best pieces of work to rise to the top?"

"And when everything is made by an AI?"

George shrugged. "Then it's just another reason why humans have to get their egos in check. I think we've been ruined by the fact that we've been at the top of the food chain for so long. Technology is the future. It's here to stay. It's not going anywhere and we should embrace it as tightly as possible, because it's only going to make our lives better."

Adrian remained unconvinced, but sadly for him he could not make a strong argument against anything George was saying. He kept returning to that primal instinct of his to protect his humanity, but was that just a reckless survival instinct that had no basis in reality? The last thing he wanted was to accept that he was arguing from a losing position, but it certainly seemed that way. Even when he left George's company and returned home with Mia it was still weighing heavily on his mind. They slipped into bed and he stared at the ceiling.

"Go on then, tell me what's troubling you," Mia said.

"It's just an argument that George and I were having. He's adamant that we should embrace technology and throw away all the things that we think are special about humanity, because anything an AI can do they can do better than humans."

"I'm not sure about that."

"Me neither, but I don't know if I'm just arguing against it because it feels wrong, not because it's actually wrong."

"Is there a difference?"

"There is."

"Well, I don't think you should spend too much time thinking about it. At the end of the day I don't think it's going to matter much."

"Why do you say that? Technology is such a big part of our lives now."

"Yeah, but can you really imagine people accepting it taking over other aspects of our lives? We're too insecure for that," Mia said, rather pragmatically. Adrian laughed and nodded, suspecting that there was a lot of truth to her words. "Besides, I'm sure there are things that we can do that AI can't, no matter how well developed it is," she added. He was about to ask what she meant, but the words were stolen from his mouth by a deep kiss, and suddenly he forgot all about his argument with George as the cold, emotionless technology was replaced by soft, warm flesh.

*

Adrian and George had been born in the same hospital ward to two women who lived in the same street. After they left the hospital, these women began spending more and more time together, and thus the boys developed a strong bond. They grew up in an era where technology was accelerating fast, and where it was becoming far more involved in day-to-day life. It just so happened that they began a rivalry as well. It started when Adrian and George were given gaming consoles for their birthday. Adrian was given a Super Nintendo, while George was gifted a Sega Megadrive. Their parents had discussed this and thought it was better for them to have different consoles as then they would be able to have a wider range of games, and George would be able to go to Adrian's house to play on the Super Nintendo, while Adrian would be able to go to George's house and play on the Sega Megadrive. While this did happen, what their parents couldn't have anticipated was that the boys would start defending their consoles. George thought Sonic was far cooler than Mario. His games were kinetic and flashy, while Mario's were slow and plodding. But Adrian argued that Mario's cast of characters were far more interesting, and that the Super Nintendo had a better range of games. They spent hours playing and debating, sometimes enjoying the debates more than the actual gaming.

Then, when they were a little older, Adrian was gifted a Nintendo 64 while George had a PlayStation. Sega had suffered a downswing in popularity, which George felt was undeserved, but with the PlayStation he had a new champion. With its sleek compact discs instead of Nintendo's archaic cartridges and the superior graphics, the PlayStation was a far more attractive prospect to teenagers than the Nintendo 64, especially with that console's strange shark fin controller, an abstract design that seemed wrong when anyone looked at it. While there were some fun games on the Nintendo, this round definitely went to the PlayStation, especially considering that many of Adrian and George's classmates owned the latter. The talk was of Metal Gear Solid and Final Fantasy and Spyro, despite Adrian and George spending hours and hours shooting each other in Goldeneye.

Adrian was not willing to accept defeat so heavily though, and remained loyal to Nintendo even in the Gamecube era. Adrian also suffered a humiliation here as he had returned for a brief fling with Sega's Dreamcast, a disaster that put the company on a brink of bankruptcy and ended its involvement with the console scene. It would only be a publisher of games thereafter. Adrian lorded this over George as Nintendo was the behemoth who had won the console wars against its old foe, but it too was suffering against Sony, especially when the PlayStation 2 came out. George reaffirmed his loyalty to Sony and crowed as the GameCube suffered an ignominious death, forgotten now by all but the most loyal of gamers.

Of course, while the 90s had mostly been defined by game consoles, as time went on there were other pieces of technology to get their hands on. Mobile phones became far more prevalent and more accessible. George had a stalwart Nokia, while Adrian had a Motorola phone that flipped like the communicators in *Star Trek*. On a purely aesthetic basis Adrian won this particular contest. They challenged each other to having the best ring tones and scoring highest in certain games, as well as vying for the best contracts. Whenever a new edition of a phone was released they rushed out to try and get it. George managed to get one with a colour screen, while Adrian managed to get his hands on one with a camera. At the time George had scoffed at this, wondering why on earth anyone would need a camera on a phone, but of course as the years continued to turn the phone became an all-in-one device. As smart phones were developed George stuck his flag to Apple, while Adrian preferred the adaptability of Samsung devices. Yet again the friends were on opposite sides of the technological divide. George had an iPod and iMac and iPad, surrounding himself with the gleaming silver devices, so sleek and sharp, vaunting the joys of having Apple products. Adrian always thought George was full of hot air though, for in his opinion Apple was more like a cult, charging people far too much entirely because of the brand name rather than the technology.

But then George had always been like this. Even when it came to personal computers as well. They had taken on a challenge to build their own gaming PCs. George chose to install Windows as his operating system, while Adrian opted for Linux, wanting more freedom as a user. George had always been more willing to put his trust in the huge corporations though, never suspecting that they would have an alternative agenda. Adrian was more cautious. He was a late adopter of online shopping because he did not like the idea of his financial information being stored in servers that could be hacked. George never had such qualms though, and often came around to Adrian's house showing off the latest package he had received from Amazon. He went through a period of ordering strange things just for the sake of it to see what he could receive through the post.

Eventually Adrian caught up, once it became clear that it was practically impossible to avoid online shopping.

As the years passed, they spent inordinate amounts of time comparing their devices with each other. They somehow always found themselves on opposite sides. Even when they spoke about things they both loved, like *World of Warcraft*, they still found things to argue about. It was such a natural part of their relationship that they did not see anything wrong with it. Occasionally they would get a little too tense for comfort, but even then they would just need a few hours to cool off and then they would pick up on something else, never mentioning the animosity again.

When they started dating Mia and Tabitha, it was difficult for the women to come to terms with this dynamic. It wasn't quite anything like what the two of them had experienced before. They were certain that after a bad argument the two would never talk to each other again, and offered kind words and supportive shoulders, only to find that the following day or even sometimes just a few hours later, that Adrian and George were acting as though nothing had happened. Eventually Mia and Tabitha understood the relationship, but it never came to them easily.

Adrian and George discovered that two houses had come on the market at the same time, that were adjoined to each other. They though it made sense to live next to each other as they were such good friends, and so as with everything else they moved at the same time. Mia and Tabitha knew there was no sense protesting, although by this point they had become friends and so were glad to at least have some companionship of their own.

Adrian and George continued their arguments through to the modern era. Now Adrian praised that versatility of the Nintendo Switch, with its ability to be played on the TV or in a handheld mode, as well as the quality of the games. George scoffed at the size of it though, and mocked Adrian for all the games he would never be able to play on it. It was an eternal debate that neither of them were ever going to win, but winning wasn't the most important thing, the argument was. It was the glue of their friendship and things would not have been the same without it.

However, this argument about the nature of technology felt like a fundamental shift in their discourse. Before they had always debated the merits of pieces of technology, of things, of objects, but this was something that would change the very fabric of humanity. It was a philosophical debate that may never have any conclusion, but for the first time Adrian was worried that his friend was beginning to lose his mind. There was so much to be thankful for technology for, but Adrian was convinced that a line had to be drawn somewhere, otherwise humanity would just slip away and nothing would be left.

This debate had mostly started when the next step in gaming came to the fore in the form of virtual reality. The early headsets were exclusive to PCs, because only they had the processing power to handle the graphics. The headsets were ungainly things, having to be fastened to the ceiling with wires extending from the black helmets back to the PC, like exterior veins. As with everything else, the two friends had opted for different headsets. Adrian had chosen a Vive headset, while George had picked an Oculus Rift.

They were both good, and at first being virtual reality was genuinely like taking a step into the future. It did become rather unwieldy though, and the software did not move at the same pace as the hardware. Many of the games were repetitive, but the potential was there for something truly special. Sometimes they would link up their headsets and watch a movie together, which confused Mia and Tabitha as they could have just as easily watched a movie in the lounge. Adrian and George insisted that it was a different experience in virtual reality. They played ping pong together, darts, went bowling together, as well as shooting zombies and robots. It allowed them to enter a world where anything was possible.

George was convinced that this was going to be the next evolution in the world. He was not a gambling man, but he often declared that he would have bet his house on the fact that a virtual world was going to be created where people could live second lives, better lives.

It hadn't quite arrived yet though. It was coming close, especially considering that Oculus was bought by Facebook. Once again George felt superior as now with the hands free Oculus Quest headset he was no longer bound to his PC. Adrian would often see George outside in the twilight evenings playing on his virtual reality device in the garden, watching with envy as he tried to keep the mass of wires untangled.

It did indeed seem as though the world was heading towards a precipice from which it would not be able to back away from. At some point they were going to have an opportunity to step away from reality, but Adrian wasn't sure. He liked virtual reality, but again he worried that leaving reality behind was going to be abandoning something precious.

*

This discussion came up again one evening as they were sharing dinner. Mia and Tabitha were drinking wine and sharing a private joke, while George was talking to Adrian about the latest developments in the MetaVerse.

"It's going to be great, you're going to be able to own your own piece of land there and you can do with it whatever you want. I mean, when you think of what the actual world is like this gives people a chance to own something tangible," George said.

"Except it's really not tangible, is it? I mean, they literally can't touch it, and it only exists in the realm of virtual reality. They can't really visit it. If the servers ever go down then it will just blink out of existence. Why would anyone want to put their money into that?"

"Because they get to be a part of a growing world! It's like being a frontiersman of old, exploring the Wild West before there were any settlers. You get to be the one to lay down a marker and make history."

"The Wild West wasn't managed by a huge corporation," Adrian muttered.

"You really need to get this bee out of your bonnet. Corporations aren't these evil monoliths that you keep thinking they are. All they want to do is make money."

"And that's such a great thing?" Adrian challenged.

"I'm not saying it is, but it does mean that in order to make money they're going to have to make the best product for the consumer, otherwise they're going to leave. So they have to do what's right and what's best in order to earn that money."

"I really wish that was the case, but I think you're being a little naïve there. Anyway, I don't get how they can charge for property in the MetaVerse when there's not going to be a lack of space. Like, in the real world I can't just add an extra bit of land to England, but just a line of code can change things there. Why does it cost any money when there's no scarcity?"

"Well… it takes up server space and there are going to be communities built, so you would want one to be in a community that you identify with, and one that is close to the action."

"I don't know, feels like we're just going to be rats in a maze at that point. I just feel like they're harvesting everything about us until there's nothing left," Adrian said.

"I feel the same way. I wouldn't want to live my life in the MetaVerse," Tabitha said. George had been about to say something, but now his mouth hung agape, unable to believe that she had just said this.

"But I thought we talked about this last night. I tried to explain it to you. I thought you understood," George said.

"I understand just fine," Tabitha replied, "and it's just not for me. And frankly I don't really like the idea of you doing it either. I mean, this promise of a second life, it makes me think that there are going to be a lot of people on there who are trying to make up for things they think they missed out on. I mean, are there going to be people who are looking for a second wife as well, or a second family?"

"You know I'd never do that," George shook his head vehemently.

"I'm sure you wouldn't, but what if one day you were watering your MetaGarden when you look over your MetaWall and you see

218

some MetaNeighbour waving and fluttering her eyelashes at you, and suddenly you're in her MetaBed MetaFuc-"

"I would never do that," George said sternly, glaring at Tabitha. A moment of awkward silence descended upon the table. Tabitha put her hand to her mouth as a small yelping burp bubbled between her lips. It was followed by an uneasy laugh, and clearly she had had a little bit too much wine. "That's not what this is about. It's a way to begin a new world, where we can leave these old tendencies of human nature behind. It's a purer, better way to live."

"Well if you want to live it then you're going to have to do so without me there because I'm not turning myself into some digital construct. My body is just as much a part of me as my mind, and I don't think we should ignore that. I don't get why people are so eager to escape from the flesh we've been given," Tabitha said.

"Because the trappings of mortal flesh are weak and impermanent. If we can upload our minds to a digital server then we can live forever and we don't have to ever suffer the indignity of death," George replied.

"That's assuming that there is nothing after death," Tabitha shot back.

"There isn't any evidence to suggest that there is. We don't remember anything before birth. We are sprung from the void, and to the void we must return. The only way to live forever is to make sure that our minds are uploaded to a server. At the end of the day all we are is data, and that data can be preserved."

Tabitha then looked at George with steely eyes. Her words trembled as she spoke. "Really George? Is that what you think? Are we just data?" They locked gazes with each other and unlike the arguments that Adrian and George had, this one didn't seem as though it would fade with time. Sometimes disagreements between married couples were far sharper and cut more deeply than anything between friends. George did not seem too sympathetic to Tabitha's concerns, however.

"This is the way forward Tabitha. There's no point in trying to turn away from progress, because then you just get trampled on," George spoke in a low, solemn voice.

"Isn't it funny how people claim that things are progress when it always means that other people get trampled on? Maybe moving forward isn't the most important thing George. Maybe it's about looking around at what you have and understanding that it's special, that you have everything you need here rather than trying to find something in some MetaVerse that doesn't really exist."

"Just because you can't touch it doesn't mean it doesn't exist. Our thoughts are just as real as any other part of us," George said, but Tabitha was already rushing away from the table, overwhelmed by emotion. She had her face in her hands to try and hide her tears. Shallow wine remained in her glass, while Mia rose to walk after her. George had a stern look on his face and then shook his head. He cut into his steak savagely, carving it apart with his knife.

"Just think about how many animals are going to be saved as well. If we managed to find a way to hook us up to a nutritional drip then we wouldn't need to breed animals for food," George continued, as though the bomb had not been dropped on their evening.

"Is that really all you can talk about now George? Don't you want to speak about what happened?" Adrian asked, not willing to engage in an argument about how living in the MetaVerse would be better for the animal species on earth.

"Don't worry about her. She just doesn't understand. I really thought that I could sway her mind, Adrian. I thought she understood the way I think and how this is going to be better for us. I always thought in a marriage you're supposed to be a team, but right now I don't feel very supported."

"Then maybe you should start seeing it from her point of view. With all this talk about the MetaVerse she probably thinks that you're unhappy with the life you've built. The problem with looking towards the horizon is that you never actually look at your current surroundings. You keep striving for something more George, and you think it'll get to the point where humans don't have to push themselves to do anything other than laze around and enjoy the beauty of the moment, but you could do that now and you aren't. When was the last time you spent an evening in the arms of your wife? I think all she wants is to be close to you, when all you're doing is pushing yourself away."

"It's not about that Adrian. I wish she would understand that it's about keeping us together, beyond this flesh," he pinched his arm and then stared at it, as though it was a fleeting thing that didn't matter at all. Adrian looked at his friend with fear in his eyes, worried that he had lost sight of what was truly important. Was it possible that he was going to lose his wife as well?

*

Later that evening, Adrian was in bed with Mia again.

"I can't believe that happened tonight. I'm really worried about him. I tried talking to him about it, but he's so tied to this idea that the MetaVerse is the future. He can't seem to understand why anyone would disagree with him. I'm worried that one day he's just going to enter that world and then never come back," Adrian said, his words heavy with fear.

"Isn't there something you can say to him? You've been friends for so long, you must have spoken about this kind of thing before. You've always managed to pull him back when he's had one of his crazy ideas."

"Yeah, but this time there's something different. I just can't quite put my finger on it. It's as though he's become obsessed. He won't listen to any reason other than his own, as though he's convinced that this is the only way forward. I know he's always been fanatical about the companies he supports. He even went to one of the vigils they held after Steve Jobs died, but this is something else, and I just don't understand it. Like, he seems to want to just plug himself in at some point and enter the MetaVerse, but the technology isn't there yet. It can't support everything he wants it to do, and I get that he wants to be at the cutting edge of it, standing at the gates of this place to welcome everyone else, but there isn't going to be anyone else for a long while. If you look at the marketing data then you'll see that the Quest hasn't sold nearly as well as they would have hoped. I think by now they wanted it to be in most homes, but people just aren't willing to adopt this technology this early. It's going to be years before it becomes a place where people actually want to spend a significant amount of time, and even then I think you and Tabitha might be right… I think people aren't going to want to give up on the world they know, at least while the sun is still shining."

"Yeah, maybe when the climate changes for good and there's no way back people will be more eager to enter a virtual world," Mia said wryly.

"I guess it takes people dying to make an extreme change to their circumstances. I just can't understand why George is so adamant to make the change now. I guess maybe he thinks if he misses out on the early stages of this that he's going to regret it, and maybe he'll miss his place in history. I'll never forget how annoyed he was when Amazon started becoming a big thing. He was so angry that he hadn't thought of the idea himself because it seemed so simple. I kept telling him that it wouldn't have mattered anyway because he didn't have the capital to invest to make it a success, but he wouldn't listen. I think he's always been frustrated that he couldn't turn his passion for tech into becoming a billionaire. When you think of all the money we've spent on it over the years it would be nice to have made some out of it," Adrian said, smiling wistfully as he thought of simpler times when it seemed as though anyone could become a billionaire.

Mia was silent for a few moments. "Adrian, there's something I think I should tell you." There was a hesitancy in her voice that caught his attention. He looked askance towards her and furrowed his brow, for she had a certain way of delivering bad news that was always notable. There was always a long preamble, but her tone of voice gave away the fact that the news was grim.

"What is it?" he asked.

"Look, I shouldn't really be telling you this because I was told it in confidence by Tabitha and… well… she did swear me to secrecy. She said that George was going to tell you in his own time, but I guess he hasn't yet and I think you should know the truth. I don't think it's fair of him to keep this from you given that you've been such good friends for such a long time. I don't want to take it into my own hands, but I am your wife and you come first so… I'm sure Tabitha will understand when I tell her. She might be mad for a while but…"

"Mia, what are you talking about?" Adrian snapped, hoping to return her attention to the present moment instead of allowing her words to wander off like a distracted dog always jerking his owner's leash in every direction.

Mia inhaled sharply. "Obviously you noticed the tension between Tabitha and George tonight."

Adrian nodded, clamping his lips shut as he summoned the patience to wait for these final few moments before she got to the heart of the matter.

"Well, there is a reason for it. It didn't just come out of the blue. You see, they've been struggling recently and it's because… well… it's because of George."

"What about George?" Adrian asked through gritted teeth.

"He's ill Adrian, really ill."

Suddenly all the tension dissipated from Adrian's body and his blood turned cold. It felt as though someone had punched him in the gut. If he had not already been lying down he would have lost all feeling in his legs.

"What do you mean he's ill?" Adrian's words choked in his throat. His chest tightened as reality crashed in on his mind. There was always the sense that life was going to continue rolling forward without ceasing, that things were always going to be sedate and steady, but then stumbling blocks and obstacles careened into view and made everything jerk to a halt. Things like this were supposed to happen to other people, not to Adrian and not to people in his world.

"I'm sorry Adrian, but it's pretty bad. I really thought he would have told you by now. It's just... I think Tabitha thought that their final days together would be spent together, when instead he keeps losing himself in virtual reality and in these dreams of things that are never going to take shape. I know it's going to be hard, but I think for his own sake he's going to need you to speak to him."

Adrian thought about it for a moment, and then he flung away the blankets and swung his legs out of the bed.

"You're going now?" Mia asked.

"When else? There might not be a tomorrow." Adrian threw on his robe and fastened it around his waist. He then stormed out of the house and went next door. He and George had each other's spare keys. He knew that Tabitha would be in bed and by the light shining in the downstairs gaming room he knew that George would have lost himself in the virtual world, so Adrian opened the door himself and closed it behind him, marching towards the room.

Once inside, he saw that George was standing there with the headset obscuring his vision. His arms waved, and to an outside observer it was an odd, eerie silent dance.

"George," Adrian called out tersely. He had to repeat the word again and again, but George had headphones it, completely immersing himself in the virtual world. Adrian could have left this for later, but anger swelled within him after having been lied to by his friend, so he jerked the headset off and yanked the headphones out of his ears. George spun around, disoriented and aghast. There was a strong unspoken rule against this.

"What are you doing?" he yelled as he tried to grab the headset from Adrian's hands, but Adrian kept it out of reach.

"I could ask you the same thing! After all we've been through why the hell haven't you told me that you're ill?"

The wind was taken out of George's sails because of this. He stepped back and looked at the floor.

"Because if I told you then it would be real."

"What does that even mean? It's still real now."

"I know! But in my mind, I mean. I told Tabitha because I had to, but if I told you then there was no going back. I would have to face the fact that this could be the end. I just wanted things to be normal for a little while longer, that's all."

"So it's bad then," Adrian said, his tone suddenly shifting, the anger giving way to fear. George nodded. He sighed as he took a seat. Adrian sank to the couch as well, placing the virtual reality headset on the desk.

"They think so. My odds aren't great. I never thought it would be like this, you know? I always thought we'd live to see the future, and now... well... the future can't come quickly enough."

"Surely there has to be another option. There has to be some way to heal you."

"Not physically. That's why I've been so adamant that this is the way forward. I've been looking into so many ways that I can save my digital consciousness so that I might still exist. I thought the MetaVerse might be my best hope, but it hasn't advanced as much as I thought it would. I think I might end up running out of time."

"So if this is happening then why aren't you spending more time in the real world? I know you don't want to admit this, but surely it's better to spend time in the world that truly matters?"

"It all matters to me Adrian. I just... I want to leave something behind, even if it is just a digital footprint. I've been doing a lot of research and there's a way that I think I can get around this."

"George, you must know that you're grasping at straws here. Just accept that the world is the way it is and try and live out the rest of your life the best you can. Spend time with your wife. Spend time with me and Mia. Come on, we can bust out the consoles we used to play when we were kids. We can see if we can beat our times on Sonic."

George let out a wry laugh. "I think those days are gone Adrian. What's the point of looking back?"

"So that we can see where we came from."

"You know I've always preferred looking at where we're going, the only problem now is that I'm not going to be able to see it with you. I'm never going to know the promised land."

"But you know that you could have lived for a thousand years and never gotten to that promised land. I know you think that this virtual reality paradise is inevitable, but you're neglecting the fact that human nature is often prone to shooting itself in the foot and doing things that aren't necessarily the best for it. Surely you can see that people are stubborn enough to hold onto this reality and not ignore it for the sake of a virtual one, even if it might have its advantages. The future you want for the human race isn't necessarily the future that is going to happen."

George sighed. "I know all that, I just really thought this was a way that we could cheat death. I thought if somehow I could upload my consciousness into the cloud somewhere then I would still be alive. A part of me would still be here. I mean, haven't we always assumed that Heaven is made up of clouds? Maybe this is the way the afterlife is going to be made real. I just hate the thought of knowing there's nothing waiting for us when we die."

George stared into the void and his words took on a hollow quality. His fear was a fear that spoke to most men, a fear that we all tried to shy away from even though it lurked within the back of our minds, a silent companion that made a chill run down our spines.

"Maybe we've been arrogant in assuming that there isn't anything. We don't know that there isn't, after all. Maybe there has been some truth to the different world religions all along."

"I guess that's all a dying man is left with, blind hope that he's been wrong all this time," George replied sarcastically. His tone then turned more pensive. "I just hate knowing that it's over. I hate knowing there's nothing left."

"You still have something left George. You still have Tabitha. You should spend what time left you have with her. She's the most important thing now, more important than anything else."

"Yeah, I suppose she is. I just… I've been spending a lot of the time thinking about the old days. Do you remember when we were kids, running between each other's houses to switch between the Megadrive and the SNES? We used to talk about being inside the games, about running alongside Sonic or jumping with Mario, and we're so close to being able to make that truly believable and I'm going to miss out on it."

Adrian didn't have anything to say. He knew there was nothing he could say to make anything better. Instead, he reached out and placed a hand on George's shoulder, wanting to show him that there were some things he could get in reality that he never would in the virtual world.

"I get that you're trying to ignore what's happening, but living in the virtual world is only going to make you bleed time away, and I think life is less about aiming for what you want the world to be like and trying to make the best of what it is. In the end for as much as we can hope and dream about how our lives are going to turn out, this is all we have."

George nodded sombrely and he seemed to accept this judgment. As the old friends rose from their seats they hugged each other. Adrian felt a twitch of emotion within as he realized that the moments with George were growing short. For all the years they had spent together, all the hours spent debating various things or losing themselves in fantasy worlds, time was running out, and before too long he was going to have to know what life was like without his best friend. The grim reality of this thought shattered his usual calm and pragmatic demeanour. The men returned to their wives, and when Adrian went back to Mia he collapsed and burst into tears, unable to cope with the truth that one day soon he would have his last argument with George.

*

The days crawled by. There were moments when nothing seemed amiss at all. Things would be normal and Adrian would be able to fool himself into thinking that there had been some mistake and George wasn't ill. They would talk about all the things they used to talk about, and spend a lot of time with their wives. However, there was always the undercurrent of inevitability about life. There was always the unspoken horror that imbued each of their conversations with a futility, a subject that all of them were aware of, but none of them wanted to face. They were all trying in vain to live in ignorance, but that could only be bliss for so long.

Eventually George began to have bad days, and then terrible days, and then utterly awful days where he howled in pain and looked a shell of the man he once had been. His skin turned a gaunt shade and there were heavy bags under his bloodshot eyes. It was as though Adrian was seeing his friend wither before his eyes.

Then, late one night, there was a hammering on Adrian's door. He rose, for he knew that Mia wouldn't. It was a quirk of hers that once she was asleep she could not be stirred without great effort, and if he asked her to open the door then she would have cursed at him and pulled the blankets around her, swiftly sinking into sleep again.

"You have to do something about him. He's gone off the deep end and I can't take it. Why can't he just be normal? Why can't he just do this with dignity?" Tabitha cried. She trembled with frustration. Adrian wondered what George had gotten himself into this time. Adrian welcomed her into the house and told her to make herself comfortable while he went to see George. He breathed deeply as he entered the house and found George sitting at the computer. The glow of the screen illuminated him, and when he turned around after noticing Adrian's presence he did not seem uneasy at all.

"I just had your wife coming to me in tears. She says that you've lost your mind," Adrian said.

George laughed. "Of course she would think that. She just doesn't understand. I've found it Adrian! I've found the thing that is going to keep me alive!"

Adrian looked at him sceptically.

"Don't give me that look," George said, waving Adrian over. "Look, it's all safe and above board. I found this company. Now, it's experimental technology, but they need people to test it and, well, who better to test it than someone who doesn't have anything to lose? What they do you see is they take scans of your brain and then they implant a chip, and it reads all the neurological data and then uploads that to the server, keeping it all intact. It's immortality Adrian. They've done it! I can live forever!" He grinned in triumph, but Adrian could only look at his friend in horror.

He stared at the screen, glancing at the procedure. "George, this isn't living. This is just... it's just capturing data. You're not going to be able to touch anyone. You're not going to be able to experience anything. You're just going to be sat in a server, a string of numbers. You'll be nothing but code."

"For now, but eventually technology is going to reach a point where this code can be untangled and then placed either in some virtual world or maybe even in a robotic body and I'll be able to interact with the world again. And even here they say that they can link the data up to different programs where you can still exercise your minds. I'll still be able to do crosswords, and maybe I can even access the Internet as well! Hell, I might be able to talk to people through a messaging service. This is it Adrian. This is the next step of human evolution and I'm going to be one of the pioneers!"

He spoke so excitedly that Adrian hated to burst his bubble, but there was nothing else he could do. He had a heavy sigh and stepped away from the computer. "You sound like one of those people who thought that the way to immortality was to be cryogenically frozen. They were certain that one day the technology would arise to unfreeze them and bring them back into the world, but it never did. We're more than data George. I know that you're looking for any way to cling to life, but this isn't it. There is no way for you to stay here. I hate to say that because there's nothing I would rather do than keep some part of you alive, but you're deluding yourself. There just isn't a way, and even if there is then this isn't it. I mean, what kind of life are you going to have? We're more than our minds. You won't be able to touch anything, you won't be able to speak to us. You'll be just lost, and I can't imagine being a consciousness drifting about in the void. By the time technology advances enough to pluck you from the ether you'll have utterly lost your mind and there won't be anything left. Do you really want to be some crazed version of yourself that has lost all sense of what it is to be human?"

"I'll be more than human."

"Or less. You keep thinking that this progress is better, but it doesn't mean it is. Maybe you're going to lose some vital part of the human experience that you're never going to get back again, and even if this works, which I highly doubt, I think it's only going to be a shadow of life. This is wrong on so many levels. Please, listen to your wife and listen to me and just stop this right now. Live out the rest of your days as well as you can and I know it's not the same, but I promise that we will remember you. You may not think that you've left anything behind, but you have, in us. Our memories aren't going to last as long as a computer's, but we'll always talk about you and we'll always cry over you. Please George, when Tabitha and I think about you we're not going to want to think about your brainwaves floating in some server somewhere, isolated from the rest of humanity. Please, will you just promise that you won't do something reckless like this? You have no idea what's going to happen, or how what is left of you mind is going to be corrupted or cracked, and at the end of the day this is only going to be a copy. It's not going to be the real you. Nothing could ever be the real you."

Adrian's words were passionate enough to get George to relent. He closed the browser and stepped away from the computer, and then went to get his wife.

*

After this Adrian did not hear anything else about strange ways for George to remain alive. They spent his last days together as a group of friends, until one day Tabitha came to the door, tears falling down her face. She collapsed into Adrian's arms.

George had died.

For Adrian it felt as though one of his limbs had been separated from his body. He and Mia took the burden off Tabitha and helped arrange the funeral, but for Adrian there was a profound sense of loss. George had been a constant companion for him, and now that he was gone life wasn't the same. Adrian tried to talk about the same things with Mia, but she wasn't as interested in them as George was, and even when they spent time together as a trio it was clear that one vital element of them was missing.

George's funeral service was graceful and dignified. Adrian stood in front of the attendees and spoke of his long and strong bond with George, reminiscing about how they used to argue and play as children, and how that friendly rivalry had developed over the following years. He also spoke of his friend as a visionary and an optimist, as someone who was always looking towards the horizon and hoping for a better future.

Adrian said that he was certain that the future was bright for humanity, and that it would always be a great sorrow that George could not be a part of it. They sung and they cried and they paid their respects to a man who always looked to what was coming rather than what had been, and Adrian would always cherish the fond memories of the many times he had spent with his friend, arguing about something or another.

On his coffin, Adrian left a game controller, noting that he would not need a player 2 now, for he would be playing all his games alone from now one. Tears flowed down his cheeks as he walked away, saying his final goodbye to his friend, wishing there was some way this could have been different. He was just glad that George had passed on as a whole being, not as some fractured shard of him that he had left behind.

But then, later on that night when he was alone and sorting through George's belongings, deciding what he was going to keep, Adrian's phone buzzed. There was a message from a number he did not recognize, and when he read it his blood turned to ice, for he knew that George had not kept his promise.

I'm cold Adrian. I don't know where I am.

The Model Village

Chapter One

It felt like the night was going to go on forever, and Hilary Smith wouldn't have minded this at all. She walked along with her friends, the small cluster of them forming a line across the pavement, stretching into the empty road. She linked arms with Emma on her right and Gary on her left. Hilary's glossy red hair cascaded behind her as she threw her head back and laughed, while a plume of vapour left her breath. She could still taste the alcohol on her lips. The stars were aglow above her, and the small town around her felt like it was fading into the distance. Beyond them they could see the inky black sea reaching to meet the horizon, melting into the sky. It looked for all the world like they could walk out onto it and reach the end of the world.

"I thought that guy was never going to leave you alone," Emma said, stumbling a little as she staggered forward.

Hilary shushed her, looking to the houses around them, each one of them brooding and stern, ready to tell them off for being awake this late at night, at an hour that was reserved for witches. She then glanced behind her, feeling a paranoid itch on the nape of her neck. For a moment she thought she saw a figure there, but she blinked and it was gone. She breathed with relief.

"Some guys just don't know when to keep their hands to themselves," Hilary replied.

"You might have to deal with that a lot when you're at Uni, and I'm not going to be around to help you," Gary said. Hilary angled her head to look at him, having to tilt back because he was a giant compared to her. Over the course of the last few years it was as though his body had decided that it wanted to reach the sky, so he shot up like a sunflower and now towered above most everyone they met. She and Emma had to take two or three steps for every one he took.

"I know. I'll have to find a new big brother to protect me," Hilary playfully nudged him in the ribs. Gary pursed his lips as a strange look came upon his face.

"It's going to be strange, not being able to do this anymore," Emma sighed.

"We can still do it, it's just not going to be as regular as usual. Besides, it's going to be good for us to get away from this place. There's a whole big wide world out there, filled with all kinds of people and opportunities, and it's ready for us to take. Who knows what kind of people we're going to grow into," Hilary said with a sense of awe.

"I'm not sure I want to change all that much. I happen to think I'm pretty great as I am," Gary said.

"You're starting to sound like a prospectus," Emma teased. "I just wish that we could have all gone to the same uni, like we intended."

Gary scowled, but didn't say anything.

"Things don't always work out perfectly in life, but it doesn't mean that anything has to change between us three. We're still going to speak to each other practically every day, and we'll make sure to visit each other as well. We can be tour guides to each other. It'll be like we're having mini holidays all the time, and when we're back here things will be just like the old days," Hilary said. She took a step that was too long and felt a lurching sensation in the pit of her stomach. Her mind was still hazy with alcohol. The taste of it lingered on her tongue, becoming more bitter as the night went on.

"This place is going to seem smaller than it already is after we've left. We're not going to know what to do with ourselves once we've been in a real city," Gary said.

"I hope we don't get lost in the shuffle. There's going to be so many people," Emma's voice trembled with fear.

"You won't have to worry about that. Nobody is going to miss you. Either of you. You're both champions. We all are, and we're going to take the world by storm. We've been waiting for this moment for years, the moment when we're going to spread our wings and soar above the world and-"

"What's that?" Gary asked, interrupting her. Hilary frowned, about to chastise him for cutting off her dramatic speech, when she realized what he was looking at.

"Did we go in a circle? It looks like the strobe lighting from the club," Emma said, twisting her body around to check if they had actually been walking in the direction of home. The light was an eerie, ethereal glow appearing as if it had settled over the world in a gentle way. It was blue, interrupting the darkness of the night, quite a curious phenomenon.

"It's probably just someone playing around in their back garden with a projector or something," Gary said. Hilary wasn't so sure. She tilted her head to the side as she oriented herself. She looked up and saw the steeple of the church in between the houses. To her right was a road that sloped down dramatically towards the shore and the small wall that separated the pavement from the narrow beach. In her mind she followed the path.

"I think it's from the model village," she said.

"Why would the model village be lit up like that?" Gary asked.

Hilary shrugged. "Mom said that when she was younger Howard used to put on displays at night, even having a UFO come down to hover above the village. Maybe he's started doing those again."

"We should go! I love UFOs," Emma said excitedly.

Hilary glanced back and forth at her friends. None of them wanted the night to end. Gary would be leaving tomorrow, Emma in the middle of the week, and Hilary was planning to leave the following weekend. One by one they were falling like leaves off an autumn tree, gently floating away on the wind, carried to new pastures. This was the last night for the foreseeable future when they would all be together, and Hilary wished that it could last forever. Although she was excited about leaving for university and embarking on this next phase of her life, she was also reluctant to leave all she had known. In fact, there was something that she wanted to tell the others that she had been holding close to her chest, but now seemed like the apt time to say it.

They ambled down the slope, heading towards the model village, none of them questioning if it was a good idea or not. The evening in the club had robbed them of their sensibilities.

"I want to tell you guys a secret," Hilary began. They were still walking arm in arm, now all of them in the middle of the road. The people of the town had a tendency to sleep at this time of night, so they weren't worried that any cars would come speeding along to collide with them, and there was something uniquely freeing about being able to walk in the middle of the road without worrying about the consequences.

"I'm really scared." Hilary almost choked on the words, having to force them out and make them punch the air.

"You're not scared of anything," Emma said, her face scrunching up with confusion.

"I am about this. I just... what if I fail? Nobody is going to know me there. What if I don't make any friends? What if my lecturers hate me? What if I hate the course?" There were more worried questions that could have poured out of her, but the flow of them was stemmed by Emma resting her head on Hilary's shoulder and squeezing her arm.

"We all feel like that. I'm pretty sure every single person who is going to uni feels like that. It's why they have all the freshers' events. I bet after a couple of days you'll feel stupid for ever being worried about these things as you'll have loads of new friends. I feel the same way as well, but when I do I just try and think that this is a good thing, and it's only the unknown we're scared of, nothing else."

Emma's words made Hilary feel better. She swung her head towards Gary. "Do you feel the same way as well?"

He nodded. "It's all the worse because we've been friends for so long that I don't know how I'm going to cope without you. But I have a secret as well."

"Oh yeah? What is it?" Hilary asked.

"I need to tell you alone," Gary said quietly. Hilary furrowed her brow and then glanced towards Emma, who was gazing high into the sky, perhaps searching for a UFO of her own.

The three continued on, reminiscing about memories they had made together and experiences they had shared. They walked along the shore, past the buildings that were all ramshackle and in decline. Once upon a time this place had been a beacon of hope and happiness, with tourists flocking from all corners of the country to enjoy a break at sea. Then the world got bigger and it was easier to fly to other glamorous, exotic countries, and this seaside town, like so many others, dwindled. Windows that had been boarded up stared at her, buildings that had been left to rot stood forlornly, as though all they wanted was to be put out of their misery. It was little more than a ghost town. The salty air drifted in from the sea and the tide lapped against the beach. It would do so long after this town had turned to dust, long after she was buried deep in the earth.

Hilary couldn't decide if that was a comforting thought or an unsettling one.

They passed the funfair, which looked creepy in the dark, a mesh of gloomy metal and stalls. Without the bright lights and the bouncing music it was nothing other than shadows, and it seemed rather grim. There was another fear that crept into her mind.

"Guys, no matter what happens we have to promise to come back here, right?" she said.

"This is our home. Of course we're going to come back. My parents would kill me if I didn't," Emma said, her words floating on a chuckle.

"Yeah, but we're going to have all these opportunities and they might be better than anything we could get here. We might find that we want to spend the rest of our lives in our university towns. Maybe we'll get jobs. Maybe we'll fall in love. We might not want to come back here, and really look at this place. It's not as though it has much going for it," Hilary said.

"We're not going to let each other go. We can't. We've been together for practically our whole lives. Nothing can change that and nothing can take it away. We're still going to be the same people deep down no matter what happens at uni, and when it's all over we'll be back together and we'll be standing here, looking out at the ocean, and it'll feel like nothing has ever changed," Gary said in a philosophical tone.

"Speak for yourself. I intend to meet my husband at uni," Emma said.

Hilary arched an eyebrow. "Your *husband*? Emma, you haven't even had a boyfriend yet!"

"I had Craig."

"Craig doesn't count," Hilary rolled her eyes.

Emma brushed away her criticism with a quick flick of her hand. "I was reading an article the other day and it said that statistically you're likely to meet the person you end up with when you're at university. So that's what I'm going to try to do."

"Uni is the time when we're supposed to enjoy being free. We have our whole lives to do all those responsible adult things. You should be enjoying your extended youth a little. Just party and relax."

"I've done enough relaxing. This is the time for business. Uni isn't just about fun. We're there to study."

"Maybe you are. I just want the extra few years to figure out what I'm doing with my life," Hilary said.

"It's an expensive method to do that. It would be cheaper to see a therapist," Emma said.

Hilary shrugged. "If it does me any good then I'll pay it back, if not then I won't ever earn enough money to afford it. To be honest I can't imagine ever having that much money. Rich people don't come from places like this."

"I'm going to be rich someday, when my book gets published. I'm going to write it at uni. I'm going to have lots of spare time in between lectures and I'm going to make sure I use it wisely," Gary said.

"Am I going to be in it?" Hilary asked.

"Sure. I can name a dragon after you."

"I want to be a princess!" Emma exclaimed.

"You already are a princess, at least the way your Dad treats you," Hilary said, envy creeping into her voice.

"There's nothing wrong with the way Dad treats me," Emma said defensively.

It was then that they reached the model village. It was tucked away behind hedges, separating it from the world. Hilary used to love this place when she had been a child, fascinated by the lifelike models that showed the town in its heyday, bright and bursting with life. She used to imagine that the small figures would come to life when nobody was around and scurry around just like the bigger, real people did. In this quiet night with her thoughts turning elastic due to the alcohol, she started to believe in that childlike thing again.

There was a small sign outside the model village that replicated the sign outside the real town. The entrance was a small gate, and now that they were closer they could see the blue light emanating from the village.

"Maybe this isn't such a good idea," Emma said reluctantly, tugging on Hilary's arm. But Hilary's curiosity had been piqued, so she wasn't likely to turn away from this place now.

"We're here now, we might as well see what's going on. Maybe Howard is in trouble, or he might even appreciate people coming to see this show, if there is a show," she said.

Howard James had been running the model of Wayhaven for many years. He was the kind of man who Hilary had always imagined was old, but as she had grown older she realized he must have actually been fairly young when she was a child. He devoted his life to this model village and she never quite understood how he made any money from it. According to her father, Howard did not need to make any money because he came from a wealthy family. She wondered why he had decided to come to Wayhaven and open a model village, but she had never been brave enough to answer that question. She could think of about a hundred other things she would rather do if she had a lot of money. Even so, the model village had always been a quaint curiosity over the years and it was one of the few things that had actually remained in the village rather than being shut down. She wondered if the model village was going to last longer than the town itself. It was a sobering thought really.

As they reached the gate they unlinked their arms. Gary climbed over first, his long legs easily able to stretch over the gate. He then held out his hand and grabbed Hilary's arm. She pulled herself over and landed with aplomb, her shoes clapping against the ground. Emma was more hesitant and clumsier. Her dress somehow got caught on the gate, so it took Hilary and Gary to help her over, and by the end of it they were both holding her and almost all tumbled to the ground. But they were in. Hilary put her finger to her lips in order to remind them to be quiet. Howard was a friendly man, but she doubted he would take kindly to them trespassing this late at night. She was drunk enough to not realize that she had likely already made more than enough noise to wake Howard.

There was a small gift shop that was closed, but the path wound round leading to the village. As they crept around, they realized that the light was coming from the centre of the model village. Part of the small lawn had been peeled back. Tools and other equipment lay around, thick cables looked like sleeping snakes, so Howard must have been doing some kind of work to it. Perhaps he was finally changing it to echo the present. Hilary suspected this would make it lose part of its charm, however.

They crouched low, hoping that the shadows of the night would shroud them. The eerie blue light helped illuminate the model village, although there were also small lampposts that had LED bulbs in them as well, and shone like little caged fireflies.

The model village was separated into different sections, but most of it was visible from where they were standing, although obviously the detail was lost from far away. There was an airfield where a pilot was ready to take a spitfire up during the war with his wife looking on anxiously. There was a hot air balloon rising and descending; the arm it was attached to needed oiling because it kept squeaking. Rows of houses were lined up, each one of them reflecting a real house that existed in the actual village and, Hilary assumed, the people had been modelled on real people as well, people that Howard had known. She bent down and peered at them as they were frozen in their daily routine. Some of them were deep in conversation, others were strutting down a street, while still others were working at their trades. Bakers were kneading dough, a bus had pulled up to take on passengers, actors were on a stage performing a play. There was a football match going on, with spectators engaged with the action. Morris dancers were jigging, while a train clacked as it went around the railway, pulling into the same station in its never ending journey.

Each part of this model village was a piece of history frozen in time, with the people in it never having to worry if their life would work out the way they wanted it to, or if they would manage to keep in touch with their friends, or even if they would figure out where they were supposed to belong in the world.

The Ferris Wheel rotated slowly, the sandy beach was filled with people and even a few dogs that were chasing balls. One of them had ventured towards the sea and tentatively placed a paw in the water. Hilary was just waiting for the animal to turn and run away, but of course it never did.

"It really is remarkable, isn't it? He did this all himself. Each one of these figures is handmade, and they're all different. I know this model village isn't going to make any difference to the world in the grand scheme of things, but it must feel so good for Howard to be able to look down on what he's created and feel proud of it. The fact that it's existed for all these years is just amazing. It's a pity that more people don't come to see it," Hilary said.

"I wonder what's going to happen to it when he dies," Gary said.

"I suppose someone else will take it over. Maybe that's what you can do," Emma shot a teasing glance in Hilary's direction.

Hilary just laughed. "As much as I enjoy this place I don't think I'd want to stare at it day in and day out. Coming here once in a while is enough for me. I wouldn't want to spend my life here."

"I'm going to see the mermaid!" Emma said, forgetting to keep her voice low. Hilary glared at her and shushed her, but Emma was already peeling away, scampering up the slope across the arched bridge where there was a small pool dotted with more details. Howard had added some mythical creatures to the village as well, like said mermaids. There was also a submarine, a fishing boat, a battleship, as well as animals like sharks and whales. It was far more eventful than the sea had ever been on the Wayhaven coast.

Hilary shook her head and sighed. "I suppose we had better go and keep an eye on her. I hope she finds a responsible friend at uni. She can't handle her drink at all."

"I'm sure she'll be fine for the moment," Gary said, reaching out and catching Hilary's wrist to keep her from moving away. She turned, stunned. "I want to speak with you for a moment, before it's too late."

"Too late?" she asked, turning to face him.

"I'm leaving tomorrow. There's something I've been wanting to say to you for a long time and now I kind of feel like it's now or never," he said with a nervous laugh.

"This is your secret?" she asked.

He nodded. "And I know that if I don't tell you now then I'm probably never going to, so I just need to get it out," he shook his hands and shifted his weight from foot to foot as he psyched himself up. When he started speaking the words came out quickly. He barely took a breath. "It's just that we've been friends for so long now and over the years we've grown and changed together and we've shared so many things. I honestly don't think there's a happy memory in my life that you're not a part of. And I just… I'm going to miss you a lot Hilary, but I've always thought that there was something else between us as well, something that could make our friendship even better. And I know that maybe this is the wrong time to be saying this because if you do agree with me then we've wasted a lot of time, but if you don't then I guess it might make it hurt a little less because at least I'll be leaving tomorrow. And maybe that's cowardly of me, but I've never been good at this kind of thing and I don't even know how to say this really. It's just that I, well, I think I… I mean, I *know* that I love-"

Before he could finish the thought there was a scream and a splash. Hilary's heart had been seized by fear as the truth behind Gary's secret dawned on her, and this was not something she wanted to think about right now. She peeled away from him, saying that they needed to help Emma.

Gary was hot on her heels as they ran over the bridge and found Emma sitting in the lake, completely wet through. She wasn't hurt though. In fact, she was smiling.

"I think I lost my balance," she said in between her laughter. Then she looked up at the sky. "I don't know where the UFO is," she said in dismay.

Hilary gasped around her. When Emma fell into the lake she had broken the ships and models in it, but it was worse than that. She must have stretched a leg out and she kicked through some of the houses. It was as though a giant monster had rampaged through the model village and left a trail of destruction. Some of the figures had been turned over and smashed, all this hard work had just been destroyed in one blaze of clumsy violence.

Gary and Hilary pulled Emma up. She dusted herself down. Water dripped from the hem of her dress and she left wet footprints behind her.

"Oh no," she gasped when she realized what she had done. The train was coming around too, but she had stepped on some of the tracks, snapping it. There was nothing they could do to stop the train, so it shunted around and then fell off the tracks, looking like a lame horse that had fallen to the ground.

Its wheels spun helplessly. It would never reach the station again.

"Should we tell him what happened?" Emma asked.

Hilary's fight or flight response kicked in and she shook her head. "There's no point. As far as we're concerned we were never here. Come on, let's go," she whispered, and dragged them away. As she looked back, however, she saw a light go on in the house that overlooked the model village, and as they slipped back over the gate she saw a figure standing in the window. A god was looking down at the world he had created, and Hilary just hoped that he was not a vengeful one. Either way, they had escaped without him seeing them, or so she thought...

*

As soon as they had climbed over the gate the trio sprinted away back through the town. They ran until their lungs were fit to burst. They put their hands on their haunches and gulped in air, while sweat made their clothes cling to their skin.

"I think maybe we should call it a night," Emma said with a reluctant tone. "I'm going to have to tell Mum I went swimming or something," she looked down at her dress. Although Hilary wanted the night to last forever, she knew it needed to end at some point. She yawned. The dawn sun would be rising in a couple of hours and she would be one day closer to leaving.

"Should we have told him what happened? It feels wrong to leave like that," Gary said.

Hilary felt a pang of guilt in her chest, but tried to ignore it. She hardened her heart in an effort to ignore her conscience. "It won't make any difference. We're leaving soon anyway, and he's rich enough to fix the model village. Besides, we saw that he was doing work on it anyway so maybe he was going to remake some of what was damaged. We might have been doing him a favour really. Now he has the freedom to rebuild parts of the village and make it fresh and exciting. It might bring back people who think they have already seen everything it has to offer."

The mental gymnastics were quite acrobatic, but as always Emma and Gary were eager to fall in line. Their sense of self preservation was keen to protect them as well.

They walked back home. Emma was first to leave. She and Hilary promised to see each other before Emma left. Gary was next. The silence turned awkward as Emma had been a buffer between her and Gary. Now there was nothing stopping him from telling her his secret again, for they had been interrupted before. At first she thought he was just going to leave it buried in the model village, but after making a couple of uneasy jokes about what had happened he turned back to that subject as they approached his house, and once again time became a pressing concern to him.

"So I never exactly got to finish what I was saying earlier. I was trying to tell you that-"

"I know what you were trying to tell me Gary," Hilary held up a hand to stop him from speaking. She tilted her face down, not wanting to look him in the eye because she didn't want to see the crushed emotion within them.

"I just… it's not really the right time for this, is it? You're leaving tomorrow."

"I know that," he said forlornly. "I wish I had been able to tell you sooner, but it never seemed like the right time and I didn't want to make things awkward between us. But I thought if there's any part of you that does feel the same way then maybe we could try and get closer. I'm willing to travel every weekend if it'll make it work because I just... you're on my mind so much and you know me better than anyone. I can't imagine feeling this way about anyone else and I just want to be closer to you. I feel like I'm going to be a fool if I let you slip away without saying anything."

"I get that, and I get that this must be hard for you. But I just... it's a lot to take in Gary. You know that you've always been one of my closest friends. I haven't thought about you like that."

"Not even once?"

Hilary blushed, thinking back to a party where she and Gary had been drunk in the garden. It had just been the two of them alone. The moonlight had caught his eyes in a certain way that made him seem different. It had felt as though she was falling into him, and if they had kissed then things might have been wholly different. Instead, someone had come storming out of the house to throw up in a bush. Needless to say, it had ruined the mood and the moment, and such a thing had never occurred again.

"It's just hard to think about this when we're going to head off to uni. I'm not saying it can't happen or it never will happen, I just don't know if this is the right moment for it. We're both tired and drunk so I don't think we can keep things straight anyway," she said, trying to laugh to lighten the moment, but Gary was crestfallen.

"The only reason I've been able to work up the courage to tell you this is because I'm tired and drunk," he said with a weak smile. "I just don't want this to be the end Hilary. I feel like we're meant to be together."

"You always were too romantic for your own good Gary," Hilary said. She reached up and placed a hand against his cheek. He closed his eyes for a moment, enjoying the simple act of affection. The longer she left it there the more she was afraid that something might happen, something she would regret. She pulled her hand away and then stepped back, breaking whatever spell might be conjured between them.

"This isn't the end of anything Gary. This is the beginning of something new. We'll have so many good experiences at uni and we'll be all the better for it. Maybe when we see each other again we'll both be ready," she said. It might have been cruel to give him this hope, but she wasn't lying. She turned away and immediately felt the chill of the night wrapping around her. She folded her arms across her chest and rubbed her white arms, not daring to look back at Gary because she couldn't bear to see the sight of his misery.

*

When she returned home, she tiptoed through the house; her parents never liked it when she clattered and clanged around after being out. In truth they never liked her being out anyway. Her mother always warned her that bad things happened. As Hilary ascended the stairs, she heard her mother turn around. She never did sleep when Hilary was out. Hilary wondered what she was going to do while Hilary was at university. It wasn't as though she could stay awake for the entire term. Her mother had laughed it off, saying that it was a different matter when Hilary was elsewhere. Apparently her mother only worried when Hilary was at home. It made the entire thing seem futile, and Hilary just decided that her mother did not want to sleep.

She peeled her clothes off and pulled on a loose t shirt as she collapsed into bed. The mattress creaked as it welcomed her weight. She glanced around at the shadowed shapes, not looking forward to packing for uni. She had no idea whether to take everything or only minimal things. It would be the longest time she had ever been away from home, and she felt wholly unprepared. The only other time she had been on a school trip was back when she had been 11. The boys and girls had been separated and she had slept in a room with two other girls. Emma hadn't been one of them, much to her dismay. Hilary had been embarrassed and cried the first night. A teacher had heard and entered the room, but Hilary didn't find their words comforting. The other girls were either asleep or pretending to be. The unfamiliar pillow was stained with Hilary's tears as she shuddered herself to sleep.

After that she did not cry, but now she wondered if history would repeat itself when she arrived at uni. Perhaps she was the type of person who needed to remain at home, although after what happened tonight it might have been better to leave. Technically it had been an act of vandalism. Hilary had never been in trouble with the law before, and this was one of the reasons why it had seemed natural to her to flee. The thought of being in trouble was daunting, and the last thing she needed was to have something like this mar the last few days in Wayhaven. She almost wished that she had been leaving the following day.

At least Gary would be gone though. She didn't mean this in a mean way, but confessing his feelings to her had made things awkward. She closed her eyes and replayed that moment in her mind, wishing that she knew how to act. He may have thought it was difficult for him to express these feelings, but reacting to them was complicated for her as well. The last thing she wanted was to lose the close relationship they shared. The truth was she counted on Gary more than anyone else, even more than Emma. He was a sensitive soul and they had bonded over their difficulties. Emma lived a life that was sheltered from some of the harshness of the world. She might as well have lived in a fairy tale as she was doted on by both parents and never wanted for anything.

Gary's father had left when Gary was just a boy. His mother worked hard, but it meant that she never had enough time to spend with Gary. Gary lost himself in books and his own imagination, which fuelled his ambition to be a writer. Hilary's parents were still together, but she suspected it was more of desperation than anything else. Hilary had once caught her father cheating on her mother. As she had been so young she hadn't quite grasped the depths of it, but she knew that things had been tense around the house for a long time after. Now it was a thing that happened that they simply didn't speak about, as though they could erase it from history through a sheer force of will. Hilary was well aware that it had still happened though. It was there in the background, looming like some terrible monster. She had never looked at her father in the same way, or her mother really. She thought her mother was weak for taking him back, and her father was weak for letting it happen in the first place. Sometimes things seemed to be as they had always been, but that was only an illusion. It shimmered away and Hilary could see them as they were; two unhappy people who had decided to stay with each other, perhaps out of spite, or perhaps out of fear.

It had never given Hilary much confidence in the ways of love. So when Gary confessed his feelings to her, Hilary's instincts had kicked in and recoiled, never wanted to feel that kind of hurt or betrayal. Rationally she knew that Gary wasn't the type of man to treat her like this, but she was so afraid of it happening. She knew her mother must have thought the same of her father and the worst had still happened. People changed over the years anyway, became harder and crueller as life took its toll on them. It was safer and easier to be alone, to push away any chance of being in pain.

But she had always wondered what it would be like to feel a caress of passion on her lips, of eager hands slipped underneath her clothes, reaching for forbidden places. Would it have been the worst thing in the world to let Gary in, even just a little bit? Even if they had only kissed at least she would have known that her first kiss would have been with a boy she cherished, and nothing would have ever sullied the memory. Perhaps if Gary had been a different boy she might have taken a risk. He was the kind of person to hold his feelings close to his soul and nurture them carefully, never allowing any harm to come to them, never pushing them away. If he carried a flame for her then he would ensure that flame kept burning, and so she knew that if she changed her mind and felt ready then he would be there, waiting. If she thought he would turn and give his heart easily to another girl then she might have fought harder for him. Perhaps at uni he would find someone to do exactly that, and that might be better for him than becoming involved with her. Hilary thought of herself as a tangled mess of emotion and she really needed to sort it all out before she welcomed another person into her heart. Really, she was doing Gary a favour by keeping him from being romantically involved with her, as she would only have ended up hurting him.

At least that's what she told herself.

All she really hoped was that uni might be able to guide her towards her destiny, because at the moment she had no idea what she was going to do with her life or who she was going to become.

*

The morning arrived, and with it came a stinging throb in her mind. Hilary groaned as she woke and rubbed her eyes, wishing that it was easy to push away the pain. Daylight spilled into her bedroom, and guilt poured into her heart, both about the model village and about Gary. She checked her clock. It was almost midday. Gary would have left by now, traveling up the country through the snaking roads, probably annoyed with himself for telling her how he felt, worried that he had ruined their friendship. She picked up her phone and thought about calling him, but nerves jangled and inside she typed out a message with trembling fingers. The more she thought about it the more she realized she was a coward, and if she kept running from life then she was never going to settle on anything.

It felt as though something fundamental had changed as well. With Gary not being in the same village as her any longer there was a sense of finality about the world, as though she knew that everything was destined to end. There was no chance of her walking down the street to his house and finding him there. The thought of not seeing him again was chilling, and she was already missing him.

I'm sorry for how last night went. Thanks for telling me what you did. It means a lot to me. There's just so much going on right now that I need some time to think about it, but I will think about it. When we see each other again we'll talk about it properly, I promise. Have a safe trip and let me know when you arrive. I want to hear all about it! I miss you already x

Hilary debated whether to add the kiss or not. She had always added one to her messages though so it would have been noticeable had she refrained. As soon as she sent the message she tossed her phone down, and then picked it up almost immediately to see if he had replied. He had not. She let out a frustrated sigh as she did not want to fall into the trap of desperate yearning. She figured he would be busy traveling, and then busy moving in. Besides, he might just want some time to think about his own feelings, and that was perfectly fine.

Hilary headed downstairs and spent some time talking with her mother, who teased her about getting up late, suggesting that she was getting well prepared for being a student. She then asked Hilary about what had happened the previous night. Hilary thought about the incident at the model village and then the conversation with Gary. She flashed her mother a reassuring smile and then casually said that nothing much had happened at all. She had some breakfast and then decided she should make a start on packing, so she went back to her bedroom and began sorting through her belongings, trying to decide what she was going to take and what she was going to keep at home. It was like walking through a path of memories as every item had some significance, and it felt as though this was a monumental breakpoint in her life, a distinct barrier between what was and what will be.

It felt important, and yet at the same time she knew that thousands of people all across the country would be feeling the same thing, and many more had gone through it previously. This somehow dampened what she was going through, lessening her own importance in the world to the point where she wondered if she should be emotionally affected by it at all. Then she checked her phone again, and saw that Gary still hadn't replied, which only served to put her in a worse mood. She huffed and tapped her fingers and chewed the inside of her mouth, and then she became so annoyed that she called Emma to talk about the situation.

Emma didn't reply either.

She must have still been hungover from the previous night. Emma had never been able to hold her liquor, often falling into a drunken state and staying there long after she should have recovered. Sometimes Hilary suspected that she put it on. Hilary typed out a quick text message and the cast her phone down again, waiting and waiting for one of her best friends to get back to her.

Was this what her life was going to be like now? Was it going to be a long wait between messages, a chasm between her and Gary and Emma that would never be broached again? She had continually said, and believed, that they would always be friends, but what if she had been wrong? Her face paled as she thought about a world in which she was left behind, where Emma found a husband and began a new life, where Gary wrote a bestselling book and rocketed towards fame. There was always one member of a friendship group who never achieved anything of note, who remained in a rut, and perhaps this was all she had been destined for.

It became such a prevalent thought in her mind that it felt as though her brain was being squeezed. The day continued, and as there had still been no reply from either Emma or Gary, Hilary found herself getting more and more paranoid.

So as the afternoon bled into the evening Hilary strode out of her home and made her way to Emma's house, hoping that she had not confessed to what had happened the previous night.

Hilary rapped her knuckles on the door and waited a few moments before Emma's mother answered. She was the spitting image of her daughter, or perhaps the correct phrasing was the other way around. Hilary noticed that tension was pinched around her lips and there was a glazed look around her eyes. She blinked frantically when she saw that Hilary was standing there.

"Can I help you?" she asked in a tone that was like that of a receptionist. She usually friendly and warm, and Hilary felt uneasy. Perhaps Emma had spilled the beans.

"I was just wondering if Emma is around. I know she's probably busy packing, but-"

"I'm afraid I don't know who you mean," she said, the smile straining again, stretching under the weight of something that Hilary could not fathom.

Hilary checked to make sure that she had the right house and the right person. "Maggie, it's me. It's Hilary. Is this some kind of weird joke? Where is Emma? I know that we were late coming in last night, but it was our last night all together before we left for uni. I'm sure you can give her a little bit of leeway for that."

"I'm sorry, but I really don't know who you mean, and I don't know who you are. I think you should move on. You might have gotten the wrong house. You're terribly confused. I'm afraid that I just can't help you." The words tumbled out of her mouth in a fast, nervous rhythm. She backed into the house and closed the door as she spoke, shutting Hilary out. Hilary was so stunned she didn't have the wherewithal to put her foot in the door or try to force her way in, but she did have another plan. She crept around the back of the house. There was an extension to the house that she had used to sneak in and out of Emma's house plenty of times during nights when sleep did not come easily to either of them. It led to right outside Emma's bedroom window. Hilary moved with feline agility and made her way up to the window. She pressed her face against it and peered in, expecting to see Emma there.

The room was empty.

She frowned with confusion. She had no idea why Emma's mother would have acted like this. Part of her wanted to march into the house and demand answers, but she didn't think that would work, and she did not have enough confidence to pull it off. The fact that she even said she didn't recognize Hilary was troubling too. Was she really that mad that they had been out last night? She hadn't seemed angry... it was all so confusing, and Hilary really didn't know what to think.

As she left, she tried calling Emma again, but again there was no answer. She tried Gary again as well, but he too was lost behind a haze of silence. As she headed home her attention was caught by Gary's mother coming out of her house. She was supposed to be with Gary, traveling up the country. Had something gone wrong? Had Gary decided not to go today?

Hilary crossed the street and waved towards her. "Julia, did Gary not leave today? I thought you'd be at the other end of the country by now."

Julia looked at her with the same kind of shock that had been on Maggie's face. "I'm sorry, I think you must have me mistaken for someone else. I don't know who Gary is."

Hilary stared at her, dumbfounded. "He's your son," she said.

A worried gaze flashed in Julia's eyes. "I don't have a son," she whispered, straining to maintain her composure. But Hilary could see the glistening sorrow within her eyes and heard the unease in her words. Hilary stepped towards her.

"Yes you do. You know you do. He means the world to you, and you mean the same to him. How can you deny this? Did he tell you to not speak to me? Look, I admit that what he said took me a little by surprise, but he doesn't need to act so wounded about it. If he's in there then I should speak with him. I did send him a message, but if he's not going to answer it then he can't act like I'm being indifferent. If he's still here then he should come and talk to me."

"I already told you that he's not here. He's not here because I never had a son. I wish I had, but this talk is very painful for me and I would appreciate it if you could move on and trouble someone else with whatever this strange little game is," she glanced from side to side as she pushed past Hilary, hurriedly walking away. Once again, she was in such shock that she could barely believe this was happening. Hilary simply stared at her, agog as she moved away, wondering if the entire world had changed while Hilary had been asleep.

As Hilary staggered back home, she tried to make sense out of all of this. Gary and Emma had both been with her the previous night, but now they had seemingly disappeared off the face of the earth and their parents were denying they had even existed at all. Even if they were trying to block communication with Hilary this was quite a drastic step to take, and Hilary couldn't understand what the reason behind it could be. After all, they were going to be separated by uni soon enough anyway, and Gary should have left already. The look in Maggie and Julia's eyes was almost akin to fear, but what were they afraid of?

*

Hilary pondered the matter for a long time after she returned home. She aimlessly packed her things and kept checking her phone, hoping against hope that either Gary or Emma would get back to her. Neither of them did. She sighed and then stomped downstairs, having to rely on her parents because there was nobody else she could turn to.

"Mum, Dad, something weird is happening with Gary and Emma and I don't know how to figure it out. I don't even know what's going on. We only saw each other last night, but now their parents are acting like they never existed and the only thing I can think is that they're upset at me for something, but I thought our friendship meant more than that. I've tried calling them and texting them, but I'm getting nothing in reply. Gary was supposed to leave today as well, but Julia was at the house and she couldn't have made the journey back yet. I just don't know what could be happening. Why would they pretend like they don't know me? Why would they pretend like Gary and Emma never existed? It doesn't make any sense."

Her mother and father glanced at each other. Their faces paled.

"What exactly happened last night Hilary?" her mother asked.

Hilary shrugged. "Nothing much, we just went to the club and had a few drinks. Then we walked around the town and went down to the seafront. We just wanted to make the night last as long as possible because it was the last time the three of us were going to be together for a while."

Her father licked his lips and wore an uncertain look in his eyes. "Did you go near the model village?" he asked, his voice a hushed whisper. Hilary swallowed a lump in her throat. How did he guess that?

"We might have snuck in for a little while and, well, there was a little bit of an accident you see. Emma lost her balance and she fell over and, well, she caused some minor damage to the village…" she trailed away, annoyed that she had to let the truth slip out so easily. Perhaps it was for the best, however.

"Oh Christ," her father bowed his head and stretched his hand across his forehead, massaging his temples. They both looked shocked.

"How much damage?" her mother asked.

"It doesn't matter how much Rita," her father snapped, and he turned his attention back to Hilary. "Of all the times to do this... how could you be so stupid?"

Anger rose within, bubbling up her throat from the molten core of her body. "Maybe I get that from you," Hilary spat. Her father glared at her.

"You have no idea what you've done. You should have left that place well alone. What were you even thinking going there at night?" he thundered.

"We weren't thinking really, it just seemed to be a good idea at the time. Maybe that's how you felt when you cheated on Mom," Hilary spat. She couldn't resist tossing the grenade, but the explosion didn't happen in the way she thought it would.

"We don't talk about that Hilary. You should know that by now," Rita said.

"I don't see why not. If I'm being ranted at about being stupid then maybe we should list all the stupid things that each of us has done," Hilary replied.

"That's not going to do any good. We're going to remain calm, that's all," Rita placed her palms out on the table and spoke in a calm tone, as though she was mediating a dispute between warring clans. Hilary's father was still huffing, a dark look etched upon his face.

"There's no sense in remaining calm! She doesn't even realize what she's done!" he cried.

"What? What have I done? What's so special about that model village? I mean, I figured that he's rich enough to repair the damage. It was just some kids messing around at the end of the day, and what does this even have to do with Gary and Emma's parents anyway?"

Rita arched her eyebrows. "You need to go and speak to Howard right away. You need to apologize to him, and you need to mean it," she said. Hilary began to protest, but this wasn't a request from Rita. It was rare that her mother was ever as stern as this, and it caused an unsettling feeling to churn within Hilary's stomach.

"Does this have anything to do with Gary and Emma?" Hilary asked.

"Just go to him and try and fix this. Do whatever you can, and go now before it's too late," Rita said. Her lower lip trembled and she leaned into her husband, clasping his hand. They both looked stricken with fear, just as Maggie and Julia had, and suddenly that feeling surged through Hilary as well. Her chest became tight as she realized that something grim was happening to her, something that had happened to Gary and Emma as well, and there was only one way to stop it. She pushed herself up from the table and then made her way back to the model village.

Somehow it was at the centre of all of this, although she wasn't quite sure how.

*

Hilary's skin tingled with fear as she approached the model village. She wished that Gary and Emma were by her side. Somehow the world seemed more fearsome without them accompanying her. The blue glow was softer than the previous night, and Hilary wished that it had not acted like a beacon to them. If there had been no glow they might never have approached the model village in the first place.

The scent from the hedge was sweet and there was a sign saying that the model village was closed due to repairs. Hilary's heart sank. She still had no idea how Howard was involved in this, but she had been unable to ignore her parents' insistence that she come here. It was rare that they agreed on anything, so this must have been of some importance.

Hilary climbed over the gate again. Without Gary's help it was a difficult task and she had to take a leap of faith to throw herself to the ground. She landed with a thud, and the impact shot through her bones. She was trespassing again, but she had already committed a sin in this place and now it was time to make things right.

The model village looked much like it had the previous night, although now the entirety of it was on display as the light shone upon it. The blue core was still visible, with cables trailing across the field, and the damage had not been repaired. Hilary winced as she looked at it. It seemed worse than it had last night. Howard was not anywhere to be seen, so she walked up to inspect the damage more closely and thought that perhaps they should have stayed here to clean up. She turned to face the house and made her way along the path towards the door, all the small figures looking up at her, perhaps wishing her well.

The door was painted red and there was a small bell that tinkled when she rang it. She stepped back and admired the façade. It seemed like a large house for one man, and she wondered if Howard ever grew lonely here.

Just as she was looked up at the glinting windows the door opened. Howard was standing there. She couldn't remember the last time she saw him. It must have been when she was just a girl. Then, he had seemed like a giant, but now she realized that he was merely a man of normal height. His hair had thinned, and his scalp appeared shining and smooth. He wore spectacles that rested on the bridge of his nose, and he was clean shaven. He wore a crisp, pale blue shirt and trousers, but in his eyes lurked a steely glare.

"Yes?" he asked. There was an edge to his voice. He must have known that Hilary was involved in the crime, and so she was on the back foot. There was no sense in trying to deny anything here. She needed to be straightforward and honest, remembering her mother's insistence to apologise.

"I'm Hilary and I just wanted to come by and say that I'm sorry. A few of my friends might have caused some small amount of damage to your village last night. It wasn't anything we intended. We had just had a little bit too much to drink and I know that we weren't supposed to be here, but we just got a little carried away and I came here to offer my deepest apologies. If there's anything I can do to make it up to you then please let me know because I feel really bad, we all do."

He arched an eyebrow at this. "You all do?"

"I'm speaking on their behalf, we're all in the process of moving off to university you see. It was actually our last night together."

"So you thought you would vandalize someone else's property?"

"I- no, it's not like that. We just wanted to have a look around. We saw a blue light actually and we wondered what it was."

"It's just some work I'm doing to the village. It's nothing that should concern you. What should concern you, however, is the cost of the damage you caused. Do you understand how much time it takes to create these intricate models and arrange them in such a way that is pleasing to other people? What you destroyed was hours and years of work on my behalf. This place is my life. I have spent decades curating the model village, work that you and your friends demolished like that," he snapped his fingers. "And what's worse is that instead of coming to me and owning up to your crime you fled like common criminals."

Hilary shook at this. A knowing, smug look came upon his face.

"Ah yes, I did see you last night Hilary. I think perhaps you had better come in so we can talk about how you're going to make this up to me. This village is a cultural landmark, and it should not be treated as some playground for you and your drunk friends." He turned his back and continued talking as she followed him, looking around warily. "Do you know how much sweat I have put into this place? It may not seem like much to you, but that village takes as much work to maintain as a real one. The weather can be brutal, and I have to make sure that the villagers are brushed regularly so the colour doesn't fade. I have spent my life making this place special, and you and your friends almost destroyed it in one moment. As with everything it is easier to destroy than to create," he shook his head and put his hands on his hips.

"It was hardly destroying everything. I mean, it was only a little area. And I can help you build it if that's what you like."

He barked a laugh and narrowed his eyes. "As if I would let you get your grubby little hands on my village. You'd only end up making things worse. That place is a utopia compared to the real world, and you just made it a great deal worse."

Hilary was beginning to think that Howard took his model village far too seriously. She held up her hands and tried to force her voice into an apologetic tone. "Look, I'm really sorry about what happened. It was a stupid, clumsy mistake that shouldn't have happened because we shouldn't have been here. I wish I could go back and prevent us from coming here, but please, if there's any way I can make it up to you then I would love to know about it. I'm supposed be to leaving for university at the weekend, but until then I can come here for a few hours a day if you like and help you mend the damage we caused. I'll even do it with your strict supervision if you're that worried that I'm going to damage anything else."

A sly smile crept upon his face, like a slithering snake that sparked a primal fear.

"Oh, I don't think you'll be leaving for university at all," he said in an oddly quiet voice. It was such a strange thing to say, and at first she did not quite believe it. She angled her head and tried to think about what might have happened to Gary and Emma. Had he killed them? Suddenly the hackles on her back rose. What if he was some sick serial killer and her parents knew… but then why would they have sent her to apologise to him? What kind of thrall did he have over the town?

She began to back away, but the door was farther than she realized. "Okay, look, I don't know what's going on here, but I just came to apologise and I've done that. I have my own life to live. I'm going to go now and I think that you should probably get some help. I'm just…"

"You're not going anywhere," Howard said. He reached into his shirt pocket and pulled out a small figuring, pinching it between his index finger and thumb. "The damage you caused does give me an excuse to make a few new additions to the village. It's a strict balancing act you see. I never wanted to make it overpopulated as then it would suffer the same fate as the real world. All I want is for my models to live a happy life in a world that is never going to end, and I want people who visit my village to be reminded of how perfect the world can be. But I also want to make sure that criminals like you never trouble this place again. Let me show you how perfect the world can be. Your friends already know."

He gestured to a table at the side of the room. Hilary followed his hand and her eyes went wide with fear and confusion as she saw what he was pointing at. Her mouth was agape. The table was littered with various bits of scenery for the village, but amid all of that were two figures. Her attention had been so focused on Howard that she had missed them previously. But now she saw them the horrible truth unfurled in her mind, but it couldn't be…

The models looked just like Gary and Emma.

"No…" she gasped.

"My handiwork is good, yes? I always try to capture the likeness of the person I am modelling. I did hear your friend say that she wanted to be a princess, so I think that I shall put her in a pretty tiara and have her by the mermaids, or perhaps you would all like to be together for eternity? You did seem distressed when you mentioned that it was your last night together. I can make it so you never have to leave."

"No… no this can't be real. What the hell have you done with them? Where are they? Did you kill them?"

Howard let out a soft chuckle. "Oh no, not at all. All the people in my village are alive, and alive they shall always be. It's what gives it its unique charm. When you visited before were you not amazed at how lifelike they all were? Did you not look into their eyes and wonder how I could capture that quintessential depth of a soul?"

"But that's not possible."

"Really? And why is that? I am an artist, a creator. There is nothing I cannot do, and I have chosen to make my own little world here, a world free of strife and poverty, a world that is not afflicted with illness or hunger. Every one of my people are free of pain. Anyone who comes here sees that. They all wish that they could live in a world like the one I have created. It just so happens that you get to have that wish granted."

Horror filled Hilary's mind. She had no idea if this was truly possible or if the man was just insane, but in that moment a thousand thoughts rushed through her mind. There were the strained lies that Maggie and Juliet had told her; had they been so afraid of suffering the same fate that they just went along with this lie? Were the other people in the model village ones who had angered Howard? She thought about other people who had disappeared over the years and all the shops that had closed. Had the people really gone out of business and moved away, or had they become a part of Howard's grim little village? Her parents had been so eager for her to make this right. They must have known as well. But why hadn't they told Hilary before this? Why was this not a part of the local folklore?

But she knew she would not have believed it anyway. And now apologising was the last thing on her mind. All she wanted to do was run. She could think about saving Gary and Emma later, if there was any way to save them. For now, all she wanted was to get to uni and be away from this place, to get as far away from Howard as she could and only return when she had a way to stop him.

She was near the doorway now. The outside world beckoned with its fresh air and sweet blue sky. Trembling breaths shuddered through her lips as she cursed and yelled at him, and his soft, unnerving laugh became a cacophony in her mind.

"Do you really think you can escape me Hilary? Do you think anyone can escape me? I have you all in the palm of my hand," he said. She looked in horror as he held the figurine of her in his hand. Time slowed, and she couldn't help but appreciate the artistry of the thing. It was like looking at a reflection of herself, albeit one that was miniscule compared to her. And then she watched as he placed his fingers around the legs. She angled her body to turn away, ready to sprint as fast as she could, but there was no running from the fate that he had in store for her. There was a snap as he broke the legs on the model, and then she felt an excruciating wave of pain pass through her as her own legs crumpled, bent and twisted in an unnatural angle. She fell to the floor as though she was a puppet whose strings had been cut, and given the situation she found herself in she thought that was an apt description. Tears filled her eyes and she gasped, trying to brace herself through the pain. She clawed her way to the door, dragging her broken, limp legs behind her. Pain flooded through her and she shuddered, but she knew that if she didn't stop then she would never escape and everything she had ever wanted in life would be taken away. She now felt stupid for ever being afraid of moving forward. She should have embraced the opportunities that uni was going to give her. She should have told Gary that she loved him. Why oh why hadn't she made more of her life?

A shadow fell over her as Howard loomed large, stepping in front of her. She angled her head up to him, choking on her own breath. A dark circle wanted to envelop her mind, the pain wanted her to pass out, but she looked at him through watery vision and cursed him.

"This is for the best Hilary. This way you never have to leave. You never have to say goodbye to your friends. You can stay here together in this perfect world, and you can see how I'll rebuild the damage you caused."

Hilary reached up towards him, but then she lost all strength and her hand fell to the ground. Her body twitched and spasmed, only half of it working now. She was on the floor like a helpless fish out of water. Howard then walked outside, humming as though this was just another day. Hilary cried out for help, but she was too far from anything else to be heard. She watched as Howard went to the middle of the village.

"You're all going to get some new friends," he said to the other villagers, all mute in reply.

He looked like a god striding over the world he had created, all of his subjects below him and beneath him. He reached the glowing blue core in the middle of the village. Hilary wondered if she would ever understand the mystery of it.

Howard placed her model on this core and then he fiddled with something that was beyond her view. She then began to feel something pulling at her. It seemed to reach beyond her flesh. Invisible tendrils grabbed her soul and started to drag it out of her body. She whimpered and shook her head, trying with all her might to stop this horror from happening, but she was utterly powerless against it. It was beyond her understanding, her comprehension, and she knew that she too would be lost. All of her essence was being sucked out of her body, and within a moment her perspective changed.

No longer was she on the floor whimpering helplessly, but she was locked in this small body, looking up at Howard's giant face.

"There we go," he said, his words deafening, echoing around her in a cacophony. "You're all done."

The world moved up and down as she was carried back into the house. They passed over her body. He held her aloft. "Take one last look at the person you used to be," he said. Hilary tried so hard to stretch out and reach her old body, but nothing would move. She was frozen, locked into this new form, and although she could think she could not take any actions, not even when Howard fixed her legs. She was then taken outside and placed into the model village, and she never did find out what happened to her body.

*

Howard's sick mind had dressed Hilary in a wedding dress and put her in the church, with Gary as her groom. She stood there silently, losing all sense of time as she stared at her best friend. She tried and tried to open her mouth, but not even a whisper would emerge. In Gary's eyes she saw the same kind of pain, but it did not make her feel any better for knowing that he was suffering too. Her mind was trapped and the thoughts ricocheted back and forth, unable to escape, driving her into a mad frenzy. She still had a view of the world, and could see shadows flickering as people passed by. Occasionally she noticed her parents, who huddled together and gazed down at her, but they never spoke, and they never tried to take her home.

And then, one day, they stopped coming at all.

Howard was still there, however. He seemed to be fixed to this village as much as any of the figures or the buildings, and he always seemed to look the same. Often he would walk through the village by himself and take notice of all the people enduring this deathless and lifeless existence, caught in a limbo from which there was no escape, and Hilary's heart was filled with hatred and rage until she grew exhausted.

The night they came into the model village had been the last night she, Gary, and Emma were still together. Life had been frightening with all she wanted to do, and she had ended up not doing any of it. There was no book written for Gary, no husband for Emma, and nothing for Hilary.

The world continued to spin for so many other people who got to laugh and love and live.

*

"Look Mummy, she's beautiful! I want to be just like her one day," a child said, pointing to the bride with glossy red hair and ruby lips. "I don't understand why she's so sad though. It looks like she's crying."

"It's just the morning dew dear," her mother said. The girl stared at the bride though, thinking to herself that it was the middle of the afternoon so all the dew should have gone. She couldn't understand why a bride would be upset though. The mother walked on, while the child remained by the church. In the distance the train chugged around, whistling just before it stopped in the station. A girl in a princess outfit was waiting to board the train.

"Why are you so sad?" the girl asked, staring at the bride. For a moment the girl thought that she saw a flicker of emotion in the model's eyes, but decided it must have been her imagination. Then her mother called her away and she turned her back, clasping her mother's hand. It was the perfect little town in the middle of nowhere, and there it would always remain.

Full Life Term

Year One

There had been a shift in public opinion surrounding the subject of death. This was due in part to a new wave of philosophical thinking, as well as the objective evidence of people aging around everyone else. With the lifespan of humans continually increasing and others watching their relatives turn into frail and feeble things, their old minds decaying into what amounted to a living ghost, the thought of living being this precious thing to which to cling was quickly becoming a thing of the past. No longer did people want to live forever as they saw the future that awaited them, one where they were dependent on other people to eat and clothe themselves, one where they would lose the independence they had cherished. In most cases their minds would be sacrificed as well. The quick witted would become dull, and memories would become like an egg with holes poked into its shell, or a jigsaw with missing pieces that would never be found again. Bones turned to brittle things, breaking at every impact, and the more people saw this the more they realized that it was not any kind of life at all.

Existence itself did not remain a revered thing, but youth did. People began to fear losing their faculties more than they did death. Taking care of all these people put a great strain on the health care systems of the world, as well as making it less and less likely that the young could move out of their homes and begin their own independent lives. More and more structures and resources were given to keeping the decrepit people alive, even though many of them wished for death.

There came a point where it was impossible to ignore. The government, wanting to appease its people, had two ends of the spectrum both angry at them. The old wanted to be freed of the chains of existence, while the young wanted the opportunity to leave the nest and not feel as though their wings had been clipped. And so, eventually euthanasia laws were passed so that people could die on their own terms, with dignity. It had struck many moral philosophers as odd that modern life was vaunted as being one of freedom and liberty, yet the one thing that you were certain to own above everything else, your life, was deemed illegal for you to take. It was a holdover of our primal survival instinct, a cry from the DNA inside us that wanted nothing more than to exist and sense the world.

And that cry needed to be snuffed out.

People were simply tired of living. The world creaked under the weight of a swollen population and until this point there didn't seem to be a way out of it. But as soon as the law was passed people were given relief. Those who suffered from dementia were able to say goodbye to their families while they still remembered them. Those who were bedridden and forced to stare out of the window, comforting themselves with a memory of what it was like to feel a summer's breeze caress their cheeks, could put an end to their misery. Those whose bodies had betrayed them could now choose when they wanted to take control of their own destiny, rather than waiting for their body to fail entirely.

There was opposition to this, of course, as there were still many people who thought that life was all there was, and people should grasp it as tightly as if it were a possession. But the general thinking had shifted. Life was not something one owned or had, it was just a state of matter, a state of being that should be enjoyed for as long as it remained enjoyable. There was no sense in people putting themselves through extra strife just because life was lauded as this wondrous thing that would never come again. There was still a mystery as to what happened after death, but even for those who thought an eternal abyss awaited them it was still better than a life lived too long, and it was welcomed as a merciful thing. It seemed that life could only be endured for so long before people had had enough, and all they wanted was a choice.

Of course, not everyone wanted that choice. There were still some vigorous people who bucked the trend and remained agile and alert towards the upper limits of a life, but even then they had a certain wisdom that came over them, telling them that it was their time. They had done most of the things they wanted in life, and knew that by dying they could free resources for other people to use. In a packed and crowded world there was a sense of selflessness and charity that played a part in the aging process. By having a thing people knew they were depriving someone else of having it, and so they let themselves free, giving other people the chance to enjoy life for a few decades, before old age eventually caught up with them as well. It created a new cycle that was faster and quicker, and actually it made people more likely to embrace life when they knew they could control when it ended. Some people wished to blaze through it as quickly as possible, while others still wanted to eke out the years to enjoy it with loved ones. But nobody had to now fear growing old and helpless, because there was always the opportunity to make the final decision.

But this had put the scientists of the world in a quandary. For years the big problem of the world was aging. So many people were afraid of slipping away that vast resources had been pumped into select teams working on a serum against death. Mostly it was greedy billionaires who did not want anyone else to get their grubby hands on their fortune, but by the time such a serum was developed they had all died out for the most part. The serum was designed to freeze a person at a certain age, preventing the aging process. It had been tested on some animals, and while it could not be said they were immortal because not enough time had passed, they had not aged yet, and so it was ready for human testing.

However, if this drug entered the world then it would exacerbate the problems of before. Now not only would people occupy space and resources for a long time, but they would occupy them forever, potentially. They would accumulate goods and wealth and it would never be passed on to anyone else. If too many people took it then the world would become a huddled mass and there would be absolutely no room at all. It was horrifying to think about. Imagine if this serum had been around since the 1800s and all of those people who had died since then had continued to live.

It was clear that it could not be brought to the mass market, so as soon as it was announced it was heavily regulated by those in power. Thankfully there were not too many objections by anyone else, for rational people could see the dangers of this drug. Most people did not want it either, fearing that to live forever, even with all faculties intact, would still be a kind of hell. They would have to see their loved ones grow older until they faded and died, and then the next generation and the next. It was existential horror made real, for once the fear of dying was taken away then there really was no reason to live for such a long time, and the fear of living took its stead. People would much rather have a fulfilling, finite life than one that went on and on without any end.

But there were some things in the world that hadn't changed, one of which was the appreciation of, and necessity for, money. So much time and energy had been poured into making this wonder drug that it could not simply be written off. Investors needed to recoup some of the costs, but without a way to market it to the masses that made it more difficult to do. Many meetings were held and opinions were shared about how to commercialise the drug. Some people suggested giving it to select people who would become the guardians of history and ensure that civilisation learned from its mistakes, or to become living time capsules that could take note of history as it unfolded and could also be there to answer questions that future generations might have about the past. There had always been jobs that required risks and sacrifices before, but of course anyone who took this job would have to be paid for an eternal life, and nobody thought that there would be enough demand for these roles that made it worth giving them the drug. Moreover, anyone who took this job would be locked into that role for a lifetime and would never be able to do anything else because their knowledge and experience of the past was part of the appeal, and necessary to make the post worthwhile. So this idea was deemed implausible and tossed on the scrap heap along with the rest of them.

For a long time it did not seem as though there would be any traction. The scientists who had poured their lives into perfecting this drug were seen to have wasted their time, and all the money spent on it might as well have been burned.

But there was one avenue that was still left to be explored. The drug had at first been made as a salvation for people, but when the horrors of eternal life became accepted it was seen as a fate to be avoided. When thinking of it as a punishment it became natural to consider the option of using it on criminals. The first time it was suggested it was deemed too inhumane for this, but there were some heinous crimes for which people were sentenced to multiple life sentences, but never actually served them because they died before they could complete their sentences. As soon as the idea was posited people began to mull about the possibilities. They agreed that it could only be used for the most dangerous prisoners who deserved to stew in their own guilt and remorse. Some people argued that even though eternal life was not something to be strived for any longer, it was still wrong to give it to a prisoner who might endanger others if they were allowed to live.

Ultimately something had to be done with the drug though, so it was agreed to be used on a trial basis and the first person was selected.

His name was Jacob Highmount, a notorious criminal who was in jail for multiple murders. His case had caught national attention because of the nature of the crime, as many people sympathized with him. His daughter had been subjected to a sexual abuse ring and when he found out he went ballistic and killed every member he could find who was involved. It turned out that his daughter had not been the only victim, so the parents of other children who had been abused came out in support of him, treating him as a kind of folk hero who did the job that the police hadn't been able to do.

Of course, the police could not have everyone taking the law into their own hands even if they thought it was justified so their hands were tied. Vigilante justice had to be punished and consequences had to be served, so Jacob was sentenced and taken away from his family. He stood in the court as the judge read his sentence. People outside jeered and booed. He could hear them shouting that he was a hero. Jacob was unmoved. He had not tried to hide what he had done. He had never shied away from it, and now he was going to suffer the consequences. There had been no need for a jury because his guilt wasn't in doubt, and people were once again reminded that sometimes what was illegal wasn't strictly immoral.

But that didn't help Jacob escape his fate.

He was stoic as he was led away and taken to his prison cell. The expression on his face was unmoved, and he gazed into the distance. The sounds of the world wafted around his ears and he tried to appreciate them for as long as he could because he knew they would soon be absent from him. So too would his family. The only time he showed a glimpse of emotion was when he thought about what he had given up, but he knew it was a worthy price to pay. If he hadn't done anything then who knows how many other children those people would have abused. It didn't seem fair that he should be deprived of his family, but he had known what was likely to happen and he had done it anyway.

He was loaded into a van and the mob outside clapped and cheered and made their voices heard. He just hoped this brought real change into the world.

*

Jacob was taken to prison and inducted into the prison system. His clothes were stripped away and he was given a bland jumpsuit. He gave his fingerprints and surrendered what few possessions he had on him, and then he suffered the indignity of an examination. The guards looked at him with a mixture of scorn and admiration. Some of them no doubt agreed with what he had done, while to others he was just another inmate, and inmates were little better than vermin.

Before he was led to his cell he was taken to a room with a medical examination chair on it. He was told by the guard to lie down. A woman came into the room, her heels tapping against the cold floor. Her hair was tied back into a ponytail, and she wore wide glasses.

"I'm Dr. Waters," she said.

"You probably know who I am," Jacob replied dryly.

"Indeed, and I have all your information here," she held up a medical file. Jacob didn't think there was going to be anything of interest in there. He hadn't been to the doctors for years.

"So what are you going to do to me doc? I thought I was being given life, not the lethal injection."

Dr. Waters' lips twitched into something that resembled a smile. "Actually, you're not being given the lethal injection, but you are going to be subject to a new punishment technique that has been developed. You're going to be trial patient zero, so I do apologise if there are any side effects that we have not experienced yet."

"Never thought I'd be a guinea pig. What's going to happen to me then? What is this for?"

"Well, you see the law has you serving many more years than you're able to. This treatment is going to ensure that you can actually serve the full years of your term. You will be punished to the fullest extent of the law."

"I see. I didn't think things could get any worse than life in prison."

"They can't," Dr. Waters said. Jacob frowned.

"I don't understand. If I'm being given life in prison then what am I here for? What is this?" a sense of panic crept into his voice.

Dr. Waters smiled and placed a hand on his shoulder. "Don't worry Jacob. This is all perfectly cleared. There isn't any funny business going on. Tell me, how do you feel about life and growing old?"

An uneasy look appeared on Jacob's face as he shrugged. "I don't know. Same as everyone else I guess. Never really gave it much thought. Just tried to live a good life."

"I suppose you failed at that."

"I didn't," he said tersely, and met her gaze. "If you knew anything about me then you would know that I stayed true to my ideals. I did what I thought was right. What would you have done if you found out that your daughter was being used by a group of men? Would you be able to stand by while the police did one of their investigations that never amounted to anything? Would you want to see them go unpunished? I know I broke the law, and I accept that, but I will never let anyone tell me that I have not lived a good life. I removed a chunk of evil from the world, and if that's not good then I don't know what is."

Dr. Waters lost some of her composure. She gulped deeply and nodded, acquiescing to his words.

"Well, I can see you're a man of principle. I hope that these principles will stay with you through the years. This treatment is going to ensure that you do not age, and that you live your life for, well, perhaps eternity. That's the aim of the drug anyway. This is the punishment for your crimes, a life that will never end."

As she said this, she strapped his arms to the table and his eyes went wide with horror. He shook and the chair rattled as he struggled to break free, for this was something inhumane. This was a horror the likes of which he had never imagined before, and as she placed the needle against his arm his eyes bulged, but there was nothing he could do to escape it. He watched as the needle pierced his flesh and she pushed this unwanted drug into him. He had always resolved himself to living out the rest of his life in prison, growing old and dying there, but he had not prepared himself for *this*.

*

Jacob awoke the following day. He wiggled his toes and fingers, and then looked down his body. Nothing had changed and he didn't feel any different. He furrowed his brow and then went to get breakfast. The other inmates were there and he was given a standing ovation. There was nothing they liked more than someone who took justice into their own hands, especially against such vile men. He nodded at them, thinking to himself that he wasn't like them and he didn't belong here. But he supposed that was wrong. In the end he was exactly like them because he had committed a crime. It wasn't the intentions that mattered, only the outcome. He glanced down at his arm, looking at the puncture wound that hadn't yet healed. What the hell kind of thing had the doctor injected him with? He supposed there was no point worrying about it now, for it was already in his system.

Later in the day he was called to the visiting booth where his wife, Sara, was waiting for him. Her eyes were bloodshot and she looked tired. There were long shadows on her face and her skin was pale. Lucy wasn't with her. She hugged Jacob, and he held her for as long as he possibly could, wanting the moment to last forever.

It couldn't, of course.

"How was your first night?" she asked.

Jacob shrugged. "Made it through," he said.

"I'm so sorry that this happened Jacob. I wish there had been another way."

"We both know there wasn't. Those men had to pay. I just hope that Lucy will understand when she grows up. I hope she knows why I wasn't there for her," he said, choking up when he thought about all the things he was going to miss. "Did she not want to come today?"

"I thought it wasn't right, what with all the media outside." Jacob angled his head and wore a look of surprise. "You didn't know?" she continued. "They're still outside covering the story and people are out there protesting your incarceration. They're trying to get the verdict overturned."

"I wouldn't hold out hope. They're not going to change anything. It'll only make them look weak, and if they do this for me then it sets the precedent of them doing it for someone else. It'll just make things complicated."

"I know… but I didn't want Lucy to get caught up in it. I dread to think what the media would do with her."

"Yeah, she's been through enough already."

"I'll bring her when things have died down. I doubt they're going to keep on this story forever. You know what the media are like, there's always something else to capture their attention."

"Yeah," he forced a smile. "Just let her know that I miss her, and that I love her, alright?"

"I will. And I'll make sure she knows that you're in here because you protected her. I won't ever let her forget you."

"And don't you forget me too," he said, reaching out a hand. She placed hers on the table as well and they found each other. It was a gentle touch, much like the one they had shared when they had first been dating. That first touch had led to a deeper caress and more profound pleasure, but of course such a thing was not possible now, not with the guard watching on. Jacob had to console himself with just a squeeze of a hand. It was like a drop of water to a stranded man in the desert.

"So have they said anything about if there is going to be a chance of parole somewhere along the line?" Sara asked, her voice dancing with hope.

Jacob shook his head slowly. "There's not going to be any Sara. This is it. This is where I'm going to end up."

"I know we always planned for it I just… it seems so final."

"Well it's not for me."

Now it was Sara's turn to give him a quizzical look. "What are you talking about?"

"When I came in there was a doctor. She injected some drug into me, some kind of anti aging thing that means I'm going to live out all the years of my sentence and then some. Apparently it's a new thing they've concocted to make sure that prisoners serve an adequate number of years."

Sara looked at him with disbelief. "That can't be real, surely?"

Jacob shrugged again and rubbed his arm. "Felt real enough. I guess only time will tell."

"Could be some kind of lie to play on your mind. Maybe they've taken to psychological punishments in here."

"Maybe. It doesn't change anything for me though. I still miss you and Lucy." He offered her a failing smile. Now that he was here, in this moment, he began to regret what he had done. Morally he felt justified in ending their lives because he knew he had saved a lot of other people from harm, but to be stripped of his right to live a life with his family... well... it had been an easier price to pay when it had been a concept rather than reality. It was just the finality of the thing, the fact that nothing was going to change. He was only ever going to see Sara and Lucy in the confines of this visiting room for the rest of his life, all liberty stripped from him.

Year Five

Jacob rose and looked at himself in the mirror. He angled his face from side to side, looking at the beard he had grown, inspecting it for any stray grey hairs. He could see none. He ran his fingers through his hair to check if it was thinning, but it felt just as thick as ever. There were no wrinkles crinkled by his eyes, and he didn't feel the weight of the years making his back and knees ache. The more that time passed, the more he became convinced that Dr. Waters had been telling him the truth. If it was a ruse then it was an elaborate one, because she came back periodically to perform tests on him. He never learned the outcome of these tests so it might all have been for nothing, some grand ploy to torture him with the existential dread of moving through the years without growing older, but he didn't think so.

On her most recent visit he had asked her if there were any other people like him, other prisoners who had been given the drug. She hesitated a moment before she spoke.

"I'm afraid that before we could test the drug on anyone else there was a change in government and they took a dim view of treating prisoners as test subjects when the end result could not be confirmed. They seemed to think it was immoral to subject anyone to an endless life, no matter what kind of crime they had committed, so all traction in that area was stopped. But you can't put the genie back into the bottle once it has been let out, so we're still going to monitor your progress. Perhaps another government will come into power who will change their minds again and there will become other people who get the same treatment."

"I see. It sure might get lonely around here."

"I'll always be here, and when it's time for me to retire I'll make sure my replacement is just as capable as me," Dr. Waters said. It was the first time that Jacob had thought about being tended to by anyone but her. It seemed strange to think there was going to be a time when she would no longer be around. But that was the same for everyone. He tried not to think about it too much.

The day was a fine one because Lucy was coming to visit. He waited in the visiting room and then a smile broke out upon his face as he saw her come in, although he had to blink for a couple of moments because whenever he saw Lucy it was as though he was seeing a stop motion animation. She had grown so much, changing in so many little ways that it amounted to a big change. She was 11 now, her long hair tied into a ponytail, the flush of youth still upon her cheeks, yet in her eyes he could see the adult that was waiting to emerge from the chrysalis. She ran up to him and hugged him tightly. He bent down and kissed the top of her forehead, feeling the painful bliss that always accompanied her hugs, for he knew they were not going to last forever.

They sat down. Sara joined them. He kissed her on the cheek. She seemed off, but he wasn't sure why. Lucy was babbling about school. She presented a wad of papers she had written for Jacob, a mixture of stories and letters. She brought these every time she visited, and Jacob had a good collection of them stashed in his cell.

"How is school?"

"It's okay," Lucy said, "I like English, but the other stuff I just don't really get why I have to do it."

"She's doing really well in hockey though, aren't you?" Sara said, ruffling Lucy's hair.

"Yeah, but I missed that shot in the last game."

"You still scored a hat trick," Sara laughed. "Her standards are too high."

Jacob smiled and nodded, feeling like a stranger with his own family. There were so many little moments like this that he missed, and they all added up to creating a deep sense of anguish that swam in his soul.

"I just like winning," Lucy shrugged.

"Well, as long as you're enjoying it, that's the main thing. And keep trying at school, even in the subjects that you're not liking so much. It's still worth it in the long run and you never know what useful things you might learn."

Lucy nodded obediently. They spoke a little more about things, but Jacob always felt the conversations were one sided. It wasn't as though he could share anything of note, and so he felt like a leech, always seeking to absorb small parts of their life so that he could pretend he was still a part of it. He wasn't even an observer though, and if one day they decided not to visit there was nothing he could do to change it. He was utterly powerless, and the feeling left him bereft and despondent. It never seemed like there were enough time in these visits to talk about everything either, so sometimes things remained unsaid. And then the guard would inevitably call for time and he would regret not asking Lucy about this or that, or not mentioning to Sara something important. He would try and remember to ask them next time, but by the time they came again he would inevitably forget. A long life did not grant him a long memory.

As he went to say goodbye he tried to take Sara's hand. This time it slipped between his fingers and was little more than a caress, and she turned away from him quickly. As he went back to his cell he wondered if he had been imagining it, or if there was something wrong.

Since he had nothing but time to think about it, he inevitably tied himself up in knots.

Year Eight

Lucy was now fourteen. She walked into the visitation room. The first thing Jacob noticed about her was the pink streak in her hair. She flicked it back and strutted towards him with more confidence than she had shown before. She wore clothes he did not recognize. She was a young woman now, just waiting for the years to tick by to be a fully fledged adult.

He remained the same.

He hugged her tightly, as he always did. She had grown so much that he did not have to bend down as far to kiss the top of her head. He also noticed that Lucy did not let the hug linger as long as she used to.

"How are you doing sweetie?" he asked.

Lucy flicked her hair and blushed a little, embarrassed by being addressed by that term. She didn't protest against it though, perhaps because she knew that Jacob had already had so much taken away from him. "I'm okay."

"Not got any stories or letters for me today?"

"I'm sorry Dad, but I've kinda stopped doing that."

"Oh, but why? You were always so good at writing, and you enjoyed it a lot."

"I used to, yeah, but I guess I just wrote all I wanted to write. I have other things to do with my time now."

"Still playing hockey?"

Lucy nodded. "I don't know if I'll ever be able to do it as a career though. It doesn't exactly pay well."

"Do what you enjoy in life and worry about the money later. It's better to be happy than to be rich."

"Try telling that to people," Lucy said scornfully.

"Where's your mother?"

Lucy's eyes were angled to the side and gulped. "She's busy."

"Busy? With what?"

"You're really going to need to talk to her about that Dad. I'm not getting involved," Lucy sighed with frustration. Jacob was filled with questions, but he knew better than to ask. Whatever was going on, Lucy had likely been drained of it by Sara. "So how is life in here anyway? Keeping yourself busy?"

"Trying to. They have a good library here, and I've been keeping up with my exercise routine."

Lucy leaned in and kept her voice low. "What are the other people like in here?"

"Most of them are okay. They're just people. A lot of them made mistakes or let their impulses get the better of them. Some of them just didn't know that there was a better way. It makes me quite sad really about how many of them are in here because they weren't taught a better way."

"So you're making friends then?"

"Some of them, yeah, but they never last for very long. People get transferred or released, so I've learned not to make too many deep connections. I know that it's only going to get worse as time goes on."

"Did you speak to the doctor?"

"Not yet."

"Dad," Lucy gave him the kind of look that he used to give her when she didn't brush her teeth. "You know nothing is going to change unless you ask."

"I really don't think there's any point. After what I did people aren't going to go easy on me." He noticed that Lucy's gaze flickered as he mentioned the past. It wasn't something he liked to talk about in front of her as he didn't want to bring up the bad memories. She had been in therapy since she was little in a bid to help her cope with the trauma, but it was something she lived with every day, and he did not wish to exacerbate this. When she came to see him he wanted the visits to be free of any stress or drama.

"Nothing is going to change unless you do something about it. I thought you would know that more than anyone," Lucy said quietly. "You have to ask them if there's a way to reverse the process. If they came up with it then they can surely do something to reverse it. You deserve to have a normal life."

Jacob nodded, but did not respond to that statement directly. He wasn't sure anyone deserved anything. Things just happened and people made decisions and the end result was largely up in the air. "How is my crusade going?" he asked in a dry tone.

"It's died down over the years. People still care, and there are occasionally stories about you, but there are other things happening in the world that need attention. I think people realize that they're not going to be able to change anyone's mind about this. I keep trying to raise awareness, but it's not easy."

"You don't need to keep fighting for me Lucy. It's okay. You need to live your own life."

"I know Dad, but after what you did for me I have to do something for you as well."

Jacob shook his head and smiled sadly. "You don't have to do that at all Lucy. You're my daughter. I brought you into this world and when that happened I made a promise to do whatever I could to give you a happy life. You don't ever need to repay me for anything. All you need to do is find a good path, and good people to walk it with. That's all I've ever wanted from you."

"I wish you could walk it with me, Dad," she reached out her hand. Jacob took it and squeezed it. It was another one of those moments that he would cling to long after he had left, a moment that he would stretch and eke out for as long as possible, trying to make it last for the eternity that lay between one visit and the next.

They spoke for a while longer until she eventually had to leave. Jacob was lost in the abyss of silence again. He went back to his cell and then went through the routines of the day as the blurred into weeks. Lucy visited him again and again, but still he was waiting to see Sara.

It was months later when she finally turned up. His eyes sparkled because she looked good. She looked… relaxed, rather than being weighed down by stress as she had been for so long. She was a sight for sore eyes. Jacob rushed towards her and hugged her tightly. He noticed that she did not hug him back.

"Jacob, I need to speak with you about something," she began in that tone that promised doom. Jacob looked crestfallen. He had been thinking about her absence for long enough that he knew what was coming, but just because he had anticipated this it did not make it any easier.

"It's been a while since you've been here."

"I know, I've been-"

"Busy. Lucy told me."

Her head dropped and she sighed. "I haven't been busy Jacob. The truth is that I've been afraid. Afraid and ashamed."

"Ashamed of what?"

She licked her lips. They glistened, a deep shade of ruby. When was the last time he had seen her wear makeup? "I wanted to see you, but I was never sure how to tell you. I've tried to pretend, to practice in the mirror like it was some interview. Lucy has been nagging me to come here for ages and I know I should have I just… it's so difficult. I didn't want to take anything away from you."

"What are you taking away from me Sara?"

She wouldn't look at Jacob as she spoke. "I know there's no good way to say this, so I'm just going to say it. I've met someone else."

It felt as though the world was crumbling around him. Jacob was numb. He knew the pain would come later, sliding through his blood like slick venom. "Who is it?"

"Does it matter?" she snapped, but then gave him an apologetic look. Her shoulders sank.

"His name is Lee. He's a good man. I just… I couldn't take it Jacob. The loneliness I mean. It was like I was a widow, except my husband wasn't dead and I didn't know how to handle it. I wanted to set an example for others. I wanted to be loyal because I still love you, but I just… I needed more. I felt so lost and everyone is always saying how you need to make the most of your life while you can. I felt time slipping away and I didn't know how to handle it. The truth is I wasn't even looking for love. I was just on some work retreat and he was there and we got to talking. I don't know what it was about him exactly, but I felt like I could share things with him that I couldn't with anyone else. He understood everything and I got close with him and I… Jacob, you have to understand that it wasn't easy for me. I spent so long agonizing over it, over everything. I felt so guilty because I know I'm betraying you but I just… I can't live alone. I know I should have told you sooner. I'm sorry for that. I'm sorry for everything."

The words whirled around him like icy hail, peppering his skin and his soul. It was difficult to see the woman he loved in so much pain, and even more difficult to know that he wasn't going to be the one to alleviate it. Once again he was reminded how things had changed on the outside. She was experiencing life, growing older, while he was stagnant. The true horror of the punishment was beginning to dawn on him.

"You must be so angry for me after everything, after all you've done for Lucy and me," she added.

"I'm not angry Sara. You're right. You deserve to live. I shouldn't expect you to be a prisoner as well because of something I did," he forced the words out. They were bitter on his tongue, for a part of him felt like she should have been in here as well. After all, she had been there when he had suggested this course of action. She was the one who hadn't dissuaded him, who had angrily declared that something had to be done, only he was the one who had done it, not her. And now she could leave the guilt behind. She could leave him behind. But he was not so cruel as to make her feel guilty about it. He still loved her, after all. And she was right, if she could take some happiness out of life then she deserved to make it so. She left in tears after not knowing what to say. He rarely saw her again after that, although they never divorced.

*

"And how are you today Jacob?"

Weeks had passed since the visit from Sara. The dull pain hadn't gone away.

"My wife left me," he said. Dr. Waters paused and wasn't quite sure about what she should say.

"I'm sorry to hear that. I suppose it is expected in these situations. One can't wait around forever," she said in her usual clinical tone. For a doctor she wasn't the most empathetic, but he presumed that was why she specialised in research rather than general practice.

"I need to ask you a question doctor. Is there any chance that this process can be reversed? Are they ever going to find a serum that will counteract the effects this has taken? The more I think about it the more I don't want to live this long."

"I'm afraid not. You see, it's not really going to be cost effective. The amount it would take to treat just one person, especially one with your… history, well, financially it would not make sense, nor would it from a reputational point of view either. I'm afraid you're stuck like this."

Jacob did not say anything in reply. He merely stewed in his frustration and lamented the fact that the years were stretching out before him without any end.

Year Twenty

Jacob looked at the sea of faces across from him in the canteen. So many of them were young. So many of them were new. There was a constant stream of them and while he did not know much about the circumstances of the outside world, what he did know was that nobody had ever managed to deal with the problem of crime. There was never a shortage of criminals, some of them came back more than once. And Jacob sat there like an old tree while the environment changed around him. The face that stared back at him was the same as it had ever been, still with no signs of slowing down. He had chopped off his beard just for the sake of a change, although he regretted this because it only served to make him appear younger.

But today was when Lucy was visiting. The time between her visits had grown as she devoted more time to her own life. While Jacob knew deep down he wanted this, he still wished that she visited more often. However, he tried to take joy in the moments they did share with each other.

The pink streak had long vanished from her hair, put down to an embarrassing urge to mark her identity as a teenager. Now her hair was dark and sleek, cut to a length that was just beyond her shoulders. Her smile was wide and her eyes sparkled. His little girl was all grown up, a fully fledged woman. Here was another snapshot of her life, and in these brief moments he was made aware of all the moments that he had missed out on. He tried not to dwell on them, though.

"I have some good news!" she cried, and immediately thrust her hand towards him, showing him the sparkling ring that adorned her finger. Jacob grinned.

"He finally asked you then."

"Yes, he did, and he told me that he came to ask you for permission as well. Thanks for granting it."

"It was a nice gesture."

"Matt is a sweet guy. He really makes me feel special. He would do anything for me. He reminds me a lot of you, although I'm not going to tell my therapist that. I don't want to unravel that thread," Lucy laughed. It was a bubbling sound free of tragedy or trauma, and it was music to Jacob's ears.

"I'm just glad you've found someone who can make you happy. When is the big day?"

"In the spring. We wanted it to be sunny, but not too hot. Everyone is chipping in to make it special, so I think we're going to have everything we want."

"I'm sorry I can't help," Jacob said. The smile fell from Lucy's face.

"I didn't mean it like that Dad."

"I know."

"I'll make sure to come and show you the pictures and the videos. I have written to just about everyone I can think of to try and get you a day release, but they're just not having it. In some ways you have been the most important criminal case of modern times."

"Well, I did always want people to remember me," Jacob said dryly. Lucy flicked hair away from her face and wore a solemn expression.

"Dad, I've been doing a lot of thinking recently. Getting married is this huge thing that has made me reflect on my life and I just wanted to say thank you again. The more I live the more I realize everything you gave up for me and I just… I know I'm never going to be able to thank you enough for it. You always have been and always will be my hero. I really wish there was more I could do to give you back what you gave up for me, but I am trying to live as good a life as I can, just like you wanted me to."

"Good," Jacob gave her a small smile and blinked away the tears that were forming in his eyes.

"Without you I don't think I would have been able to move on properly. If I knew that those men were still out there, still alive… I never would have been able to leave the house. You made it possible for me to live properly Dad and I just wish that you could do all the things you're supposed to do. I'm sorry that you can't be at the wedding."

"I'm sorry too," Jacob said. He tried to pretend that everything was fine, but it really wasn't. The more years that passed, the more he saw how much he was missing out on, and he actually began to pity the men he had killed. At least they were just dead, meaning they did not have to suffer the pain of seeing all these moments slip by without being able to enjoy them.

Year Twenty Seven

Lucy and Matt came to visit him with their son, Jake. It was touching that he had been named after Jacob, but Jake was shy around this man who was little more than a stranger to him.

"You really don't need to bring him here. I can't imagine what this place must seem like to him," Jacob said.

"I think it's important that he knows you," Lucy said. It was difficult for Jacob to see her now. She was the same age as he was when he had been incarcerated. They looked like they should have been brother and sister rather than father and daughter. He noticed the way she looked at him sometimes, as though he was a photographic man, frozen in one moment of time.

Jacob tried to interact with the boy to little avail. He tried not to think of the fact that one day Jake was going to be the only family he had left. Jacob asked about Sara. She had been struggling with an illness, but other than that she was fine.

"She says that she wants to come see you, but she doesn't think she has anything good to say. She thinks it's better if she stays away."

Jacob nodded, understanding that Sara did not need to be tethered to the past like he was. Jake was skittish and nervous. Eventually he burst out crying and his parents were forced to take him away. Jacob could understand. Sometimes he burst out crying too.

*

Dr. Waters moved slower than she once did. Her hair was the same colour, although Jacob suspected this was out of a bottle now. Her features were pinched and creases marred her face, creases that would never adorn Jacob's face. There was something noble about an aged face, some kind of majesty that created a sense of pride and awe. Yes, I have endured the world for this long. Yes, I am still standing. These are the marks of my triumphs and my failures, look upon them and be inspired.

"I need to ask you a question doc, and I don't want you to dance around the answer. Just tell me straight. Can I be killed? I know that this serum you put inside me keeps my body in this state, but if someone stabs me will I bleed out?"

"Are you thinking of doing something you're not supposed to?" Dr. Waters asked. Jacob remained silent at this. He would have been lying if he claimed the thought had not crossed his mind, but he had endured so many moments of solitude there wasn't much he hadn't thought about. Dr. Waters continued, realizing that he wasn't going to answer her question. "I wasn't sure if I should tell you this or not. One of the animals we tested on was released back into the wild and monitored. It got into an unfortunate accident, and it did not die. It seems that the serum makes the body react to death as though it is an attack on the immune system. At the point where it realizes it is going to shut down completely it puts the body into a kind of stasis, and the serum enables the body to repair itself far more efficiently than normal. So aside from being obliterated before the body has a chance to respond, no, I don't think you can die. It would certainly be impossible in a place like this, unless the very walls fell on you."

"I see. So I'm stuck like this then."

"As was the plan," Dr. Waters said. Jacob returned to his cell and stared at the ceiling. He had thought about starting a fight with one of the crueller inmates in the hope that it would free him from this torture, but now he realized there was no point. He would have all of the pain without any of the freedom. He was approaching almost three decades in prison now, three decades that he could have used to accomplish so many things. He should have been there at his daughter's wedding to walk her down the aisle, he should have enjoyed romantic nights with his wife, he should have taken care of his grandson. Instead all of these things had been denied him, and at night the pain gave rise to choking sobs that would never let him rest.

Year Forty Five

Jacob was an old man, although he did not feel it. He should have been entering the twilight of his years now, preparing to ride off into the sunset leaving behind a legacy of good memories and cherished relationships. Instead the days were the same as they had ever been. Even if he had grown old in prison at least he would know that things were coming to an end, but he was locked in a purgatory from which he would never escape. Usually when someone looked to the future there were fewer days ahead than there were behind, especially someone at his age, but this was not the case for him. The years carried on slipping by and he remained the same. The only thing he could do to give himself the illusion of change was to change his appearance slightly, but even then the same eyes stared back at him, tired and weary and wanting to sleep.

Lucy had continued visiting regularly. Jake hadn't. She sometimes brought him, but Jacob knew that he had been forced to come, much like when he had been younger. Jacob wasn't his grandfather. He was just a man who was related to him by blood. There were no shared memories there, no good ones at least. All Jake remembered was being dragged to some brooding building when he was a kid, a scary place where everyone was in a bad mood. It was no wonder that he wanted to stay as far away from that as possible.

And while he enjoyed seeing Lucy, she had confessed to him that it was hard for her to see him as she remembered him and not as he should have been. She was older than he appeared now, and she was even older in life experience. She had pursued her dream of hockey and had played in the Olympics, winning a few gold medals during her career. After this she then coached the team, adding to her medal haul, although she was looking to wind down her career now. He was filled with pride to know that she had lived such a successful life though, and was constantly amazed that she had been able to achieve so much.

She had kept her promise to never forget him as well. He had seen and read interviews with her, and whenever they asked a question about her greatest inspiration or who she was most thankful to for her success she always gave the same answer; her father. Some people did not like her speaking about this because they would rather forget that Jacob existed, but Lucy kept trying to rally people to his cause and make them see that his treatment was inhumane. Nobody did change their minds though, not that he expected them to.

However, on this occasion it wasn't Lucy who visited him when the announcement was made, but a man he had only seen in pictures. His name was Lee, and he was the one who had won Sara's heart.

He looked distraught. Jacob gestured for him to sit down. "I wish we could have met in other circumstances," Lee began.

"What happened to her?" Jacob asked, knowing that Lee wouldn't have come here for any other reason.

"She died. It was... she was struggling with an illness for a long time. The doctors tried all kinds of medication to give her a few more years. It didn't seem right that she should die just yet. She wasn't ready. I wasn't ready," his voice cracked on emotion. "I always thought we would grow old together and then leave with dignity, but that wasn't her fate. They could have used a machine to keep her alive, but what kind of life would that have been? I just thought I should come here and tell you, face to face. I didn't want to leave it to Lucy. She's dealing with enough already."

"I can imagine," Jacob said. It was strange to think that he was never going to see Sara again. Of course, it had been years since the two of them had shared the same room. Their relationship had been over for decades, and yet he had never truly moved on. When they married he had promised to love her forever, and that was just what he had done. But now he would never get to see her again.

"Did she have a good life in the end? Was she happy?" Jacob asked.

"Yes, she was. I tried to give her everything I could," Lee replied. His words were becoming lost in choking sobs. "I'm sorry. I know this is strange. She was your wife and maybe it doesn't seem right that I should be sitting here talking to you like this-"

"It's okay Lee. You loved her for longer than I did. You got to spend more time with her than I did. It's only natural."

"She never forgave herself you know, for the way she treated you. She felt so guilty about moving on while you were stuck in here. It's a hell of a sacrifice you made. I don't know if I could have done the same thing. I think she would have liked to see you again, just one last time, just to put things right."

Jacob forced a smile. "Things are already right Lee. Wherever she is, she doesn't have to worry about that. I don't begrudge her for living her life. It wasn't right that both of us should have gone through this. I'm glad what you did for her, and what you've done for my daughter as well."

Jacob sat across from this man who had lived the life that should have been his, but he didn't feel envious or resentful. After all, there wasn't anything he could have done about it. He just had to get on with things and wait for the next tragedy to strike.

Year Eighty

Jacob sat opposite an old woman. Her hair was fully grey and wispy, while her once supple skin was wrinkled. Her eyes were enlarged by her wide glasses, and her shoulders were hunched. She had waddled into the visiting room with the help of a cane. Her frail hands shook, and she looked diminished from the woman she had once been. Her smile was the same though. Some things never changed.

She looked around the room.

"I wouldn't like to say how much time I've spent in this room," Lucy said, wheezing as she laughed.

"Not as much time as I've spent in my cell," Jacob said. He meant it to sound more humorous than it ended up being. "How are the kids?"

Lucy shrugged. "Getting into trouble. I keep trying to get them to come and visit, but they just... I don't know. I'm sorry Dad. I feel like it's the one area in which I failed."

360

"I don't blame them. I wouldn't want to be there if I had to be. It's got to be hard for them as well, to see a man they don't know and who never changes. It must be hard for you as well."

"I got over that a long time ago. But this is the last time I'm going to see you Dad."

Jacob's eyes flicked up. "You made a decision then," he said, fighting against the lump in his throat. She inclined her head.

"It's time. Life after Matt has been… lonely. The kids have their own lives. There's not much else that I want to accomplish. The only thing keeping me around is you," she smiled sadly. Her eyes became watery. "I can already feel things getting worse. There are times when I forget things that I should remember, and I can't always get around by myself. I never want to be dependent on anyone else and I know that if I don't act soon it's going to be too late. I've tried to hold on for you Dad, but I can't do it any longer."

Jacob closed his eyes and took her hands. It was strange to feel them in his, so small and frail and weak. But when he looked at her he could see past her age. She was still his daughter.

"I'm going to miss you so much Lucy. I don't know if you can comprehend how deep the pain is going to go."

"I'm going to miss you too Dad. I know it should be the other way around, and I'm sorry it can't. I'm sorry that I couldn't make a difference. People just wouldn't listen."

"Don't you worry about that. Of course you made a difference to my life. You never forgot me, Lucy. You kept visiting all the time. I really appreciate that. It's not going to be the same without you."

"No, it's not. I'm going to make my grandkids come no matter what. I'll put it in my will. They're not going to get anything unless they come and visit you at least once a month," she said, half joking. Jacob didn't want anyone to come and visit him because they were obligated to, but he appreciated the sentiment. Her soft chuckled faded into silence, a silence of which he became acutely aware. It was the kind of silence that grew between them and took on a life of its own, the kind of silence that couldn't easily be pushed away. He knew that this silence was going to stay with him forever.

This was the kind of moment he wished would last forever, the kind of moment that he wanted to cling to with all his might. But he knew that it was impossible.

"I'm glad you've lived a good life Lucy."

"I did Dad, and it was all because of you. I'm sorry that I couldn't do the same for you," a shade of guilt adorned Lucy's face.

"You don't have to feel guilty Lucy. I did what I did and I was prepared to face the consequence. I suppose I just didn't realize that the consequence was going to be this far reaching."

"They have to let you go at some point Dad. They can't expect you to stay here forever."

Jacob looked away, because he knew that was exactly what they intended.

Lucy stayed with him for as long as possible. Eventually the klaxon sounded, indicating that visiting hours were over. It might as well have been the toll of a bell for it signified the last time he would ever see his daughter. He rose to embrace the old woman, taking her into his arms just as he had done all his life. He squeezed her tightly and felt the salty tears trickling between his eyelids.

"Thank you for coming to see me all these years Lucy. I love you so much," the words choked out of him. There were not enough words in the world to express how fond he was of her, and he knew there were still things that he wanted to say, things that he wished he could leave her with, but he supposed that in life there were always things left unsaid. As she drew away he saw that she was crying too, and then she turned and walked out of the door, out of the building, out of life itself. He would never see her again. All the memories of her formed a tapestry that flowed within his mind, a tapestry that had now reached its end.

The two people who had meant more to him than anything else in this life were now gone. Sara, the woman he loved who had turned away from him, and now Lucy, the resolute daughter who had never forsaken him. He had done an unspeakable act to avenge her, and now he was still here paying the price despite the fact that she was going to die. He was just glad that she had a good life though. That was why he had done what he did. That was all he had wanted for her. It was perhaps the only thing that could console him.

Year One Hundred and Thirty

Jacob had long been the oldest person alive, but what point was that life when it was lived behind stone walls and iron bars? There were no great achievements to look back on, no experiences to share, nothing except the same thing day and in day out. It had gotten worse since Lucy had left. She must not have been able to secure the stipulation in her will that enforced her children to visit Jacob, for none of them did. Lucy had been his family, but they had not been. They had another family, a family who was present. He was just some strange man who they spoke about from time to time, a man who probably scared them because of what he had done.

Barely anyone remembered now. There were whispers of course, but the new breed of inmates who came into the prison always asked him what he had done. When he found himself telling the story it was difficult for him to remember the details that used to be burned into his mind, like the faces of the men twisted in horror, or the scent of blood.

Eventually everything turned into a hazy memory that was more like a dream than anything else, and although life might have been a dream, Jacob was not going to be able to row his boat to the farthest shore.

"How are you feeling Jacob?" Dr. Halliwell asked. She was even more procedural than Dr. Waters, if that were possible.

Jacob sighed. "I ache all over. I just feel so tired all the time. I'm exhausted of living. I want it to end. There's nothing more I can do. I don't want to keep waking up to the same thing every day. Please, can't you find some way to undo this?" his voice was more emotional than he intended, and his eyes were watery. They did not have an effect on the stoic doctor, however.

"I'm afraid there is no such solution," she said in a cold tone. Jacob turned his gaze back to the ceiling and let out a long exhalation. After this he went into the prison yard to do his exercises. The other inmates were having a conversation about what they were looking forward to most when they got out. They were talking about things that he didn't understand, new technologies that the world had progressed to using that were far beyond his comprehension. He turned his back on them and kept to himself, confining himself to a solitary life because what was the point in making friends? They would only die, and he could not bear the pain of bringing someone close to his heart again.

Year One Hundred and Seventy Seven

Jacob was told that he had a visitor. At first, he thought it must have been a mistake, or perhaps his mind had finally cracked and he had gone insane. He had longed for the day when he lost his mind, believing that if he went crazy then he would not be aware of his miserable plight and might actually be able to find some semblance of happiness in a broken and fractured world. Unfortunately, whatever drug had given his body so much fortitude had also strengthened his mind as well, so he was stuck with the rational outlook on the world that caused him so much pain.

He dragged his weary limbs to the visiting room where he saw a dark-skinned woman sitting on a table by herself. As soon as she saw him her eyes lit up and a smile appeared on her face. It had been a long time since he had seen anyone smile quite like that. She raised herself to her feet and gave him an enthusiastic handshake.

"Jacob? Jacob Highmount? Is it really you?"

"The one and only."

"I can't believe that you're actually here!" she squeaked, looking as though she was about to burst with excitement.

"Where else would I be?" he arched his eyebrow as he sank into his chair. He hoped this wasn't one of those crazy women who wanted to marry him. He had received letters from strangers proclaiming their love for him even though they had never met him. He had never replied to any. "And you are?"

"Debbie, Debbie Parker. I'm with the Herald."

Jacob looked at her blankly.

"The Herald is the most popular news blog in the world."

"What's a news blog?"

"It's…" her smile faltered. "It's a way to share news and opinions all around the world."

"I see, and what kind of story are you hoping to find here?"

"You. I want to find your story."

Jacob snorted. "I think you're looking in the wrong place. There have to be a million more stories out there."

"But none like yours. You are the oldest man alive by some way. You have seen the world grow and change. You are a living piece of history! I've long believed that one of the drawbacks of our short lives is that we never get to truly learn from our mistakes, as a species I mean. By the time people realize that something they've done is wrong, there is already another generation ready to make the same mistake. But through you we can see how one man has witnessed the evolution of the world, both for good and bad. That is, if you'd be willing to talk to me?"

Jacob turned his head from side to side, then he shrugged. "It's not as though I have anything better to do."

Debbie beamed. "Okay, I thought I'd ask you about what you think of the current state of the world. Do you think we're better off having these unified continental governments, or do you think it was better when countries were governed individually? Obviously people tend to get annoyed that the bureaucratic machine moves slowly, but was it really any better in the past?"

Jacob looked at her blankly. He had heard that the way governments work had changed, but he had never paid much attention to it. It wasn't as though it affected him. "I'm sorry Debbie, but I don't have an opinion on it. I never took much notice of politics even when I was a free man, let alone in here."

Disappointment flickered across Debbie's face. "Okay... well, how about the environment then. Did you ever think it was possible that the world would come back from the brink of climate devastation? Were you proud when it was announced that a new balance had been achieved?"

Jacob's cheeks flushed.

"I wasn't really aware that this had happened," he said. Perhaps Lucy had mentioned it in an offhand comment once, but it had never made a great impact on him. Debbie tilted her head to the side and furrowed her brow. Clearly she had thought Jacob was going to be able to provide more insight.

"What about-" she began, but Jacob cut her off before she could ask another question.

"Debbie, I appreciate you coming down here today, but I'm not sure it's going to be as revealing as you would like it to be. I'm not a great thinker. I'm not a philosopher. I've never been concerned with current affairs. Before I came to this place I just wanted to live my little life without bothering anyone at all, and then something happened that snapped inside me. I was willing to live out my life in this place, and instead I've been forced to endure an eternity. My wife and my daughter died so long ago that they're just relics now, and I haven't had any family to think of since they passed. For almost two centuries I've been in this same building, staring at the same walls, watching people come and go, streaming in and out like the flowing tides. If you want a comment from me then it's going to be about that. Clearly the world you live in is a lot different from the world I left, but things haven't changed all that much, have they? Aren't people concerned with preventing crime? Why are the same punishments still in effect? Am I supposed to believe that everything has progressed in society apart from the way we treat our criminals? But then people like us have always been the forgotten ones, and I doubt that is going to change. I'll probably be having the same conversation with some other reporter in another couple of hundred years or so," as he said this the abyss of the future dawned on him and his throat tightened, choking his breath. His entire body went rigid with tension as he realized there was never going to be any escape. There was never going to be a way out.

Debbie looked forlorn. "I'm sorry Jacob," she said. Then she turned and rose, and just like everyone else in his life, she was gone.

Year Two Hundred

Two centuries had passed since Jacob had first been incarcerated. The daughter he had defended had passed away a long time ago, and he wondered if he had truly made a difference to the world. The strain upon his mind was terrible, and he spent his days clawing at his scalp, wishing that he could rip his skull open and see his mind spill upon the floor. The days blurred into each other, and time had lost all meaning for him. Existence was one long elastic thing, being stretched and stretched and stretched, but for him it would never reach breaking point. He had been robbed of all the things he could, and perhaps should, have done. He had read so many books that he had seen the same themes presented over and over again. It seemed foolish to him how so many people strove for meaning in life when the meaning was in the living. Having that taken away showed him that the only point to life was life itself. There was nothing else.

Yet how many words had been strung together by thinkers pontificating about some deeper level of existence? It had all become too much for him to bear and he could not stomach reading these trite thoughts any longer, so even one of the last few pleasures that could help him while away his time had been taken from him.

Without these external forces he was left a hollow man. The only thing he possessed was consciousness, unending thoughts that were tired and burned out. He had not accomplished anything in life and he was now ready for it all to end, but it never would. The same face stared at him every time he looked in a mirror, this face that had been frozen in time.

And then one day he was told he had a visitor again. This time it was special enough that he was taken to one of the private offices used by the staff. The doorway was flanked by two guards wearing sunglasses. Inside the room was a tall, slender woman who reminded him of an actress he had seen in a film two hundred years ago, someone who had died a long time ago, and he couldn't quite capture her name.

"Mr. Highmount, please take a seat," she said, gesturing with an open palm towards a chair. He did as she asked.

"My name is Gabrielle Baker and I am a Senator in the Eurasian government." He blinked as she introduced himself. When he did not react, she took a chair and joined him at a table. She clasped her hands together and tilted her head. "Mr. Highmount, do you remember some time ago a reporter came to visit you here?"

Jacob nodded.

"And are you aware that she wrote an article about you?"

Jacob's face twisted in confusion. "I didn't think I could give her what she was looking for."

"I think she might have found something else. She called her article 'The Forever Man,' and used some direct quotes from you. She wrote about your plight, about how you have been alienated from the world and she reflected on the fact that the way we treat prisoners has not changed. It created quite a stir and began a movement where we looked at our justice system. There is a sense among many of us that we have allowed things to stay as they are simply because we are used to them, but habits should never be accepted without question. Frankly, after reading the article I was struck by your plight. I think what has been done to you is completely barbaric. This punishment goes beyond the pale, and it is high time that an amendment has been made for your release. I cannot see the logic in you suffering through more years of this punishment. I fail to see what good it could do, or how you could be further rehabilitated by spending more years in jail. If anything it would only make you condition worse, and at that point your incarceration is tantamount to torture. So I took it upon myself to fight for you, and I'm here to tell you today that I have won. You have been granted your release."

Jacob stared at her, not quite understanding what she was saying.

"I thought you would have had more of a reaction than that. Do you understand me Mr.

Highmount? You will no longer be a prisoner here. You will be a free man again."

"But… but what am I going to do for a job? What am I going to do for money?"

"There is plenty for you to learn. Every citizen of Earth receives a basic income to allow them the resources they need to survive. I have already arranged a place for you to live. I'm sorry that you had to endure this for so long, but I'm happy to say that it's over now. It's been an honour meeting you Mr. Highmount," she shook his hand and then walked out of the room, leaving the door open.

Jacob was stunned. Was it really as easy as all that? After so many years his stay in the prison had ended.

It didn't seem real.

But it was.

He was shown out of his cell. The possessions he had turned over when he had first been incarcerated were given back to him, and then he was taken to the entrance of the prison and let out into the world. He stepped out and breathed in the sweet air of freedom, but when he opened his eyes after the inhalation he was stunned by the sight that greeted him. The city was before him, bathed in neon lights, the buildings rising as high as mountains. Small airplanes that he would quickly identify as hovering cars whizzed around in designated lines, and the bright lights glittered, as though stars had fallen to the sky. Then he looked up at the sky and saw huge cities floating among the clouds, tethered by great cables to each other. Wide billboards flickered with various advertisements, while people walked around with electronic attachments to their faces and limbs. It was as though they all had a personal TV. It was all so immediate, as though while he had been in prison the world had exploded and reached out into every nook and cranny of the world, itching to cover every space. It was so big, so massive, and he let out a whimper because he was overwhelmed.

He turned back to the prison, only to find its large iron doors closed and impassable. Jacob sank to his knees and cried again. The world he had known had died a long time ago, and now he was alone in this new, alien world. At least in prison he had a routine and he recognized the four walls. Here he was utterly lost, and he did not truly want to live in this new world. He did not want a new life.

He just wanted it to end, but it never would.

Magic Grandma

Angela skipped along happily. Her red cloak billowed out behind her like a cape, while strands of dark hair fell over her eyes. There was an itch that she ignored, because the itch always hopped around her body like a frog so there was no point in giving it attention. Angela just had to ignore it as best she could. Her gaze was focused on the pavement, her feet darting as she sought to avoid the cracks. Grandma had told her that if she wasn't careful and stepped on the wrong crack then she might fall out of the world itself. Grandma always had good advice. Angela hummed and sang to herself, a song that had been with her for as long as she could remember. There were two high notes, then a few low ones, and then some high ones again. It might have had words once, but she had never been taught any, but the noises were enough.

A smile widened on her face as she approached Grandma's house. It was a quaint little thing, nestled in a small crook of the world. She kicked the plant pot away with her foot and picked up the key, sliding it into the lock. The door opened effortlessly. She had always told Grandma that she needed to find a better hiding place for the key because any thief might find it. Grandma replied by saying that she didn't have anything worth stealing anyway. Grandma was always like that, pragmatic.

Angela entered the lounge and was delighted to see that Grandma was already ready in her mobility scooter.

"How did you know I was coming?" Angela asked, her voice soft and innocent as an angel's. In fact that was why she had the name she did, although her parents were not religious at all so they could not stand have a child named after something linked to the Christian faith, so they added an 'A' and that seemed to make everything better. But Grandma had always called her an angel. It was their little secret.

"Because you always come at this time of the week. I may be old, but I haven't lost my wits yet. Now, where are we going today?" Grandma asked. Her eyes were milky, her skin creased and wrinkled, but her expression was a kindly one. Her voice was ragged. Once it had been melodious and lilting, but it had been weathered by the years. However, Angela knew it was similar to hers. Sometimes it sounded like an echo.

"To the palace!" Angela cried, reaching a hand in the air and pointing a finger to the ceiling. Grandma rolled her eyes.

"You always want to go to the palace," she said, with mock frustration. "Well, come on then. Help me get out of here."

Angela took her position behind the mobility scooter. Once upon a time she had ridden in Grandma's lap, but Grandma had told her she was too big for that now. So Angela held onto the back and walked behind. It wasn't as though the mobility scooter went very fast anyway. There was a ramp leading out of the door, which was just wide enough for the mobility scooter to fit through.

"I'm glad I'm so thin," Grandma joked. Angela giggled. "Now, do you remember what I told you about what happens if we see any strangers?"

"Yes Grandma," Angela rolled her eyes. Grandma always asked her this, every single time they went out. And Angela had never seen any strangers at all. Well, apart from that one time. But she didn't like thinking about that.

"I saw that. If you keep doing that one day they're going to roll into the back of your head and they're never going to come back."

Angela wasn't sure if she believed that, but she was just scared enough to stop.

"I won't speak to any strangers. I'll hide from them. I promise," Angela said.

"Good girl. That's my angel. Well, let's go to the palace then!" Grandma exclaimed, and Angela suspected she might have been as excited as Angela herself.

In truth, Angela never had to worry too much about strangers. The streets around her neighbourhood were always quiet, so much so that sometimes Grandma drove her scooter in the middle of the road, when the roads were smooth. Sometimes there were cracks and pot holes and other things that got in the way, but she was able to move quite swiftly, shrieking with girlish glee as the wind whipped through her hair. Angela had to struggle to keep up.

By the time they reached the palace, Angela was out of breath. She stopped for a moment, drinking in the sight as she caught her breath. Sweat trickled down the side of her face and made her clothes cling to her skin. It didn't help the itching sensation any, and she couldn't help but reach her hand under her clothes and scratch her stomach. She winced a little and then wiped her fingers on her cloak. The itch was still there, although now it had travelled to the base of her spine. She sighed, wondering if there had ever been a time when she hadn't itched.

But this itch was not enough to prevent her from enjoying the palace. It was a vast building with huge iron gates that swung open to allow her entry. The courtyard was filled with chariots, and the tower rose high into the sky. Angela tilted her head back and back until she almost toppled over.

"Do you think the Queen will be here today?" Angela asked.

"There's only one way to find out," Grandma said. Angela walked forward and nodded to the two still guards standing at the doorway. They never moved or blinked, not even when Angela jumped up and down in front of them and waved her hands in front of their faces. She had thought about staying up all night to see if they ever slept, but she had always gotten too tired. Inside she walked along the marble floor and gazed at the fountain before her. Huge rooms spiralled off in every direction, offering amusement and wonder in abundance. She thought she could spend her entire life in this place and still not see it all.

"It doesn't look like the Queen has returned yet. Maybe next time we come. I'm sure she wouldn't mind us poking around though. Where shall we go first?" Grandma asked.

"The banquet hall," Angela said. This was always her first port of call. Grandma's mobility scooter whined as they headed towards a huge entrance and passed through it. Before them stood all kinds of different foods displayed for them to take. There was a banquet every time Angela came to visit, and she often stuffed herself so full she thought she was going to explode. Today was no exception. She had crackers and biscuits and sweets, chunks of meat in jelly, bread, and tangy crisps. Her stomach ached even after she had eaten, and she looked towards Grandma with a mixture of guilt and shame.

"Don't you look like that my angel, there are a lot worse things you can do in this world than enjoy yourself. You fill your boots up with whatever you like. It's only going to go to waste otherwise, and I'm sure the Queen would want you to enjoy it."

Angela's guilt was alleviated. "Would you like anything?"

"Oh, perhaps just a bite, but you know I can't eat as much as I used to. You can have my share, you're a growing girl and you need it," Grandma said. She was always kind like that.

Once Angela had eaten all she wanted, she and Grandma left the banquet hall and ventured back into the main entranceway. Angela looked all around before she decided where she wanted to go this time. She wanted to go into the Queen's closet, although the word closet was something of a misnomer as it was a huge room that was filled with all manner of clothes, and not just for the Queen either. There was attire for her servants and maids and guards as well, and that was not counting the jewellery. Angela always felt wary of coming in here, but the guards had never stopped her yet and Grandma kept insisting that as long as the Queen did not tell her otherwise, it was okay for her to be here.

"You're special Angela. You're one of the Queen's favourites. I think she would want you to watch over her things in her absence," Grandma would say. Angela agreed. After all, the Queen had taken all her servants with her wherever she had gone and left only two guards and a cook, although Angela had never seen the latter. It was important to make sure that nobody else ever came to this place. Angela walked around the closet with Grandma, who would comment occasionally when she saw something that would look nice on Angela. The Queen was so rich that she had multiple copies of the same outfits. Angela would try different things on, but she would only take Grandma's opinion of how she looked. She did not like looking into the mirrors that offered her a glimpse of her reflection.

Nothing felt as good or as comfortable as her cloak though, and soon enough she grew tired of trying on these clothes. Her attention was drawn to the shining jewellery. She played with the rings and necklaces and tiaras, most of which did not fit quite right. She would have to wait until she was older, although that felt like it was going to take forever.

"You can take one home with you if you like. I'm sure the Queen won't mind," Grandma said as Angela eyed a particularly beautiful ring. It had a ruby set into it, as red as blood, and was perhaps the purest thing that Angela had ever seen. A pang of guilt entered her heart, however. She shook her head and put it back among the others.

"I can't Grandma. I'm not a thief."

"Well, you just ask the Queen when she comes back. I'm sure she'll say that it's okay."

Angela thought that was a good compromise. She wasn't going to take anything without permission.

They continued walking around the castle for a while longer, peeking into various rooms. These were mostly unchanged from the last time Angela had been here, and she wondered if the Queen was ever going to return. Grandma chatted idly, before Angela decided that she had had her fill of the castle for one day. They emerged outside. Angela thanked the guards, and they passed through the courtyard back to the gates. The day was still light, so there were plenty of things to do.

"Where to now?" Grandma asked. With her magic scooter there were no end of possibilities. Angela turned her head this way and that, scrunching up her face as she tried to think about where she wanted to go. Then a thought struck her.

"Space!" she cried out.

*

Stars twinkled around her as she floated in the vastness of space, safe in her rocket, peering out of the window. Grandma's magical scooter protected her from the cold harshness of space, so neither of them had to worry. There was special equipment in the rocket as well. But for now Angela was enjoying the sights. In the distance there was a huge planet looming before them, looking like a giant cloud of red and gold, with hints of green. It looked like a marble that had been blown up a million times its original size, and it was utterly beautiful. Angela pressed her face to the window, thinking that she must have been the luckiest girl in the world to be able to see these things. She had the best Grandma ever, because nobody else would ever be taken to these different places.

She decided to go on a spacewalk. She got into her spacesuit and connected her helmet, making sure that it was all secure. She had plenty of oxygen left, but still she was filled with trepidation. Space was a dangerous thing, and anything might happen, especially when she did not have the luxury of a crew. She thought back to a time when she had a second in command, but then bile entered her throat and she thought she was going to choke. Sometimes it was better not to think at all.

She tethered herself to the rocket and tested the wire, pulling it taut. One of her greatest fears was spiralling out into space forever without the hope of ever stopping. But at least if this happened she had Grandma. Grandma would whiz after her and catch her.

Angela took a deep breath to quell her fear as she stood at the airlock. It opened down to a silver ramp. This was it, she thought, before she released her grip and let herself go, surrendering to the pull of the abyss. The exhilaration washed through her and she giggled with glee as she went tumbling down. She moved slowly, waving her arms through the air, turning and twisting as there was nothing to keep her down.

"You look like you're dancing!" Grandma said.

Angela moved completely around her. The rocket became smaller and smaller in the distance, and the inky blackness of space was oddly beautiful, but she barely had a moment to enjoy it because suddenly a warning light flashed on her spacesuit. She was losing oxygen. There must have been a leak in the suit. Angela could hear a hiss as she started to panic. She gripped the tether, but the hiss was becoming louder and she wasn't sure if she was going to make it back to the rocket in time. The tether was like a long snake, waving and slithering and she found it hard to keep a grip.

"Grandma, save me!" Angela cried out. There was a frantic beeping all around her as she found it hard to breathe. Her chest was tight and she became disoriented. There was no way to get back to the rocket at all… but then Grandma came whizzing in to save the day. Angela placed her hands on the mobility scooter and Grandma put the thing into overdrive, charging away from space, away from danger.

Angela ripped off her helmet and collapsed to the ground, holding her chest.

"That was a close one," she panted, her voice hoarse and ragged. It felt as though she had been talking all day.

"You know that I'm never going to let anything happen to you dear. I'll always be here for you," Grandma said. Angela nodded and felt comforted by this. She pulled herself up. "Now, is there anywhere else you'd like to go, or do you think that's enough adventure for today?"

It was rare that Angela ever agreed that enough adventure had been had, and Grandma knew this. There was a twinkle in her eye that suggested as much. "I think I want to go to the submarine," Angela said. Grandma's eyes widened.

"Okay, but only if you're sure," Grandma said.

*

They crept up to the submarine. If Angela was ever going to run into any strangers then she thought it was going to be here. She scanned the area carefully, keeping as quiet as she could. There didn't seem to be anyone around though. She and Grandma made their way to the submarine. It was a long, metal thing that was half out of the water, making it easy for Angela to enter. Unfortunately, it was not large enough for Grandma to enter, so she had to stay behind. Angela made sure she was safe though, and warned Grandma to not go rushing off. Grandma just laughed.

Angela turned to the submarine. It was white, and she wasn't sure if all submarines were white or just this one. It was halfway in a wide river, its nose plunged deep beneath the surface as though it had paused in the middle of submerging. The tail was pointing out of the water, and there was an entrance to the rear. Angela approaching, gagging a little at the smell of damp. There were passengers already aboard, their heads tilted back in the seats as they slept. Some things hung from the ceiling. They looked like masks, but Angela wondered if they might have been hats as well. Angela had to be careful as the submarine was at an angle, and if she had not been careful then she would have slipped all the way to the bottom, and it could have been very difficult to make her way back up. But she had been here before. Grandma had given her the good idea of forming a chain with loose seatbelts. She gripped onto these as tightly as she could and made her way down.

The bottom of the submarine was drenched in water, and Angela thought that the masks hanging from the ceiling must have made it possible for these passengers to breathe. She wished that she had kept her spacesuit, although in its current state it would need repairing. She couldn't reach the masks, not with her short arms. Like so many other

397

things she would have to grow before she could use them properly. It was taking forever though, and she wondered if she would ever get older and bigger. It would make the world easier to navigate. Bigger and stronger people could do more things, they could protect others and they weren't so helpless, not like her. She was lucky because she had Grandma, and Angela didn't know what she would do without her.

Angela carefully descended the declining slope, feeling the grey seatbelt cords bite into her palms. Water slowly swam through the bottom of the submarine. As Angela approached she looked at the people around her, so still and silent in their sleep. They looked like Grandma, but none of them spoke back to her. She wondered if they all had to sleep during the voyage. It might have made things easier. After all, Angela liked sleeping, when it occasionally came to her.

She bent low and kept a hold of the seatbelt as she lowered her head below the surface. Bubbles emerged from her lips as she looked at the people there, frozen. Their mouths were open as though they were fish, their eyes unblinking. Angela had tried to keep her eyes open for that long before, but they always started to sting. They must have blinked whenever she didn't look at them. She waved to them and smiled, but they just stared vacantly at her. Perhaps when they reached their destination they would be more alert. Behind them were buttons, like the controls on the rocket ship, but there were no blinking lights. There was a woman there as well, a pretty woman with shaded lips. Angela had tried to get her hair like hers, but it was too thin. If there were such things as angels then this lady must have been one, Angela thought. Angela would have loved to be as beautiful as her one day.

Angela's lungs burned and so she lifted her head out of the water, gasping as she did so. She shook the excess water away and swallowed the rest, and then her heart leapt into her throat. She heard voices outside.

Strangers.

Quickly, she pulled herself up the submarine as panic filled her heart. This was even more raw than when she had run out of oxygen in space. This time Grandma was in trouble. What if strangers had gotten to her? Angela couldn't let it happen. She wasn't sure how she was going to stop them, but she had to. She was bigger than before, bigger than when it happened with Kyle.

She ascended the slope like a monkey and crouched at the back end of the submarine. Her eyes narrowed as she saw two people standing around Grandma. They wore heavy clothes. She looked around and saw a sword at her feet. She picked it up, her muscles straining, but she wasn't going to let Grandma be hurt by these strangers.

"Leave my Grandma alone!" the mighty words bellowed out of her young throat as she wielded the sword, waving around the air maniacally, rushing towards the strangers, willing to do everything she could to drive them away, even if it meant killing them.

*

The sky looked like sludge had been smeared across it. There was a nasty, toxic haze to the world, a mist that shrouded everything in a dim, almost sepia-like tone, although it was not as nostalgic. Emma coughed and spluttered.

"Thought a lung was going to come up then," she muttered, spitting out a glob of saliva. It was flecked with blood. She tried to ignore it. It wasn't like there were doctors around anyway.

"Maybe next time," Dennis said. It should have been a joke, but his words were humourless. His face was shadowed, his eyes bloodshot. They trudged forward, their limbs aching and tense, their eyelids heavy. Was there ever going to be any respite?

"It's a hell of a thing, isn't it, that that's all poisonous to us now," Dennis continued, glancing towards the river they were following. It bubbled along without a care in the world. Emma tried not to look at it because it tempted her. Her throat became dry and scratchy, and there was a whisper in the back of her mind telling her to drink, telling her that it would be okay.

She knew better though.

"This whole planet is poison to us now. Makes me wonder if we were ever supposed to be here in the first place. I mean, think back to before; the oceans were made up of salt water. Did nobody ever find that strange?

Why would there be an abundance of something that we couldn't drink?"

"Maybe God was playing a joke."

"If he existed then he had a funny sense of humour."

"You'd have to, if you were him. I mean, imagine dealing with all those prayers all the time. It must have driven him insane."

"Maybe it did. Maybe that's why all of this happened. Could be a plague sent by him so that he could start again."

"Nah," Dennis said. "If he wanted a clean start then he would have just swept us all away. There's no reason why he should make us suffer."

"Why not? We made plenty of things suffer. Hell, we made our own species suffer. It's pretty messed up when you think about it. Humans have always been awful."

"Just the way of the world."

"Guess it won't have to worry about us anymore," she sighed and gazed towards the water. "I think I might just dive into the river.

Dennis's eyes widened. "Wouldn't do that. You know what could happen."

"Do you really think there's going to be anything at the end of this river? I feel like we're chasing a rainbow expecting to find a pot of gold. We might as well give up."

"Could do, or we could keep going until the last breath."

"Why, because that's what heroes do?"

"It's all there is left to do. Might find something, might not, but it's worth trying," Dennis said. For such a droll, dry man he could be strangely optimistic. Emma thought she might love him, if there was room in this bleak, dying world for something like love. She coughed again, the sensation jarring the thought from her mind.

They followed the river along, passing through what used to be a city. The buildings that used to rise into the sky so triumphantly were now crumbled, cut off like a sail at half-mast. It was a grim sight, and there was no escaping it, no matter where they looked. They had just passed an old shopping centre. The beaming face of a woman still smiled. 'Queen Jeannie's Emporium,' the sign read. It was a dark place. Emma and Dennis went inside to scavenge supplies. They passed through broken iron gates and a car park, which was littered with abandoned vehicles. By the entrance stood two sculpted guards, the paint flecked and worn.

Shadows abounded inside. Glass crunched under their feet. Their first stop was the supermarket. A place like this would once have been teeming with people, but now it was deserted, at least at this moment.

"Looks like someone's been here," Dennis said, glancing towards the packets of food that had been strewn around. Emma inspected them. Boxes of biscuits had been open and crumbs had been left. Her stomach turned at the thought of eating them though, for they were all dry and hard. The bread had mould on it.

"Could be animals," she suggested.

"Animals couldn't have gotten into that." Dennis pointed towards the floor. Emma gagged when she saw the cans of dog food peeled open by a ring pull, the jelly trickling on the floor. Whoever had eaten here had been desperate, and she pitied them. They grabbed a few things that might still have been edible, although that word certainly had a far more expansive definition than it had before all this, and continued on their way.

They passed a park. In it was an old play area built to resemble a spaceship. The rocket was the main hub. A slide extended out of what would be the air lock. A faint smile appeared on Emma's lips. She remembered playing in something like that once, a long time ago. Funny how childhood could seem like another life. It was almost as though that child had been killed and replaced by this jaded, broken, diseased woman who could feel time ticking away.

She didn't share any of this with Dennis though. There was no point wallowing in misery. It wasn't going to save them.

Eventually they came across something that made them gasp. A plane had fallen from the sky and crashed into the river. Half of it protruded out, its tail rising into the air. It was hard for Emma to feel pity for the passengers though. In a way she envied them because at least their suffering was over. The survivors were the ones who had gotten the short end of the stick.

"What's that?" Dennis asked. As always he looked away from the thing that should have been the focus of attention. He always liked to say that the most fascinating things were in the background. She followed his gaze to see an old trolley, one that had probably been taken from the shopping centre, standing near the fallen plane. But there was something inside. They walked up slowly and noticed that one of the wheels was askew, pointing in a different direction to all the others. The stench was palpable, impossible to escape even when the entire world reeked of doom.

Then she gasped. Someone had put a dead body in this trolley. The flesh had decomposed and rotted, turning greenish black. The eyeballs had long since melted away, leaving sunken pits. It was like staring into an abyss. The flesh was flaking, what little hair remained was wispy and grey. Bones could be seen through tattered clothes and torn flesh, while the lips had been peeled back and formed a permanent, eerie smile. It was a ghoulish sight and it almost made Emma vomit. A hacking cough came instead. Blood splattered against her hand.

"Who the hell is this and why are they here?" she asked.

"Maybe they died in the trolley," Dennis said.

"But why? And look, these tracks are recent," Emma pointed to the muddy ground. Grooves led right up to the trolley. "Why would anyone want to cart a dead body around?"

The legs were extended in the trolley, although some of the toes were missing. Everything was a repugnant mix of flesh and bone and clothes, and it looked as though horror had been brought to earth. Was this the fate that awaited all of them? Was this what they would all turn into? It was a wonder that humans had ever been able to delude themselves into thinking they were a beautiful race. This was what they really were, rotten to the core.

"We should keep moving," Emma said, feeling a shudder pass through her. The more she saw of this world the farther she thought they were from God. If he had ever had anything to do with this place then he must have abandoned it a long time ago, and taken all the angels with him.

"Leave my Grandma alone!" a rasping, high pitched voice came rising through the air. Emma and Dennis turned in surprise as a young girl who could have been no more than eleven came running towards them, struggling to keep hold of a piece of shrapnel they had taken from the plane. She wielded it like a sword, and there was venom in her bloodshot eyes. She screamed as she ran at Dennis, who went to meet her.

"Dennis, wait!" Emma said, but almost before she spoke he had already clamped his hands around the metal as the girl swung it, catching it because she hadn't had any strength to put into the swing. He wrenched it from her hands, almost lifting her off her feet in the process. He shoved her back and she fell to the ground, her blood-stained cloak billowing out around her.

"She's just a kid!" Emma glared at Dennis, who kept the shrapnel far out of the girl's reach.

He shrugged. "She's feral."

"She's not feral, she's just scared." Emma crept towards her. "Hey, I'm Emma, we didn't mean to startle you. What's your name?"

"A-Angela, but don't speak to me. You're strangers. I can't trust strangers."

"Well, I'm Emma and this is Dennis. Now we know each other's names and so we're not strangers anymore," Emma said, nodding and smiling as much as she could. The world might have been cruel, but that didn't mean she needed to be.

"S-stay away from Grandma," Angela said. Her voice was shredded.

Emma turned slowly. "That's your Grandma?"

"Yes," Angela said, then her voice changed. It became strained ragged, a twisted approximation of what an old person would have sounded like.

"I'll take that as a compliment dear. I never did look my age," the words came from Angela's mouth, but she was speaking for her Grandma. Emma glanced towards Dennis. It was clear what had happened. The poor girl had lost her mind. Angela pushed herself up to a sitting position. The hood of her cloak fell

409

back. Emma stifled a gasp. She had the sickness alright. Her skin was peeling too, coming off in flakes as she scratched. Her skin had a yellow shade, and some of her teeth had fallen out. Her lips were dry and chapped. Emma thought she had been wearing lipstick at first, before she realized it was dried blood. Her hair was so thin that Emma could see her scalp, and this too was covered in sores and welts. They wept with puss and blood.

"Angela," Emma spoke slowly in a low voice. "I need you to take a really good look at your Grandma for me. I really want you to see her, to see how she truly is."

"Emma," Dennis said in a warning tone.

Angela looked up and smiled at her Grandma. "She looks fine to me. You're all good, aren't you Grandma? She looks after me, you see. We go on adventures in her magical scooter. She can take us anywhere." There was a dreamy quality to her eyes, a deliriousness that spoke to the fact that her mind had gone.

"Angela," Emma began again, but Dennis grabbed her arm and pulled her to the side, speaking in a low voice so that Angela couldn't hear them.

"What are you doing? Why are you wasting your time with this?"

She wrenched herself free from his grip. "She's just a kid Dennis. Maybe we can help her. God, look at her, she's young enough that this is probably the only world she knows."

"And it's not going to change any time soon. Look at her, she's too far gone. She's probably been drinking that water because she doesn't know any better, and nothing is going to repair her mind. There's nothing we can do for her. Better to leave her be."

"So she can die?"

"We're all going to die Emma, but what good is making her see the truth going to do? It's not like there's anything better waiting for her, is it?" he gestured around with his arm, encompassing the entire world. He was right. She knew it in the depths of her heart, and yet it seemed so wrong to deny the truth. Her shoulders sagged and a long breath escaped her lips.

"It just doesn't seem right," she said forlornly.

"Nothing's right anymore. There's only what is, and we can't drag her with us, especially if she doesn't want to come."

"Have you seen Kyle?" Angela asked. Emma and Dennis turned back towards her. She gazed up at them and through the gruesome mask of disease Emma could seen an innocent child, one that was too pure for a world like this.

"Who is Kyle?" Emma asked. Dennis clucked his tongue and rolled his eyes, clearly annoyed that they were still wasting time.

"You shouldn't roll your eyes young man, one day they'll go so far back into your head that they won't come back," Angela, as Grandma, said. It would have been funny if it hadn't been so tragic.

"Who is Kyle?" Emma repeated.

"He was my friend. But one day strangers came along and they… they took him. I wasn't big enough to save him. Even Grandma couldn't help."

Emma's throat tightened. She knew exactly what had happened to Kyle, even though she dreaded to think about it. "I haven't seen Kyle, I'm sorry. But if Grandma can take you anywhere then perhaps she can take you to wherever he is and you can bring him back," Emma said. It broke her heart to keep this fantasy going, to force Angela to remain in her delusion, but Dennis was right. It was the only thing they could do. Perhaps, in a world like this, it was the humane thing as well.

Angela's eyes lit up. "Why didn't we ever think of that before?" she said.

"Well I had, I was just waiting for you to catch up," she said, as Grandma. It was eerie hearing the old woman's voice coming from such a young child. Emma looked back towards the body in the shopping trolley, almost fearing that it would have twitched back to life. "Would you like to come back for some tea?"

Emma dreaded to think what Angela would conjure as tea in her mind. At best it would be imaginary, at worse it would be some of the toxic muck slithering through the gutters.

"I'm afraid we can't. We're on a journey so we can't really stop for long. Would you like to come with us?" Emma asked.

"Can Grandma come?" Angela tilted her head. As unhealthy as the world was, Emma knew it wouldn't be safe to travel so close to a dead body. Just thinking of what kind of diseases that thing was carrying... and then as she thought this a maggot crawled out of an eye socket and dropped down to Grandma's lap. Emma took a step back. Dennis muttered a curse under his breath.

"I'm afraid not."

Angela looked despondent. "Oh, well, I can't leave her. Grandma needs me, and I need her."

"I'm sure you do. You should run along then. It was good to meet you Angela."

"You too," Angela called out, and her earlier trepidation had vanished completely. She walked away from Dennis and Emma, heading back towards the trolley. She placed her hands on the rail and pushed it away. One of the wheels whined.

"See Grandma, I knew that not all strangers were bad," she said. Emma didn't hear what Grandma said in return. She watched Angela disappear along the street, making a whizzing sound as she pushed the trolley. She noticed that her cheeks had become sticky with tears.

"Come on Em, it's not going to do any good crying," Dennis said.

Emma turned away and looked towards the bleak horizon, one that was decaying before her eyes. She coughed again and groaned as she looked at the blood. Maybe Angela had the right idea. Maybe we should all live in our fantasies, because the real world was just too much to bear.

Will He or Won't She

Marylyn

Marylyn applied the finishing touches to her makeup. She powdered her nose, and wondered if she had used too much mascara. Was it unbecoming for a woman of her age to doll herself up like some young ingénue? She thought about wiping it all away for a few moments, but then decided to let it remain. It wasn't as though she could wipe away anything else, either. She stared into the mirror, trying to reconcile the face she saw with the one she remembered from her youth. It was lined with wrinkles now, time leaving her diminished compared to what she once was. Her voice was lighter and wispy, her eyes cloudier than before, as though they were awaiting the bleak future rolling forth on the horizon.

Gosh, she was acting like she was on her deathbed. She forced a chuckle and shook herself from the alluring mirror, telling herself that she was only 70, and she still had plenty of time left. This was supposed to be the beginning of the rest of her life after all, for she had finally reached retirement age. Of course, over the years the retirement age had risen and risen, and there were rumours that it was going to be raised again. It seemed as though the world just wanted people to keep working until they their bones were grinded into dust. Well, she thought, they weren't going to grind her soul.

She pulled on a flowery dress and ran a brush through her thinning hair. The dye she used gave it a yellow tint, echoing the blonde locks she used to wear. The doorbell chimed. She glanced at the clock.

He's early, she thought.

She walked through her flat and opened the door, wearing her most pleasing smile. Her eyes twitched with anxiety, worried that something would be amiss in the flat, that she would have forgotten to clean up some small mess, or that he would see a stain on the settee. A bead of sweat formed on her temples. It was cold and trickled down the side of her face. Had he seen it? How could he not see it? Suddenly her chest tightened and she found it difficult to breathe. Was this it? Was death going to come and dig its bony claws into her, dragging her down into the depths of Hell before she could enjoy her retirement? It didn't seem fair. Then again, when had life ever been fair?

"Marylyn? Is it okay if I call you Marylyn? I'm Jimmy, from the *Globe*, I'm here about the interview."

Marylyn blinked, shaking herself from her stupor. "Of course," Marylyn said, smiling, hoping that her voice did not sound too cracked. She needed to remember to speak. Speaking was what people did with each other. "It is my name after all. Please, come in." She held the door open and Jimmy walked past. His fragrance was bitter, but the scent familiar. It brought back many memories, painful ones. Was it just chance that he was wearing this? He was here to talk about the past, after all. She tried to focus.

"I have some tea all ready for you, and there are some biscuits if you like. Please, make yourself comfortable," Marylyn gestured to the small coffee table, upon which sat a teapot, two cups, as well as a plate of biscuits. She tried to remember how her mother had entertained people as a child. It was a skill, like any other, and this particular skill had waned over the years. Like a muscle that had not been used it had atrophied, and now Marylyn was completely at sea. She was tempted to make an excuse for the state of her small, humble flat, before reminding herself that Jimmy probably didn't care at all. She smoothed her skirt under her legs as she sat down, taking her seat beside a window. The window was open, and it looked out upon the city, its sprawling network of roads and buildings looking like an insect hive. The sky was grey, with ominous clouds swirling in the distance. The sun was a soft glow behind the shroud, as though it was hiding. Sometimes it seemed little more than a dream.

Jimmy was a man of below average height, shorter than Marylyn. He wore a long sleeved shirt and a brown leather jacket. It was tattered at the shoulders, and the cuffs were loose. His hair had been shaved and she could see a tattoo that curled around his scalp, reaching all the way to the back of his skull. He was young, too young to etch something upon his skin that would last for the rest of his life, but then she supposed she had been young once too. Every decision mattered. Every decision lasted.

He helped himself to a biscuit and then placed his pad on the table. Crumbs collected in the corner of his mouth as he explained how he was going to record her.

"I'll have to be careful about what I say," Marylyn said, tittering after she spoke. Jimmy gave her a reassuring smile, at least she thought it was reassuring. What if he was actually judging her? He probably thought she was a silly old woman.

"Don't worry, just speak the truth. That's what I'm interested in. That's what all good news is about, isn't it?"

"I'm not going to say anything to that. I've lived through too many scandals."

Jimmy cleared his throat and he looked abashed. Marylyn wondered if she had said anything to upset him. "Yes, well, we hold ourselves to a higher standard nowadays. Believe me, if I try to misrepresent anything I won't be around to explain myself. But this is mostly a puff piece. All I want is to hear about your experiences growing up in a changing world. As I explained on the phone, we're trying to capture as much of history as possible and it's only going to be possible if we speak to those who remember it. Previous generations never gave as much attention to history as we should have. If we can learn from how things happened then maybe we can do better. And it'll still be worthwhile to see how attitudes change over time."

"Well, I'm not sure if I'm going to be much help because I haven't done anything of note during my life. I will try though."

"All I want is your story Marylyn. That's what we're really interested in."

Marylyn reached up and touched her hair. She blushed a little. She couldn't remember the last time anyone had been interested in her story.

"Where should I begin?" she asked.

"Well, let's start with an easy one," Jimmy said with a wry smile, indicating that the question wasn't going to be easy at all. "Do you think the world is in a better place now than it was when you were younger?"

Marylyn glanced out of the window and puffed out her cheeks. "I suppose that's difficult to say. I think people have more rights now, which is certainly a good thing, but it has seemed to come at the expense of doing anything with those rights. There are always so many things to be scared of as well. They say that they have fought back against climate change, but how can we really be sure? What if they've just kicked the can down the line and we're going to have to deal with it all again in a few years? I suppose it's not really my problem for much longer, but you have to think of the children. Did you know there is a conspiracy theory that says the world has long gone past breaking point and the governments of the world aren't telling anyone because they know that it'll result in widespread panic?"

Jimmy's mouth formed a thin line. "I am aware of such a thing, but as I said we're only interested in truth today. As far as I know there hasn't been any proof about that. Speaking of children, do you have any?"

Marylyn's heart caught in her throat. "One. I have a son. I... I don't speak with him though. There was a, well, a difference in opinion within the family."

"I see, is that a personal matter, or is that something to do with the changing times? I know that sometimes different political opinions can have a profound impact on relationships."

"All of the above?" Marylyn offered and averted her gaze. She reached for a biscuit and took a bite. It crumbled in her hands, falling all over her dress.

Jimmy suggested they get back to the topic at hand.

Hamish

"Go on!" Harry cried out, pointing wildly with his finger. His flushed cheeks puffed out and his hair, slick with sweat, lay lank across his head. He backed away, allowing Hamish to run through on goal. The ball spun at his feet. The net loomed large before him. Hamish secretly cursed under his breath. He had hoped Harry would keep up with him so that he could square the ball, but this moment of glory was going to be his and his alone.

Come on Hamish, you can do this, he thought to himself. *Don't cock it up.*

The goalkeeper made himself big, stretching himself out like a sail that caught the wind. The grass was dark and muddy, the ground pitted with marks from the football boots. Breath like knives in Hamish's chest. His legs felt leaden, as though he was going to collapse at any moment. But all he needed was to see this moment through. All he needed was to make this moment count, and it would be glorious. He blocked out the cheers on the side line. It was easier when he didn't have to think about letting anyone down. There was only one man between him and glory, and he could make up for all the other mistakes he had made during the season.

But then he could sense the ball rolling out of his control. It was all slipping away, just like it had before. Damn Harry, why couldn't he just have kept running? There was no other choice. Hamish had to go for it now, before it was too late. If fortune was on his side then maybe he would be able to score. He swung a heavy leg at the ball, his momentum twisting his entire body around. He felt the connection reverberate up his shin and thigh. He turned, falling down, his palms slamming against the ground. His messy blonde hair fell across his eyes, which he shut, clamping them tightly and praying that it would all be alright, praying that it would go in.

He waited to hear the rush of excitement from the crowd, the cheer that would swell among the cluster of people who had come to see this muddy, amateur match. He waited to feel the vibrations of the stampede as his teammates came to congratulate him, bundling on him as though he was treasure that they were all trying to claim.

Instead, there was a groan. Harry plodded over.

"Never mind Hamish, you'll get the next one," he said in a beleaguered tone. Hamish groaned and turned to look at the goalkeeper, who was bounding away behind the goal to fetch the ball. It had soared over the bar, and once again Hamish was the reason why the team had lost. Harry stuck out his hand to help Hamish up.

"Why didn't you keep running with me? I could have squared it to you and you would have had an open goal," Hamish said with a hint of accusation in his eyes.

Harry shrugged. "I thought you deserved the opportunity. I thought it might make you feel better."

"Well don't make the same mistake twice. You know I always choke. I can never see these things through, not when the pressure is on," Hamish turned away before Harry could say anything reassuring. They were only words, and words wouldn't help the gnawing feeling in the pit of Hamish's stomach. He trudged off the pitch and guarded himself against the muttered curses and insults of his teammates. How quickly allies could turn to enemies when they felt betrayed, but it wasn't Hamish's fault. He had been betrayed as well, by his own body. It was so ungainly and awkward and clumsy. It had always been this way, ever since he had transformed from a cherubic boy into this... hairy thing. Sometimes he wished he could retreat back into the cocoon and try again or, even better, go back to the way he had been before. Life was simpler then.

Everything was simpler.

He had a quick shower and then left the changing room, wishing that the water had been enough to wash the shame away. He looked at the remnants of the crowd. There was only one person there for him. She looked lonely. Once upon a time there had been a whole group of them there, especially his mother. She had been his best cheerleader, but then... well... then his troubles had started.

*

"Are you going to sulk all evening, or are you going to let me cheer you up?" Madeline

428

said. She leaned against the frame of the door. Long, red hair fell to the middle of her back. She wore a loose t shirt that clung to her figure, and nothing on her lower half. Hamish knew that most men would have killed to be where he was now.

"I'm not sulking. But it doesn't feel great knowing that yet again I made a mistake and we lost. If I hadn't made so many errors then we would have gotten further in the cup, and we might be pushing the league leaders. The team would be better off without me," he moaned.

"Don't say that. You're just going through a bad spell, that's all, and you don't know that other people would have done any better in your position. It's not like your all world beaters. Who are they going to get to play for you instead? Blind Tommy?" she sauntered into the room towards him. Something was playing on TV, but Hamish hadn't been paying attention. It was just a blur of noise and sound. He was perched on the bed. She slipped beside him, trailing a fingertip along his chest and up his neck.

"I think you just need to relax and think about what really matters in life," she dropped her voice an octave and leaned into him. Strands of copper hair fell across his cheek and her sweet breath was like a tidal wave. He clenched tightly, feeling something knotting inside him. Her hand spread out along his chest and roamed across him.

"To be honest Hamish," she continued in a breathy voice, punctuating her words with kisses, "I don't really give a damn about the result. I just love watching you running all over the pitch. Your legs move like pistons, and you look so sexy when you're galloping all over the place. You're so manly, it gets me so turned on," she kissed him as she said this, and her hand made its final descent into the depths of him, that shadowy realm in between his legs, where the forbidden thing existed. She gripped him and he immediately tensed up and pushed her away, squirming out of her grip and away from her kiss.

She shrank back. Her eyes were heavy with hurt.

"Are you not even going to let me touch you now?" she asked. Her voice trembled with emotion. Hamish wished he could say and do the right things, but something was broken inside him.

"I just can't Madeline. I'm sorry. Not right now. It's just… I have too many things on my mind."

"Then let me help you get them off my mind. That's what I'm here for Hamish. Let me be your girlfriend."

"I know, and I'm sorry. I'm glad that you're here. I know how lucky I am it's just… I find it hard to get things off my mind."

She looked him straight in the eye. "Is this about your mother?"

He looked away and shook his head.

"Because if it is," she continued, "you need to see someone about it. This can't keep happening. If we're going to have a life together then you need to sort out the past. I want to help you. I love you, for some damn reason, but you're not making it easy and I need to tell you that I can't just keep doing this. I don't have infinite patience. I get that you're going through something, but there are parts of a relationship that I can't live without. I want to be close with you. I want to be intimate with you. If you're not going to let me in then I don't know what we're really doing."

Hamish could feel her slipping away. It was as though the chasm between them was getting wider as every moment passed. He wanted to reach out and take her hand, but he couldn't. He couldn't move.

"It's my body Madeline. It's not my Mum. It just won't do what I need it to do. Even today, I didn't feel like I was in control. I don't feel like myself."

"I love you for who you are, Hamish. You're a good man, and I know that we can get through this. It's just going to take time and patience," she said softly, evidently trying to make up for her earlier outburst, "but if you need to see someone then see someone. If playing football is only going to make you feel bad about yourself then don't play football anymore. And when there's something I can do other than be here for you let me know. I don't mean to be cruel and I don't mean to give you ultimatums I just... I know that we're so close to having everything we could ever want. I don't want anything to get in the way. I'm ready for our lives to begin, together and forever."

She pressed her forehead against his and they shared a breath. He closed his eyes and nodded. He wanted that too, badly, but there was something inside him that didn't seem right, and he wasn't sure what it was.

Marylyn

"Did the world turn out how you thought it would?" Jimmy asked.

Marylyn sighed. "Well, yes and no. When I was younger there was so much turmoil in the world that I think it led to us becoming the most jaded and cynical generation there had ever been. With the global economy in the toilet and the gap between the rich and the poor getting ever wider we didn't think we had much to look forward to, so I suppose the future didn't have very high expectations to meet. I still wanted to hope for the best though. I wanted a roof over my head, food on the table, and some company now and then."

"And has that happened?"

Marylyn tried to ignore the emptiness that surrounded her. "For the most part. I didn't really have the family I wanted."

"Some other people I spoke to mentioned that they felt lonely. Do you think this is a generational thing?"

"Of course," Marylyn said without any hesitation. "We were the generation raised on mobile devices. We were the generation of moral outrage and social media. It's poison, utter poison."

"So, you're not a fan then," Jimmy said dryly.

Marylyn folded her arms across her chest and dusted the crumbs away from the crook of her elbow. "That place just allows people to be mean. I don't care how much they regulate it, it's always going to be the same. It's a place where bullies are allowed to gang together and be cruel to people without any consequence. They can flit about like butterflies and spread their misery as much as they like before they disappear into the darkness again. Once I actually believed that people were good, deep down, that it was only the vocal minority that was a problem. But what's the point of a majority if its silent? There's no escaping the cruelty of the world. People are mean, and social media gives them access to everyone of all ages. Everyone is a target and there's nothing you can do about it except stop using the service."

"So you don't use any social media?"

Marylyn shook her head. Jimmy arched his eyebrows. She knew it was a surprising admission. Everyone was interlinked in the virtual realm, shifting their experiences to that place so they could ignore the crippled environment and the industrial cities that had consumed lush nature. "You should know that it has changed over the years. Behaviour is heavily regulated and now that everyone's avatar is linked to their actual identity people can't just get away with being trolls. There are rules and punishments. It's as heavily policed as the real world. You should give it another try."

"It'll be a cold day in hell before that happens," Marylyn said, blinking away hot tears as awful memories threatened to push their way to the surface.

"Do you think that this lack of social interaction has been a detriment to your happiness?"

"Of course," Marylyn wore a sour look, thinking that it was a stupid question. But she had agreed to this interview so she might as well answer anything he wanted. Besides, she was lonely enough where this interaction filled a hole in her soul. "Before us people had bars and community centres and clubs to attend. Our lives were all sucked down a virtual hole. We had all these different things to occupy our time with, all these games and movies and TV shows that gave us the illusion of being a part of something that was bigger than ourselves. God help me, this is going to sound pathetic, but I actually used to believe that certain fictional characters were my friends. When I watched them on the screen I believed that we were hanging out. I guess it was the only way that I could cope with being alone. Other people had different ways to cope. Some of them were able to play games with others online, but that was never me. And as for communicating via text, well, that just seemed to me like people were shouting out into the void. There was never even an echo coming back. And people just seemed to look for others who agreed with them. We all segregated ourselves in likeminded communities where we could share the same thoughts over and over again without fear of anyone disagreeing with us, and then because of that we forget that we could actually like people who didn't share the same opinions with us. I'm not blameless in this either. I made the same mistakes. I read a very good book though called *I'm the Main Character*. It was all about how people began to look at themselves as though they were, well, as the book says, the main character. They only saw other people as vessels who could affect their lives, and other people didn't have any worth other than that. It was quite humbling actually. I realised that I had made the same mistake along the way, although not to an extreme degree."

Marylyn flicked back a few locks of hair and took a breath, along with a sip of tea. "But yes, I think we have been lonely. We haven't had much of a break either, so we don't even have national pride to believe in. I hope that things are getting better for your generation."

Jimmy smiled. "Things seem to be turning a corner, thanks. I don't know if they're perfect yet, but I certainly feel like the world is getting better."

"Then it seems that I was definitely born at the wrong time. Too young to enjoy the boom period, too old to take advantage of the rebuild. I think they should start calling us the lost generation, or the cursed…"

Jimmy cleared his throat. "And how do you think the pandemic fifty years ago affected things?"

It was actually fifty and change, but Marylyn wasn't going to correct him. She assumed he would be more exact in the article. "Well, it felt like the world reached a breaking point really. Tension had been building and then that happened and we were just stunned. I mean, you got through it because you had to, but none of us knew how long it was going to last. A lot of people thought it was going to stay that way. I guess that's another reason why we were lonely. We learned how to be alone. We had things taken away for us, and of course it was all for the greater good, but we also heard about people dying as well. There was government corruption, money being misplaced, people breaking the rules who weren't punished and we basically lost a couple of years of our lives. But I'm not going to blame everything on that. It was a global event that we managed to muddle through. It's what happened after that that was bad, with all the fraud and the rising costs of everything. People had to put their plans on hold. I remember that there was a great outcry about the world's population getting smaller. Of course it was! We could barely afford to feed and clothe ourselves, let alone a child. It would have been irresponsible for most people to bring another life into the world without knowing if they could have taken care of it."

"So that wasn't the case for you? I mean, you did mention you had a son."

Marylyn looked away. "Yes, well... I'd rather not talk about that if it's all the same to you."

"Of course, whatever you're comfortable with," Jimmy said. Marylyn clasped her hands together to stop them from trembling.

Hamish

"Come on, don't do this," Harry protested.

"I have to Harry. I'm not happy anymore. And the rest of the guys don't want me either. We all know that you'll be better off without me. I've done more harm than good."

"That's not true. So you've missed a few chances, who hasn't? It's not like we're asking Graham to quit. He's let in more goals this season than anyone else ever has! We're not world-beaters. This is just a bit of a laugh."

"Yeah, well, I can't remember the last time I laughed. It's for the best."

Harry put his hands on his hips. "Look, how about you just give it until the end of the season. There are only a few games left, and we can't register a replacement for you now. Just last a few more games and then think about it over the summer. There's no sense making a rash decision. I get that it hasn't been as fun for you, but football has been a part of our lives since we were kids. Do you remember going to that run down park round the back of yours, using that small fence as a goal? Always being afraid that we were going to lose the ball over the garages?"

Hamish smiled and nodded. It was a fond memory. "We always dreamed about going to Wembley."

"Yeah, well, we can still dream about that." Harry put his arm around Hamish's shoulder. "Is everything else alright?"

Hamish pursed his lips. "Has Madeline said anything?" he asked curtly.

Harry looked guilty. Hamish rolled his eyes and pulled away from Harry.

"She was only trying to look out for you. She hasn't said anything specific, just that you've been having a hard time, just that you've been down recently. Is it just football, or is there more to it?"

Hamish stared at Harry. They had been friends all their lives, and yet there were still certain things that Hamish hadn't been brave enough to share with Harry. He glanced around to make sure that nobody else could hear them and then sidled closer to Harry. Uneasiness had settled into his heart and he wasn't sure where to turn. He had to talk to someone about these things, otherwise it was never going to settle in his heart.

"Alright, look, I'll share something with you, but you have to promise me you won't tell anyone," Hamish added extra emphasis to the last few words. Harry nodded. Hamish paused before he spoke again. "Look, do you ever… do you ever find it difficult to, you know… be intimate with Claire?"

Harry recoiled. Hamish immediately felt self conscious for asking the question. Harry furrowed his brow. "I mean, sometimes I get tired, but mostly I don't."

"Right."

"But I'm sure other people do."

"Well, that's what's wrong with me. I just don't feel the drive like other men do."

"You're not…" Harry looked around, "gay," he whispered. Hamish rolled his eyes and shook his head.

"No, I'm not. I worked that out a long time ago. I'm definitely straight I just… whenever we go to do it I feel uneasy and I just… I'm not sure how I'm going to get past it. The longer this goes on the harder it gets, and she says that she's there to support me but I know she's feeling the toll of it too. And the thing is it's not that I don't love her, I do, I love her with all my heart. I want to marry her. This isn't about her at all. It's about me. There's something broken inside me and I don't know what it is," he said, his voice cracking with emotion. He wasn't sure he had ever been this vulnerable in front of Harry before. He actually sobbed, and quickly choked back the sound.

Harry looked confused and unsettled, but he put his arm around Hamish's shoulders, bringing him closer towards him. "It's going to be okay Hamish. You probably just need to speak with someone. It's not that bad. It's never going to be that bad. Things are going to be okay, you're just going through a bit of a bad patch. We'll see that you get through it alright, okay?"

Hamish nodded, although he didn't find himself convinced.

*

Later on, when he was alone, he was deep in thought about his state of mind. There was definitely something wrong with him, but how was he supposed to figure out what it was? The thought of going to a therapist was interminable. What was he supposed to talk about, his relationship with his mother? God, was that going to define the rest of his life? Things had been said, nasty things, but it didn't mean that was the only thing that mattered. Whatever was wrong with him ran far deeper than that. Even so, he did look up a few different therapists and baulked at the price. Why did it cost so much to be healthy? They'd probably just give him some trite advice anyway, maybe some pills. He didn't want to be on pills though. He wanted to figure this out himself. There was a point in the past when he had been happy, so why couldn't he just get back to that point?

The thought of going back to football filled him with dread. Maybe he should go against Harry's advice and just quit the team altogether. He was certain that waiting a day or a month or a year wasn't going to make any difference. Every time he had to play football he felt a twisting knot of anxiety deep in his stomach. It made him feel sick, and then a thought occurred to him. Maybe him missing all those goals and making so many mistakes was his subconscious' way of telling him that he shouldn't play any longer. Maybe he was making himself a liability.

While this lifted his spirits, he wasn't sure it was going to change things with Madeline. The thought of being with her... it wasn't a pressure to perform exactly, more like this feeling that he shouldn't be making love to her at all. But it was such a paradox because he wanted to be with her. He cared about her deeply. She was the only person he had ever felt close to and he would have given up his life for her if he could have, so why couldn't he do something that came so naturally to people? It was one of the most fundamental aspects of nature and it was eluding him, and in the end he was afraid of it ruining everything he held dear.

There had to be reason, and so he made the effort to book himself in with a doctor. He made the effort at least, he was not successful. The patient lists had bloated and the healthcare service was unable to cope with the demand. First he was forced to call up the surgery and hope that he got through to a receptionist. There was no dial tone, no holding pattern, either he got through or he didn't. There was no online service either. It seemed as though appointments were going to be given based on how determined people were to make it through that initial phone call. His fingers became numb due to the amount of times he was calling the surgery. He spent just over an hour ringing them, always redialling as soon as he was cut off in the hope that he would be able to make one. When he eventually got through he thought he was hallucinating. He stammered on the phone, stumbling over his words as he asked for an appointment.

Two months.

Eight weeks.

Sixty-one days.

What was he supposed to do if it was an emergency? He asked.

Was he hurt? There was a phone line he could call for advice, or there was A&E at the hospital, but his problem did not have any pressing physical issues. His life was not in danger, only his relationship was, and the GP could do nothing for that. He made the appointment anyway, although he wasn't sure if there was any point. Would Madeline still be around in eight weeks' time if he didn't sort himself out?

No, there had to be another way forward. There had to be something he could do in the meantime to figure out what was wrong with him.

So he turned to the Internet in the hope that some answers would come his way. He typed in the way he was feeling and he stared at the faint blue glow of the screen, his eyes darting across the words as he read about his issues, and other people who had suffered the same thing. He started to be comforted. He started to realize that all hope may not be lost.

Marylyn

"What do you think is the most important issue that people could learn from the history you have lived through?" Jimmy asked.

Marylyn blew out her cheeks. "I suppose to be kind to each other, to remind each other that there is a real world out there, one where fresh air can blow on your cheeks. I would hope that people also learn to trust in one another and always look into the truth behind a story rather than just the headline. The world is filled with people who want to make you think one thing or another. There's always some kind of agenda to push." She thought for a moment and then leaned forward. "I don't mean any offence by that."

"None taken," Jimmy said. "Do you believe that history is going to repeat itself?"

"I hope not. I look at the world around me and I can see the strides that people have made. There have been efforts to fight against corruption in politics, and to stabilize the world's economy. I think that broadly we have become a more tolerant and accepting culture, although I hope that we still remember that it's okay for other people to have difference opinions. I'm glad that some people have been able to find a safe space for themselves online as well. I do wonder if things might have been different for me if something like that had been available to me when I was younger."

"Do you think it would have given you advice to help mend the relationship with your family?"

Marylyn nodded. "The problem was that I didn't have many people to talk to, certainly not in real life, not with the same problems as me. The trouble was that nobody tells you how to figure these things out. They just expect you to have all the answers and sometimes you have the wrong ones."

"Have you tried to make amends with them? I'm sorry if it's a personal question."

Marylyn swept away his concerns with a swift hand. She leaned forward. Her features became pinched and she stared at the cold cup of tea sitting on the table before her. "I have tried, yes, but unfortunately what I did was, well, it's unforgivable. There's no going back. That's just about true of anything."

"There's just one final question, and then I'll be on my way; do you think you've made the most of life? Have you lived the life you wanted to live? Are you happy?"

"Three questions for the price of one," Marylyn said wryly, cocking an eyebrow. She took a deep breath as she considered the matter. "I think that in life we can never have everything we want. It's all about compromise, sometimes for big things, sometimes for small things. I think you're asking me if life has turned out the way I wanted it to, and no, it hasn't. I never thought I would be spending my retirement alone. I thought I would be surrounded by friends and family, but I suppose sometimes you're just fated for things no matter what you try and do in life. At least that's the only thing that makes sense to me because I tried to be a kind person. I tried to be true to myself, but I ended up hurting people and people ended up hurting me. As for happiness, well, that's a sliding scale, isn't it? I don't know if any of us are truly, truly happy. I don't know if such a

451

thing is possible. Isn't it human nature to want something more, no matter how much we have? As for the global side of things, well, when I was younger I used to think I would have more say in that. I've voted over the years of course, but have I really affected anything? I'm not so sure. I've had to trust that other people have been able to take care of things and guide the world in the right direction. I thought that maybe I would do something more with my life, that maybe I would be remembered. I suppose that's the saddest thing really... knowing that people are going to forget me."

Marylyn gave him a quick smile. "I know what you're going to say, that if I become part of the virtual world then a piece of me will live on forever, but I'm not bothered about that. I'm not sure I have much of interest to say anyway."

"You may think that, but I've enjoyed talking to you. I have a feeling that there's a lot you've left out. There's something you're not telling me, isn't there?" he asked, his natural curiosity getting the better of him.

"Perhaps, but that's not the story, is it?"

Jimmy looked into his lap and wore a rueful expression. "No, I suppose it's not."

"And I'm not important enough to have an entire article written about me."

"I like to think that everyone is important. Some people have more important roles in the world than others, but intrinsically everyone's soul is sacred."

"That's a nice sentiment. If you want to suggest it to your editor then I might well tell you my story, if you'd like to come back. I could always use the company."

"I'll keep it in mind," Jimmy said. He collected his pad and slurped down the last dregs of his tea. He asked Marylyn if he could take a biscuit for the road, which she was happy to offer as they would only go straight to her hips otherwise. She showed him out of the door, wondering if there was anything that might entice him to stay. Perhaps she could tell him all the details of her personal story, but then she reconsidered it. Such a thing would be an act of ego and vanity, and would not be ladylike at all.

She bid Jimmy farewell and closed the door. She pressed her ear against the door and listened to his footsteps fading down the stairwell. She was surrounded by silence once again. It was a constant companion in life, always threatening to swallow her whole. Soon enough she thought it might well succeed. She sighed as she cleaned up the mugs and biscuits, putting them back in the box. Most of them would probably go stale before she had a chance to eat them. She ran a finger through her hair and stared out of the window, thinking about the past and all the mistakes she had made. There was plenty of blame to go around, but perhaps it had been long enough to let it lie. She was an old woman now, retired, counting down the rest of her dwindling days and did she really want to let them to be defined by loneliness? There were few chances to fix things now, so perhaps it was time to make reparations.

Hamish

Hamish stood in front of the mirror. He had sequestered himself away, shrouding himself in darkness. If there were any prying eyes out there in the world then he wouldn't let them in. The curtains were drawn, doors were closed, and he was entirely alone.

Nerves swam under the surface. His heart beat fast and he could feel himself trembling. He stared at his reflection as he peeled his clothes away, almost as though he was taking off a second skin. One by one the garments fell away, falling to the floor like autumn leaves.

He was naked. He stared at his muscular physique, so manly, so desirable, according to Madeline. But he was repulsed by the thick torso, the forest of hair, and that long thing that dangled between his legs. Bile rose in the back of his throat. He wanted to turn away, but that's not what the advice suggested. He had to look.

He licked his lips and steadied himself, calming his nerves. He put one leg forward and then crossed it, bending slightly, tucking his manhood between his legs. Suddenly something changed. It was as though dawn had broken after a subdued and solemn winter. He stared at himself without the male genitals, and for the first time he felt like he was seeing himself as someone he wanted to be. He took one of his trembling hands and ran it down his body. He skirted around the area at first, but then he closed his eyes and allowed it to roam over the smooth surface, giving the illusion that he did not have anything male at all.

And it was perfect.

He realized then that this was always how he had wanted to feel.

Elation burst in his heart. The joy that came from this understanding was something that he had never experienced before. It was as though he had been a jigsaw and someone had slotted the last piece into place. It made sense. He knew why he had never felt at ease in himself, and why it was time for change.

It wasn't going to be easy to tell others, but he could not go on living a lie. Madeline would understand, surely? She said she loved him, that she supported him. He was intoxicated by the joy of his new discovery and longed to tell her. He drove over to hers, singing and smiling widely. She looked at him with admiration.

"Well, you're certainly in a good mood," she said.

"I am, I feel like I have a new lease on life. I feel like I know what's been wrong and I'm ready to start the new chapter," he gathered her in his arms and he kissed her, whirling her through the air. She laughed giddily and looked delighted.

"I'm so happy for you," she said.

"But we need to talk about it," he added. The smile faded from his face. A grave look overcame him. She wore a faltering smile.

"Okay. I hope that this isn't anything to do with me," she laughed nervously.

"It's not, but it does involve you. It involves a… a change," he said. They sat down on the couch. He dipped his head and clasped his hands together to keep them from trembling. Thinking about telling her was one thing, but actually doing it was something else entirely. In the back of his mind he kept telling himself that this was all going to be okay, that she had already promised to stand beside him and walk into the future together, so what did he have to worry about?

His throat was dry as he forced the words out. "We both know that there's been something wrong with me for a while now. I'm sorry that you've had to put up with this, and I want to tell you that I appreciate how supportive and patient you've been. I know it hasn't been easy and you could have walked away before this. You would have been well withing your rights to, and I'm just incredibly thankful that you haven't because I do love you with all my heart and I want us to build a future together."

"I want that too," Madeline said, a wide smile upon her face. Her eyes sparkled with delight. Hamish hoped that this glint was not going to disappear.

"But there is something that has been wrong and we're going to have to work through it together. I have to apologize again because I know you never signed up for this. It would be much easier for you if you were going out with someone normal, and I wish that I was different. But I'm not. This is who I am, and I hope that we can continue standing by each other and working together to find the future that we both want."

"Okay Hamish just… just tell me what's wrong. We can work it out," she put a hand on his and smiled reassuringly. It was clear that she was cautious about what he was going to say. His throat was dry and he wished he could have just said the whole matter was done with, but he wanted to do things properly.

"I'm telling you this because I want to be open with you. I think it's important to be honest. We don't wany to have secrets from each other, right?"

"No, we don't," Madeline said. She was looking guarded now. Hamish thought he had better speak more quickly before she accused him of having an affair.

"I think the world has become a lot more open and accepting of different things, of different ways to live, and as a culture we're becoming more away that sometimes people don't always feel comfortable with the way things are. Sometimes what we consider normal isn't what's best for people and I think that's what's been happening with me. I haven't felt comfortable for a while now, and I haven't been able to put my finger on it, but I've been doing some research and I've discovered that it's because this body isn't the one I want."

Madeline furrowed her brow. "What do you mean?"

Hamish spoke slowly. Heavy emotions rolled through him and he didn't want anything he said to be misinterpreted. It was also the first time he was admitting this out loud as well.

"I mean that I've never really felt at ease. And I think it's because I was meant to be someone different. I think I was meant to be a woman, or at least have a woman's body. That's why I've found it so difficult to have sex with you. It wasn't because I didn't want you, it's because every time I looked down I saw my body and I just… I was repulsed by it. I didn't want to see all these hard angles and muscles. I want to be soft and smooth like you. It's like I've been walking around all these years in clothes that are the wrong size for me."

"But that… it doesn't make sense. We've had sex before, many times."

"I know, but it never felt like it should and I guess the older I get the worse it gets. I can't go on living a lie like this. I can't keep being someone that I'm not. I need to accept myself and I hope that you can accept me too."

Madeline blinked slowly. A few moments passed, moments that dripped with silence and that seemed like an eternity. The longer it lasted the more uneasy Hamish felt. Had it been too much to hope for her to embrace the news with open arms and embrace him as well?

"So… so now that you know this what happens? Is it enough to be at peace with yourself? Because, you know, I happen to like this body."

"I know you do, and I know that this is going to be an adjustment, but I've been looking at different treatments and I think I can get the body I want. It's going to take time, but it's going to be worth it in the end. I can be the person I've always been meant to be and I won't have to feel this tension inside. I can just relax."

"Okay, but what does this mean for us?"

"Well, it's like I said, it'll be an adjustment. But I'm still going to be the same person, the same person that you love, that you want to build a future with. That hasn't changed. I have the same morals and the same beliefs. I'm sure that our love will survive it."

"Are you," she said in a dry, cracked voice. Hamish realized he had grossly underestimated her tolerance for something like this. In his elation at discovering this new aspect of himself he hadn't thought through what it would mean for Madeline. He decided the best way forward was to be assertive.

"Yes, I am, and I know that it's a lot to take in. I'm sure that once you've had a chance to think about it you'll see the same thing too. I want you to know that I'll be patient with you, just as you have been, and I'll try and work through this together as well. We can make it through this Madeline, I just know we can," he held her hands tightly and pressed his forehead to hers, trying to share the same breath again, the same heartbeat.

"Okay Hamish, if this is what you need," she said, albeit hesitantly, but Hamish would take that. She was not as enthusiastic as he hoped she would be, but at least she had not turned him away. He wrapped his arms around her and led her to bed. They made love as man and woman. He found that he was able to enjoy it more knowing what was to come. He thought about how their bodies would twine together as two feminine halves becoming whole, and the images were so intense that they allowed him to enjoy loving Madeline more than he had done in a long time.

*

He didn't tell Harry or the rest of the team about it at first, He wanted things to be right with Madeline. He was so buoyed by his good spirits that he was swept up in a wave of glee and was blind to anything else. Obviously, Madeline wasn't completely on board with it at first, but he was certain she would get used to. After all, the world was a different place than it had been. People were far more accepting of people like Hamish in the modern world. They were allowed to flourish and grow, and Hamish felt like a flower in bloom.

When he attended his doctor's appointment he told them about his wishes. They began the course of treatment, hormones and cosmetic surgery to make him into a woman. Hamish could have cried, he was so happy.

The results would take some time to show, but in the meantime, he had gone shopping, picking out clothes for himself. People in the shops had smiled at him, saying what an attentive boyfriend he must have been to spend so long treating his girlfriend. He just gave them a knowing smile. They couldn't begin to understand how wrong they were. He had always had an idea of what made a good outfit and he was thrilled to finally be putting this nascent skill into practise. He flitted around the shops like a curious bee, buzzing here and there whenever something took his fancy. He had a trunkful of clothes by the end of it, and realized that he couldn't afford to buy such a lot. In the end he discarded a few items and went home.

In the privacy of his own home he took of his masculine clothes and dressed himself in his feminine ones, allowing the loose dresses to descend upon him like a kiss from an angel.

He felt freer in these clothes than he ever had done in his ordinary garb. No longer were his legs trapped in tight jeans, his arms throbbing against tight sleeves. He twirled in the mirror, imagining what his body would be like once he had completed the treatment. He ran his hands down the sides of his body and then cupped them over his chest. Currently his chest was flat, but by the end he would have pert breasts, and all this nasty hair would be plucked away from his body, chopped away like unwanted weeds.

He then applied some makeup. He had asked to borrow some of Madeline's. Guided by tutorials on the Internet, he made an effort to add some sparkle to his face. Then he took a picture and posted it on the Internet. He had found a safe haven where people like him could meet and interact, and he had been encouraged to share a picture, offering the world a glimpse of his new self.

Quickly enough he realized his mistake. The forum had been invaded by trolls and they peppered his picture with comments, calling him a freak, a monster, an abomination. They laughed and ridiculed him for looking like he did. Tears trickled down Hamish's cheeks as he read each and every one of them, unable to turn away. He ended up throwing the phone across the floor and collapsing in tears.

It was late when he headed over to see Madeline. He had washed make up off his face and returned to his normal clothes. His phone kept buzzing with notifications. Any positive comment had been drowned out by the negative ones in this mire of repugnance. He burst into Madeline's flat.

"You'll never believe what's happened," Hamish said bitterly as he marched in. He paused when he saw that Madeline and Harry were together. Harry had his arm around her shoulder, just as he had with Hamish once upon a time. Hamish tilted his head arched an eyebrow. "Is everything okay?"

Madeline's eyes were puffy and red. Her cheeks were stained with tears and her breath shuddered through her. Harry squeezed her arm and kissed her on the forehead, as a father would a child. He turned to Hamish and gave him a sympathetic look.

"It will be Hamish, just… just be patient with her. I'll talk to you later," he said, and then left the apartment. Hamish wasn't sure what to think.

"What's going on? What is this about? Are you and Harry…" the question lingered in the air. Hamish couldn't bring himself to say it. Madeline glared at him.

"Of course not."

"So what's going on then?" he asked, slipping into the chair that Harry had just vacated.

"I don't even know where to begin," Madeline buried her head in her hands and sniffed. Hamish waited for her to speak again, but she didn't.

"Well, I have something of my own to share. Maybe this will make you feel better at least, to know that you're not the only one suffering," he said, and then shared news with her about his own tribulations. He pulled out his phone. "Do you really think this picture is deserving of hate?" he asked. Madeline took one look and then wailed again. She wheeled away from the table and leaned against the wall, her entire body shuddered. Hamish realized something really serious was wrong.

"Madeline," he asked gently, "what's going on?"

Madeline breathed heavily and managed to compose herself. She turned to face him, but kept her back leaning against the wall. "I need to talk to you and I know you're not going to be happy, but I need you to listen to me. I'm pregnant."

The words sliced through the air. It was all so surreal. Hamish was bemused at first, but then he was delighted.

"That's wonderful," he said, moving to embrace Madeline. But she stiffened and warded him off.

"No, it's not Hamish, because you're... you're changing."

"Well, yes I am, but not every part of me. I'm still the same person you've always known, and now I'm going to be a father, well, a mother."

"I'm the mother," Madeline said, the words whipping harshly from her mouth. Hamish frowned and an awkward laugh burst out of his mouth.

"Okay, I mean, it's not a competition and we don't live in a world where everything has to be so clearly defined."

"But what if I want to?"

"What?"

"What if I want to live in that world? What if I want a husband, not a wife? What if I want our child to have a father, not two mothers?"

Hamish blinked slowly. An icy feeling crawled through his heart. "But you have me. I know that this isn't easy for you, but-"

"It's not just that it isn't easy Hamish. It's impossible."

He was stunned. He staggered back as though she had slapped him.

"Impossible?"

"I'm sorry," she groaned. "I'm really sorry, but I just don't know how else to tell you this. I get that you've been so excited about figuring yourself out and I'm happy for you. I'm glad you don't have to feel uncomfortable and that you can be free, but I don't think that I can go on this journey with you."

"What do you mean? We love each other. Christ, you've just told me that we're going to have a kid together!"

"And we can Hamish I just... I just think that maybe if we're going to have a kid then you could stay the same way you are now. You could put a hold on this, for their sake, you know?"

Hamish glared at her. Unsettled prickles rose up. "You want me to just ignore this? You want me to be less than I am?" he asked.

Madeline was still breathing deeply. "I don't know, I just know that I want a husband. I don't want a wife."

Hamish paused for a moment, closing his eyes. Everything in his body went rigid. He was so close to being who he wanted to be, so close to finally solving the riddle of himself and now she was trying to take this away from him.

"You told me you would support me. You told me we would get through this together," he said in a low voice that rolled like thunder."

"I know I did," she sounded defeated. She looked it, too. "But I didn't know the reality of the situation. I didn't know you were going to take it this far. You have to be practical about this Hamish. I get that this is important to you, but you can't expect to make this massive decision and just have everyone go along with it."

"Can't I?" he asked flippantly.

Madeline wiped her eyes and glared at him. "This isn't easy for me Hamish," she snapped. "Have you even once stopped to think about how this is affecting me? I'm sure there are people out there who could take this in their stride, but I'm not sure I'm one of them. I'm sorry for that. I wish I was because then this would make the whole thing easier, but I'm not, okay, and I'm not sure I'm ever going to be."

"I'm the same person Madeline."

"Except you're not, are you. Flesh and blood is important. This is who I fell in love with. This is who I'm attracted to," she gestured towards Hamish with her hand, sweeping it up and down in a vertical motion. "I'm not attracted to her," she pointed to the phone that held the picture Hamish had taken. "I'm just asking you, for the sake of me and our child, is there no room for compromise? Is there no way that you can stay as the man I know and be a father to our child?"

"I don't think so," Hamish said, the world spinning upon his words. "Is there really no way you can get past this?"

Madeline sniffed and shook her head. It was as grim as an executioner's gesture. "I've tried Hamish. You have to believe me that I've really tried. I've looked at naked women. I've tried to make myself attracted to women, but I just can't. It's not how I'm wired. I need a man to make me feel good. The world might be fluid and open for you, but it's not like that for me. I just like things the way they are."

"I see," Hamish tilted his head back, cursing himself and cursing her, cursing the entire world. "So this is it then? I have to choose between being fulfilled and complete as a person, or being half of myself and having a family?"

Madeline nodded, unable to bring herself to speak. They both knew what a terrible choice it was. She hated herself for forcing Hamish to make it, but there had been no other way. They had reached an impasse and something had to give. Hamish looked at her, his heart swelling with love. This was the woman who was carrying new life that she and he had created.

This was the woman he thought the world of, who had stuck with him through so many things, and yet she could not stick with him through this.

And he could not turn back now that he has tasted liberation. Despite all the hatred and all the abuse he received online he could not turn away from the fact that this was who he was, this was who he needed to be, and he was not willing to stop the treatments.

"I guess this is the end then," he said, and then his world fell apart.

Marylyn

There was a bitter tang in the air. Marylyn ignored the biting cold as she walked along the barren streets. Machinery whined and churned in the distance. The world shuddered as mechanisms of industry held the world in its thrall. She ignored the towering buildings though.

She passed a football pitch, which was deserted. The grass had turned a yellowish-brown, sickly looking, as though it suffered from a disease. The nets had been taken away from the goals. So many years had passed, years that she would never get back. She made her way to a house. Her heart was pumping. Her mind was wracked with guilt and anxiety. Speaking of the past with Jimmy had brought things back to her mind, and made her want to repair the schisms that had formed between her and her family. There were fewer years ahead than there had been behind her, and she knew that if she didn't make an effort to reconcile with her son then there might never be another chance.

474

The house was a pretty little thing with a red door. Flowers lined the front garden, and a bowl of flowers hung next to the door. The bay windows were covered with net curtains, so she couldn't see inside. She pressed the doorbell. It chimed lightly. Part of her was so nervous she wished that nobody would answer, although she wasn't sure she would ever summon the courage to come here again.

The door opened. Her son stood there, looking the spitting image of his father. His blonde hair was messy, his shoulders broad, and he was about the same height as Marylyn. As soon as he saw her he recognized her. Some innate part of him knew. His eyes narrowed, his lips formed a thin lin.

"Harold," she began. It always galled him that he had been given that name. "I think you know who I am, don't you? I'm your mother. I know that things have been strained between us and we haven't had the relationship we would have liked, but I thought I would come to you now and try and repair things. I thought I would try to make things better."

"I have a mother," he said tersely, gripping the door tightly. It was only open enough for him to stand there. He didn't allow her to pass.

Marylyn sighed. "I know, I mean... you know what I mean. Look, I'm old, I'm retired, and I don't have anyone. I'm so lonely. Will you please just talk to me? Can we try and make up for the lost years?"

"The lost years? You're talking about my life! Mum told me everything that happened. I was always here. I was always waiting for you to come by. She wouldn't have stopped you."

"Things with your mother and I were complicated..."

"Life is always complicated. It doesn't change the fact that you never came to see me."

"She wanted me to stay away. She didn't want you to become confused. And I... it wasn't easy, not after what I went through."

"But you chose to go through it, *Dad*," he said, the word cutting through her like a knife. "You chose to be like this instead of being a father to me."

476

Marylyn looked away. "I didn't want you to look at me and see a man without integrity. I wanted to be true to myself and at the time the world was different. People were allowed to explore themselves and change."

"And I don't begrudge you that. I'm glad you found yourself, but in the process you lost me. You could have fought harder for me. You could have tried to convince Mum. Instead, you just disappeared."

"I had other things to fight as well. You don't know what it was like for me."

"No, I don't, but you don't know what it was like for me either, and now it's just… it's too late."

"No, please… don't say that. We still have a chance."

"I really don't know what you want from me," he rolled his eyes.

"Just a conversation. Just a chance to get to know you. I don't want to be alone Harold. Not anymore. I want to make up for the mistakes I made. You see, I never had a good relationship with my own mother. She was a difficult woman and she could never accept that I grew up. As soon as I started developing a mind of my own she started acting differently. She wanted me to do exactly as she wanted. She would have been happy if I had stayed living with her all my life, but I couldn't do that. I wanted to be free. I thought my feelings of being trapped were due to her, but they weren't. It was because of the way I was. I was only trying to be my true self."

"And like I said, I'm glad that you found a way to be able to do this. It doesn't change the fact that you weren't around for me, and I have no interest in getting to know you now."

"But I'm your mother, or your father, or however you want to think of me."

"No, you're not. I had a mother and a father. I'm named after him for goodness' sake, because he was the one who was there for me and yeah, okay, he wasn't the best man in the world, leaving his partner for Mum, but they were happy. We were a family. I never missed out on anything and I'm only angry at you because you never even made an effort to see me. Look how old I am, do I really look like a child in need? I've lived a long life. I have a family of my own now, and you're not a part of it. You never were, and you never will be. I think we're done here," he said, and slammed the door in Marylyn's face.

She turned away, her heart breaking with anguish. Her shoulders shuddered and hot tears ran down her cheeks. She had never wanted it to be this way. She thought Madeline was right and that it would have been less confusing for her son to stay away, at least until he was old enough to understand. But then the years had slipped by and her work had taken her out of the country and the constant nagging and trolling had made her think that nobody was ever going to accept her, and so she had always been too scared.

But maybe he was right. He already had a mother and a father. What could Marylyn be to him? Perhaps she could have been both, but instead she was neither. Would she have been happier if she had never undergone the transformation and remained as Hamish? She would have been a father, but she never would have felt right in herself. It had been an impossible choice and she wondered if some people were just meant to be lonely, no matter what they endured through life, no matter how much they changed themselves.

She shuffled back to her small, lonely flat and sighed as she closed the door and was embraced by silence once again. She looked out to the bleak sky and tormented herself with thoughts of what her life could have been. And then she bowed her head and wept. She pulled out old pictures of the man she used to be, the proud Hamish. She looked into his eyes and found it difficult to see a glint of herself. She had left him and everything else in his life behind, including a claim to his son. She had nothing of her own, only a sense that she was in the body that was right for her.

But it was the world that was wrong. If things had been different then maybe Madeline would have been more accepting. Maybe... oh hell, what was the point in maybe? It was all such a mess, and the worst thing was that there was nobody to share it with.

Many Thanks to:-

Robert Spake: Editing and Input.

Cover design: Scott Gaunt

Printed in Great Britain
by Amazon